The air in t to shiver

The man's body swayed, and the sway became a tremble and the tremble turned into a spasm. His eyes remained open, but they did not see. His mouth gaped open, but no words came out. He croaked a sound of pain and terror and agony.

With a faint crackling sound similar to that of burning wood, a gray pallor suddenly swept over the man's body, spreading out from the device attached to his neck. A ghastly dry gargling came from his mouth, then the gray tide covered his lips, smothering his voice. Within another pair of eye blinks, a coal-black calcified statue knelt before the podium. The silver spider seemed to have dissolved, absorbed by the same process that turned flesh to carbon.

Nausea roiled in the pit of Brigid's stomach and she swallowed a column of burning bile working its way up her throat. The little spider clinging to her own flesh suddenly seemed to weigh a ton. Her heart pounded frantically in terror, but she forced herself to raise defiant eyes to Megaera's blank golden face. Reflected firelight cast red highlights across its dully gleaming surface, lending it an expression of cold, superior mockery.

Other titles in this series:

JAMES AXLER

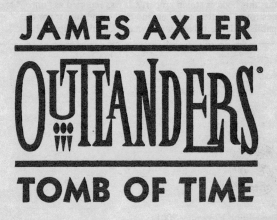

OUTLANDERS®

TOMB OF TIME

A GOLD EAGLE BOOK FROM
WORLDWIDE®

TORONTO • NEW YORK • LONDON
AMSTERDAM • PARIS • SYDNEY • HAMBURG
STOCKHOLM • ATHENS • TOKYO • MILAN
MADRID • WARSAW • BUDAPEST • AUCKLAND

First edition November 2001
ISBN 0-373-63832-9

TOMB OF TIME

Special thanks to Mark Ellis for his contribution to the
Outlanders concept, developed for Gold Eagle Books.

Time, like an ever-rolling stream,
Bears all its sons away;
They fly forgotten, as a dream
Dies at the opening day.
                    —Isaac Watts, 1674–1748

The Road to Outlands—
From Secret Government Files to the Future

Almost two hundred years after the global holocaust, Kane, a former Magistrate of Cobaltville, often thought the world had been lucky to survive at all after a nuclear device detonated in the Russian embassy in Washington, D.C. The aftermath—forever known as skydark—reshaped continents and turned civilization into ashes.

Nearly depopulated, America became the Deathlands—poisoned by radiation, home to chaos and mutated life forms. Feudal rule reappeared in the form of baronies, while remote outposts clung to a brutish existence.

What eventually helped shape this wasteland were the redoubts, the secret preholocaust military installations with stores of weapons, and the home of gateways, the locational matter-transfer facilities. Some of the redoubts hid clues that had once fed wild theories of government cover-ups and alien visitations.

Rearmed from redoubt stockpiles, the barons consolidated their power and reclaimed technology for the villes. Their power, supported by some invisible authority, extended beyond their fortified walls to what was now called the Outlands. It was here that the rootstock of humanity survived, living with hellzones and chemical storms, hounded by Magistrates.

In the villes, rigid laws were enforced—to atone for the sins of the past and prepare the way for a better future. That was the barons' public credo and their right-to-rule.

Kane, along with friend and fellow Magistrate Grant, had upheld that claim until a fateful Outlands expedition. A displaced piece of technology...a question to a keeper of the archives...a vague clue about alien masters—and their world shifted radically. Suddenly, Brigid Baptiste, the archivist, faced summary execution, and

Grant a quick termination. For Kane there was forgiveness if he pledged his unquestioning allegiance to Baron Cobalt and his unknown masters and abandoned his friends.

But that allegiance would make him support a mysterious and alien power and deny loyalty and friends. Then what else was there?

Kane had been brought up solely to serve the ville. Brigid's only link with her family was her mother's red-gold hair, green eyes and supple form. Grant's clues to his lineage were his ebony skin and powerful physique. But Domi, she of the white hair, was an Outlander pressed into sexual servitude in Cobaltville. She at least knew her roots and was a reminder to the exiles that the outcasts belonged in the human family.

Parents, friends, community—the very rootedness of humanity was denied. With no continuity, there was no forward momentum to the future. And that was the crux—when Kane began to wonder if there *was* a future.

For Kane, it wouldn't do. So the only way was out— way, way out.

After their escape, they found shelter at the forgotten Cerberus redoubt headed by Lakesh, a scientist, Cobaltville's head archivist, and secret opponent of the barons.

With their past turned into a lie, their future threatened, only one thing was left to give meaning to the outcasts. The hunger for freedom, the will to resist the hostile influences. And perhaps, by opposing, end them.

Chapter 1

The dead man seemed to be kneeling in prayer. Hunched over with both hands raised palms outward and his head tilted back, he looked as if he were seeking benediction. Judging by the condition of his body, he had received damnation instead.

The man was completely black—not only his hair, skin and fingernails, but also his teeth. His mouth gaped open in an agonized rictus, exposing a tongue the hue of ebony. His eyes resembled a pair of small onyx orbs. His clothing, which appeared to consist of a short denim jacket and zippered cover-all, was as jet-black as the rest of him. His clothing, flesh and hair had the texture of porous charcoal or black plaster. The figure looked more like a three-dimensional shadow or a singularly unattractive statue than a corpse.

Eyeing the man closely, Kane ventured, "Rad exposure?"

Brigid Baptiste hesitated a second before murmuring, "Not of a kind I'm familiar with."

"And just how many kinds is that?" asked Grant, his brow furrowed.

Brigid shrugged. "Just off the top of my head, there's X-ray, neutron, gamma, cobalt—"

"We get the general idea," Reba DeFore broke in dryly.

Brigid cast her a slightly irritated glance and gestured toward the kneeling corpse. "I don't think you do. Whatever did that to this man doesn't fit the symptomology of any recorded type of radiation exposure."

From the breast pocket of her shirt she unclipped her rad counter and stepped closer to the motionless figure. Passing the little square instrument over the top of the man's head, she kept a close watch on the LCD window. It continued to glow a steady yellow-green. The device didn't emit a warning electronic chirp, so she returned it to her pocket.

"Rad levels read within the tolerance range," Brigid announced. "Not even a hundred roentgens. It's well within acceptable limits."

"How can you be so sure it's not what it looks like?" DeFore inquired. "Just a statue some scrounger was moving and then abandoned?"

Kane answered in a flat voice, "When you come on more of these field trips with us, you'll learn that almost nothing is what it appears to be. No, this is— was—a human being."

Grant pursed his lips. "Could a chemical have done that to him? Some sort of strong corrosive?"

Brigid shook her head. "That doesn't seem

likely.'' Absently, she combed a hand through her thick hair, which tumbled in waves from beneath the long-billed olive-green cap on her head to spill artlessly over her khaki-clad shoulders like a red-gold mane. Her delicate features didn't show her inner consternation and confusion. Her complexion, fair and lightly dusted with freckles across her nose and cheeks, held a rosy hue.

Her eyes weren't just green; they were a deep, clear emerald, glittering now in anxiety. She was tall and willowy, her figure slender and taut. Long in the leg, her athletic physique reflected an unusual strength without detracting from her undeniable femininity, despite the unflattering shirt, trousers and high-topped jump boots she wore.

Kane stepped closer to the ebony figure and carefully sniffed the air. ''He hasn't been burned, that's for sure. It's more like he's coated with something.''

At a shade over six feet, he was nearly a half a head taller than Brigid Baptiste. Long limbed and rangy, he was a lean, sinewy wolf of a man, carrying most of his muscle mass in his upper body above a slim waist. His skin was lightly bronzed from exposure to the elements except for a thin scar that stretched like a white thread across his cheek. Kane wore a twin to Brigid's long billed olive-green cap over his longish, dark hair. Sun-touched highlights showed at the temples and nape. His pale eyes, blue with just enough gray in them to resemble the high sky at sunset, were bright and alert behind the dark lenses of sunglasses.

"Some kind of heat or radiation did that to him," Grant argued in his characteristic lionlike rumble of a voice. "He almost looks like he's been carbonized...or calcified."

Grant's long, heavy-jawed face was twisted in a scowl. Droplets of perspiration sparkled against his coffee-brown skin. He stood four inches over six feet tall, and was very broad in the chest and shoulders. Gray sprinkled his short-cropped, tight-curled hair, but it didn't show in the heavy black mustache that swept fiercely out from either side of his grim, tight-lipped mouth.

"In fact," he continued, his eyes narrowing to suspicious slits, "he looks sort of like all of us did after we were transported from New Edo to China."

Both Kane and Brigid regarded him in surprise, their thoughts flying back to the incident he described, nearly three months in the past. After they had been teleported through means still undetermined, all of their bodies had been covered by a layer of soot that smelled faintly of hot grease. The ends of their hair had been scorched, as well.

"Are we going to stand around here and talk about it?" Reba DeFore demanded impatiently. "Or are we going to move on?"

No one responded to the brown-eyed, bronze-skinned woman's sharp tone. Brigid, Grant and

Kane knew how anxious and fearful the medic became whenever she left the shielded shelter of the Cerberus redoubt in Montana. Her blouse showed half-moons of perspiration at the armpits and neckline, and the intricate braid she favored for her ash-blond hair had come undone. She hadn't bothered trying to pat it back into place, although loose tendrils hung about her face. The posture of her stocky body telegraphed tension.

All of them were tense, particularly since they were strolling through a hellzone, even though Chicago hadn't been a first-strike target. Still, it had taken a couple of direct hits from neutron bombs during the brief but all-out nuclear war of two centuries ago. They had been tramping down the litter-choked streets, between bombed-out ruins and collapsed buildings for the better part of an hour. Some areas were nothing but acre upon acre of scorched and shattered concrete, with rusting rods of reinforcing iron protruding from the ground like withered stalks of some mutated crop.

There were signs that some kind of incendiary agents had been dropped on the city, but they weren't nuclear in nature despite how the indicators of their rad counters occasionally glowed between the far end of the green scale and yellow. Brigid had told them that megascale radioactive deposits from nuclear power plants and toxic-waste dumps contaminated much of the soil of the Midwest, as well as the Great Lakes. With the wholesale destruction of large land areas during the nukecaust, these smaller catastrophes poisoned the ground with such virulence that they were rendered sterile for generations.

Kane, Grant and Brigid had visited several derelict predark cities, and Chicago seemed to be in better shape than most, but it still echoed with the relics of a lost civilization.

Kane started to turn away from the kneeling figure, then did a double take. He leaned forward, slitting his eyes. Where there should have been an ear on the right side of the man's head, there was only a ragged nub, looking like a crushed cigar butt.

"What is it?" Brigid asked.

"He's missing an ear," Kane replied, pointing. "See?"

Brigid squinted in the direction of his finger, then from a pocket of her shirt she withdrew the symbol of her former office as a Cobaltville archivist. She slipped on the pair of rectangular-lensed, wire-framed spectacles and gazed at the man's head. Although the eyeglasses were something of a reminder of her past life, they also served to correct an astigmatism.

Kane briefly wondered if her vision hadn't been further impaired by the head injury she suffered a few months before. Brigid seemed in good condition, and DeFore had pronounced her fully recov-

ered. The only visible sign of the wound—which
had laid her scalp open to the bone and put her in
a coma for several days—was a faintly red horizontal line on her right temple. Her recovery time had
been little short of uncanny. Kane was always impressed by the woman's tensile-spring resiliency.
However, he couldn't help but notice how she
needed her glasses more and more since the injury.

"I see it," she said, "but I don't necessarily think
it's significant."

"It doesn't look like an old wound," he declared.
"There's no sign of scarring."

With the barrel of his Copperhead, the close-
assault subgun he carried slung over a shoulder,
Kane gently prodded the side of the corpse's head.
A hairline crack appeared in the black skull and
from it curled a lazy tendril of equally black smoke.
At the same time, an astringent stench filled Kane's
nostrils, an odor of hot sulfur mixed with ammonia.

As he took a hasty step back, the crack in the
dead man's head expanded into a split and more of
the oily vapor plumed out. The smoke spread
quickly, and the kneeling man seemed to unravel as
twists of mist rose like a multitude of loose black
threads. Within a heartbeat he turned into a cloud of
vaguely human-shaped sepia mist. Clothing, flesh,
bones and hair dissolved into a foul-smelling fog.
The fetid miasma rose over the street, and a gusting
breeze wafted the cloud to one side.

In less than five seconds, the dissolution was complete. Nothing remained of the dead man except flakes and a couple of handfuls of black dust. Kane, Brigid, DeFore and Grant gaped wide-eyed, shocked into speechlessness. They watched in silence as the cloud of black vapor continued to lift and slowly disperse, floating toward the broken ramparts of the Chicago skyline.

It took Kane three attempts before he was able to husk out, "You don't see that every day."

When no one replied, he cut his eyes over to Brigid. "Speculation?" he inquired. "Hypotheses? Technobabble?"

Her intense gaze still fixed on the fading scraps of smoke, Brigid said, "I'd guess it to be a form of molecular decohesion, similar to the effect of the MD gun. I'm sure you remember that."

Kane didn't bother responding to her assumption. Although he didn't possess an eidetic memory like Brigid Baptiste, the incidents in Redoubt Papa and aboard the *Parallax Red* space station to which she referred were impressed indelibly in his mind.

"Similar, you said." DeFore's tone was skeptical. "Not the same?"

Brigid nodded. "That's right. If this is the work of a molecular destabilizer, it's a new application, but the result is pretty much the same." She snapped the fingers of both hands. "Poof."

As if the snapping of her fingers were a signal,

the detonation of thunder boomed in the distance, a long, loud roll. Kane scanned the horizon and saw billowing clouds massing over the shattered column of the Sears Tower, at least two miles away. The underside of the clouds bore a sickly green tinge, undershot by a salmon pink.

"Chem storm," he announced flatly. "It wouldn't be a stroll through a hellzone without one."

No one laughed. The early years of skydark, the generation-long nuclear winter, had been a period of nature gone amok. Hundreds of very nearly simultaneous nuclear explosions had propelled massive quantities of pulverized rubble into the atmosphere, clogging the sky and blanketing all of Earth in a thick cloud of dust, debris, smoke and fallout.

For nearly two decades, it was as if the very elements were trying to purge the Earth of the few survivors of the atomic megacull. The exchange of nuclear missiles did more than slaughter most of Earth's inhabitants—it distorted the ecosystems that were not completely obliterated. The entire atmosphere of the planet had been hideously polluted by the nukecaust, producing all manner of deadly side effects.

After eight generations, the lingering effects of the nukecaust and skydark were more subtle, an underlying texture to a world struggling to heal itself. Yet the side effects of the war were still unavoidable, like a grim reminder to humanity to never take the permanence of the Earth for granted again.

One of the worst and most frequent side effects was chem storms, showers of acid-tainted rain that could scorch the flesh off any animal caught in the open. They were lingering examples of the freakish weather effects common after the holocaust and the nuclear winter. Chem storms were dangerous partly because of their intensity, but mainly because of the acids, heavy metals and other chemical compounds that fell with the rain.

In the immediate aftermath of the nukecaust, chem storms could strip flesh from bone in less than a minute. As the environment recovered, the passage of time diluted the potency of the storms, but the lethal acid rain could still melt flesh from the bones during long exposure.

Fortunately, chem storms were no longer as frequent as they had been even a century before, but the peculiar geothermals of hellzones seemed to attract them. Although fewer hellzones existed now, there were still a number of places where the geological or meteorological consequences of the nukecaust prevented a full recovery. The passage of time could not completely cleanse the zones of hideous, invisible plagues.

The west coast of the United States was one such zone, where much of what had been California was under water. The best-known zone was the miles-long D.C.-New Jersey-New York Corridor, a vast stretch of abandoned factory complexes, warehouses and overgrown ruins. D.C., otherwise known as Washington Hole, was still the most active hot spot in the country. Kane still retained vivid and unpleasant memories of his one visit to the Hole. Only a vast sea of fused black glass occupied the tract of land that once held the seat of American government. Seen from a distance, the crater lent the region the name by which it had been known for nearly two centuries. Washington Hole was the hellzone of hellzones, still jolted by ground tremors and soaked by the intermittent flooding of Potomac Lake. A volcano, barely an infant in geological terms, had burst up from the rad-blasted ground. The peak dribbled a constant stream of foul-smelling smoke, mixing with the chem-tainted rain clouds to form a wispy umbrella stinking of sulfur and chlorine.

Fortunately, this region of the Midwest was only warm, not hot, but a hellzone was still a hellzone even if the rad levels were low. One of the mysteries spawned by the nukecaust was how hellzones could coexist cheek to jowl with "clean" regions.

There was another flash of lightning, so close that Kane could feel his skin tingle and body hair stand up. The thunderclap followed almost immediately. All of them smelled the ozone in the air.

"I think we'd better get to cover," Kane announced.

His tone was calm and uninflected, but in truth he was very anxious. It wasn't only the exertion of the long, slogging trek through the ruins of Chicago that made him nervous. His sixth sense, his point man's sense, warned of a danger far more immediate than unpredictable weather.

For a moment Kane contemplated ordering a retreat back to the Sandcat, but he knew by the time they even reached the halfway point to where the vehicle was parked, the chem storm would be upon them. There were measures against the dangers of acid rains, airtight protective suits and helmets, but none of them carried either a suit or a helmet. They were over a thousand miles away, stored safely in the Cerberus armory. His and Grant's Magistrate body armor was treated to withstand all weather, but both suits were in the Cat. As it was, neither man cared to test whether their polycarbonate exoskeletons could survive a dousing of acid rain.

Besides, the heat was surprisingly oppressive, particularly for the Midwest so early in the spring. Marching around in the body armor and its Kevlar-weave undersheathing was like walking around in a portable sauna, even in the coolest of temperatures. In the Outlands, the black armor would have been a target for jackals skulking among the ruins.

Grant removed a small map from his pants and unfolded it. He glanced from it to a small compass he held in his right hand. The map had been generated by the database in Cerberus and depicted the city's layout before the nuke. A little doubtfully he said, "According to this, we only have about three klicks to Redoubt Echo."

"Yeah," Kane agreed musingly. "But we'll have to spend some time searching for the entrance, and that storm looks like it's moving at ten klicks an hour. We've already spent a week getting here... another couple of hours won't make much difference."

Brigid leaned over to study the map. "We're in the vicinity of the Illinois Deep Waterway, so the Lake District Central Filtration Plant ought to be easy to spot."

"Why were so many of the Totality Concept installations hidden inside of other buildings?" De-Fore asked sourly.

"The old purloined-letter approach," Brigid replied. "The predark strategists thought hiding their secrets in plain sight—more or less—kept them safe from discovery."

"Don't complain," Kane replied. "A lot of them were hidden inside of national parks. At least we're not having to cover Sequoia National Forest inch by inch."

Stowing the compass back in his pocket, Grant unclipped his trans-comm unit from his web belt. He flipped up the cover of the palm-sized radiophone. Depressing the transmit key, he asked, "Domi, do you read me?"

Only the crackle and pop of static hissed from the comm. Grant opened his mouth to repeat the query, but his words were drowned out by a thunderclap so loud and explosive everyone flinched. The air shivered from its violence.

"Forget it," Brigid declared. "We're out of range and the storm is ionizing the atmosphere. Besides, she's safer than we are at the moment."

All of them glanced again at the black clouds building like a solid wall over the derelict outskirts of Chicago. The mountainous thunderheads continued to skim out of the north, blotting out the sky above the broken spire of the Sears Tower. The billowing mass thickened rapidly, casting deep shadow over the entire perimeter and bringing a sudden and oppressive gloom. The atmosphere seemed to gain weight, pressing against eardrums, making respiration labored.

The blackness slowly lowered and spread like a blanket. Strange crackles of luminescence glowed within its roiling center, like flashes of heat lightning. The underside of the cloud surged out, belling downward and narrowing into a black funnel shape. The tip brushed the top of a building like a tentative finger, and even at that distance they glimpsed debris swirling around it.

"I read about storms like this," Brigid said

grimly. "This kind has a small cyclonic center that's completely unpredictable, spawning twisters every few minutes. You can't tell where one will hit."

No one questioned her statement. As a former archivist in the Cobaltville Historical Division, Brigid's knowledge on a wide variety of subjects was profound. Her greatest asset was her eidetic, or "photographic," memory. She could instantly recall in detail everything she had read, seen or experienced, which was both a blessing and a curse.

The funnel cloud drew back up into the thunderhead, and a moment later a shifting curtain of rain fell. Even from the distance, they saw little puffs of vapor rising from the impact points of the raindrops.

Kane tried to quash his rising sense of dread and worry about Domi. If she stayed inside the Sandcat, she was completely safe. Although built to serve as a FAV, a Fast Attack Vehicle, the dual-tracked wag was armored with a ceramic-armaglass bond to shield it from both intense and ambient radiation. It would certainly be sufficient to protect her from a shower of acid rain—provided she hadn't decided to explore her surroundings. The little albino girl from the Outlands was unpredictable, often driven by impulses and whims. She had become more so over the past few months, ever since her resurrection.

Her retrieval, Kane corrected himself. Since Domi hadn't really been dead, she couldn't have been resurrected. Still, the Outland girl's behavior had become more and more erratic. She disappeared from the redoubt for extended periods, as if she needed the solitude.

Kane remembered how, during his and Domi's captivity in the Area 51 complex, the albino had shown an uncharacteristic display of compassion for the sickly hybrid infants kept there. He wondered if Domi sought solitude in the thickly forested ravines of the mountainside in order to come to terms with what she had learned about herself.

The one thing she hadn't learned was the details of her apparent death. Nobody else really knew the precise details, either. In order to learn more, they had come to Chicago, the metropolis that had once hosted Totality Concept's Operation Chronos. And so Domi, left behind in Sandcat, still didn't realize she was the main reason for the mission.

Kane wheeled around to the southeast. "Let's get the hell off the street and find a roof somewhere."

He moved ahead, unconsciously assuming the point position. Kane always assumed the position of point man. It was a habit he had acquired during his years as a Magistrate, and he saw no reason to abandon it. Both Brigid and Grant had the utmost faith in Kane's instincts, what he referred to as his point man's sense. When he walked point, Kane felt electrically alive, sharply tuned to every nuance of his surroundings and what he was doing.

He led his three companions along the boulevard

quickly, avoiding pits of thick mud that looked as if they could easily be several yards deep. Rats, some of them as big as housecats, scattered at their approach. A few of the bolder ones stopped after their initial fright and reared up on their hind legs to sniff at them as they passed by. Both Brigid and DeFore did poor jobs of repressing shudders of revulsion. Their loathing for rodents went far deeper than a simple antipathy for filth-wallowing vermin—both women had shared a nightmarish experience with plague-infected rats in the bayous of Louisiana a few months back. Kane was a little surprised that they showed enough restraint not to shoot at the creatures.

The suburb of old Chi-town was comparatively intact, though that was a relative term. It was untouched compared to Washington Hole, but it was still a wasteland. The buildings were little more than gutted shells, the streets choked with rubble and debris. Thorny brush and weeds sprouted within the walls of homes, and vines coiled around the wreckage of collapsed roofs. Scrubby grass grew in the pockets of windblown debris and weathered detritus. On some of the city blocks, the breadth of rubble was so widespread, they could see no discernible difference between the street and the ruins. The roadbed itself had a ripple pattern to it, a characteristic result of earthquakes triggered by explosive shock waves.

During the nuke-triggered quakes, rivers and lakes were often diverted. Here in outer Chicago, rivers, waterways, canals and Lake Michigan had run together to form temporary inland seas. The floodwaters broke through storm drains and levees and overlaid the entire region with layers of brackish, fetid sludge. They saw statues so deeply eroded and encrusted with dried muck it was no longer possible even to identify the subjects as human, animal or otherwise.

Kane noticed how some buildings still stood among others that were no more than ragged foundations. Wide dark bands of dried mud discolored many of the walls, from the ground to waist height. The next street they turned down looked as if it had been a residential neighborhood, a mix of stores and luxury apartment buildings. Many of them lacked roofs, but the walls still stood steadfast against the corrosive effects of time and nature.

The sky quickly turned the hue of old lead as the banks of black clouds spread, like a tapestry unrolled by a vast invisible hand. Grant kept checking their back trail but saw nothing but the labyrinth of tumbled ruins. Bits of debris fluttered in the air, skimming across their path.

"The wind is rising fast," Brigid said, her mane of red-gold hair streaming out from the beneath the edges of her cap.

Kane eyed the sky. "One of your tornadoes, maybe."

"An acid-rain tornado?" DeFore's crisp tone didn't quaver, but her stance telegraphed a mounting fear.

"Could be." Grant blinked as handful of wind-driven dust scoured his face. "By the looks of this place, it wouldn't be the first time."

The wind increased, causing their clothes to flutter and stinging their faces with particles of grit. Keeping his mouth tightly closed, Kane looked toward the storm front and saw rain sweeping slowly in their direction like a solid but shifting curtain. Faintly he caught a whiff reminiscent of rotten eggs blended with burned brown sugar, seasoned by kerosene. The deep rumble of thunder had become a constant kettle-drum roll in the background.

Brigid suddenly cried out and slapped at her hand. A second later, Kane felt a pinpoint burn on the back of his neck, and he realized the leading edge of the squall had already reached them. They couldn't afford to be choosy any longer, so the four people lunged into the first open doorway they saw.

It was a storefront with a gaping square in the front wall where a plate-glass window had once formed a transparent barrier between the street and the shop's wares. The exterior of the building was half-swallowed by creeper sand vines, saplings and green undergrowth. A quick upward glance showed them at least a quarter of the roof and ceiling was still in place.

It wasn't much, but it offered them a measure of protection from the fiery kiss of the rain shower. Through the layer of debris and detritus on the floor, Kane could just make out a mosaic pattern of timework. What had once been a huge showroom was now a broad open piazza. On the far side a corridor stretched away into darkness. The corridor was bisected by a strip of light where the sunlight lanced through a crack in the ceiling. He wasn't too anxious to enter it and find out what lay beyond the crack— he retained vivid and exceedingly unpleasant memories of what explorations in similar settings had wrought.

It was hot, even inside the building. The air was heavy and sluggish, pressing moistly on exposed skin, despite the approaching storm. Grant palmed away sweat from his forehead and muttered, "This is more like the bayou than the Midwest."

Brigid nodded in silent, grim agreement, then flattened herself against the nearest wall just as the rain began pattering down, first in a lazy drizzle then in a sheet.

Kane, Grant and DeFore put their backs against the wall and watched the drops strike the exposed floor tiles with a series of prolonged hisses and tiny curls of smoke. The chemical stench wafting up caught Kane by the throat and seared the tender tissues and scorched his nasal passages.

Clapping a hand over his nose and mouth, he struggled against a coughing fit. He was still struggling when the ragged man came stumbling through the doorway.

Chapter 2

Neither Brigid nor DeFore saw Kane and Grant flex the tendons of their right wrists. Nor did they hear the click of the actuators or the faint, brief drone of tiny electric motors and the solid slap of the butts of the Sin Eaters sliding into the men's palms almost at the same time. But they did see the blasters appear almost magically in their hands.

The official weapons of Magistrates, Sin Eaters were strapped to holsters on their right forearms. The big-bore automatic handblasters were a little under fourteen inches in length. When not in use, the stocks of the pistols folded over the top of the weapon, lying perpendicular to the frame, reducing their holstered lengths to ten inches. Cables and actuators attached to the weapons popped the Sin Eaters into Grant's and Kane's waiting hands when they tensed their wrist tendons in the right sequence.

The 9 mm blasters had no safeties or trigger guards, and when the firing stud came in contact with a crooked index finger, it would fire immediately. However, both Kane and Grant kept their fingers extended and out of contact with the trigger stud.

There wasn't any need to use a firearm on the man who staggered inside the door, then collapsed almost at Kane's feet. They caught only a glimpse of a face gaunt to the point of emaciation and staring, bloodshot eyes. His clothing hung in tatters.

Grant and Kane aimed their Sin Eaters at the prostrate form while Brigid and DeFore moved a little closer, their own weapons drawn and ready. Brigid held an Iver Johnson TP9 in a double-fisted grip. The autoblaster was fairly small and lightweight, but it was a true cannon compared to the toylike Titan FIE .22-caliber pistol in DeFore's hand. Grant had remarked sourly that the medic chose that particular gun only because the armory didn't have slingshots.

"Where the hell did he come from?" Grant demanded harshly. He didn't need to raise his voice to be heard over the steady drumming of the rain or the howl of the wind.

"You could always ask him," Kane commented.

The man lay on his face and twitched uncontrollably. Kane nudged him with a boot. "Hey, this place is occupied. We'll have to ask you to move on if you don't give us a good reason not to."

He wasn't surprised when he received no response. Wedging his foot beneath the man's midriff, Kane rolled him onto his back. Uttering a wordless snarl of horror he took a swift, involuntary step back. The man's face bore inflamed, leaking blisters inflicted by the rain, but those injuries were minor. Through a gaping rent in his pants, all of them saw how his groin had been ripped open and his genitals torn away.

The ghastly wound had then been clumsily cauterized, apparently by the application of white-hot metal. Even over the chemical stink of the rainfall, the odor of burned human flesh was sickeningly strong. A dew of agony glistened on his face.

All of them gazed in horror at the man, their throats constricting. Both of his testicles were only glazed lumps at the juncture of his thighs, the flesh seared smooth with branding irons. His respiration was rapid and shallow. From his open mouth came a wordless gargle, either a plea or an inquiry. He coughed rackingly, and pink foam frothed on his slack lips.

"Dear God," DeFore muttered. She went to her knees beside the man, placing her medical kit on the floor and raising the lid. Removing a stethoscope, she listened to the man's heart, took his pulse and examined his eyes, moving from one task to the other with a grim, brisk efficiency.

"The wound is fairly fresh," she announced flatly. "Inflicted in the last twenty-four hours or so, thirty at the outside. It isn't infected, but I hear fluid on his lungs."

Grant's brow furrowed, casting his eyes into

shadow. "He must be completely fused out from the pain to run through acid rain like that."

"I imagine he barely felt the burns," DeFore replied. "He's in deep shock."

"No shit," Grant said dourly. "Can he be questioned about who did this to him?"

DeFore took a small hypodermic syringe from the medical kit, holding it up to the feeble light. "He's completely disassociative at the moment."

She injected the amber-colored contents of the syringe into the man's arm. "I'm giving him a shot of stimulant compound and an analgesic for pain. We may be able to stabilize him."

No one asked her why she bothered ministering to the man. Even if he hadn't appeared to have all but one toe in the grave, he wasn't their responsibility. Still, they knew Reba DeFore took the Hippocratic oath seriously, even though she wasn't a doctor in the conventional sense. The man's eyelids fluttered in reaction to the injection, but that was the limit of his reaction. Even in the near dark, Kane could see the harsh lines of pain etched deeply in his face. It was grimy with dirt encrusted in the deep wrinkles and seams. Kane had seen many faces like that in the Outlands, and he pegged the man as a Roamer or a scavenger belonging to a band of Farers.

Eyeing the inflamed area at the man's crotch, Grant said lowly, "Maybe he did that to himself, or let it happen. Remember those fused-out cross-dressers we met in Russia? What were they called— the Scots Pees?''

Despite the situation, Brigid couldn't repress a brief laugh. ''The Skotpsis. It's possible there might be a similar cult practicing around here.''

Kane recalled what Brigid had said about the Skotpsis when they encountered them nearly a year and a half before. They were a religious sect that flourished in Russia in the eighteenth and nineteenth centuries. The cult traced its origins back to the pagan goddess Cybele, whose priests wore women's clothes and castrated themselves as sacrificial offerings at her altars.

Kane shuddered at the recollection and asked, ''What do you know about the history of Chicago?''

Brigid regarded him quizzically. ''Pre- or post-skydark?''

''Post would be a little more helpful at the present time,'' Kane replied with a touch of sarcasm. ''Did the *Wyeth Codex* have any intel about this place?''

''As a matter of fact,'' Brigid answered, ''it did.''

''Why am I not surprised?'' Grant muttered a little peevishly.

The *Wyeth Codex* was a document based on a journal written by Dr. Mildred Wyeth, who had been revived from cryonic suspension by Ryan Cawdor in the late twenty-first century. Many years later, the *Wyeth Codex* was spread through the ville network by Mohandas Lakesh Singh as a means of fomenting dissent against the authority of the baronial oligarchy.

Due to his actions, the document became linked with rumors of the Preservationists, the name given by the barons to a suspected underground resistance group operating in the villes. The Preservationists were alleged to be an elite group of historians who possessed a greater understanding of "true" history of the pre- and postnukecaust world. The Preservationists were, in fact, a fiction created by Lakesh as an adversary to occupy the attention of the Magistrate Divisions and the barons, while the real insurrectionist work proceeded elsewhere.

Although the *Codex* contained recollections of adventures and wanderings, it dealt in the main with Dr. Wyeth's observations, speculations and theories about the environmental conditions of postnukecaust America. It was the only real source for information about places and people of the previous century, despite the fact the journal didn't often go into great detail. In fact, some of the data was maddeningly brief.

A line of concentration appeared at the bridge of Brigid's nose as she brought an image of the document to the forefront of her mind and visualized the appropriate entry. Her lips creased in a frown. "Dr. Wyeth did visit here, but as usual, she kept her descriptions cut to the bone. She mentioned that a group of women mutants lived here in the ruins, even though she admits the term 'mutant' might be inaccurate. The women were called Midnites, and they hated men with a vengeance. They used them only to reproduce and apparently castrated them when their function was fulfilled.''

Kane glanced at the man being treated by DeFore and winced. ''So it's safe to assume this poor bastard was of no more use to them.''

Brigid hesitated and said, ''There's something else.''

Grant cast her a glance full of weary exasperation. ''You mean this gets better?''

She shook her head. ''According to the *Codex,* the Midnites were anthrophagists.''

Seeing the blank looks on the faces of Kane and Grant, Brigid declared, ''Cannibals.''

Kane sighed. ''You could have said so in the first place.''

''It's been at least a hundred years since the Wyeth woman was here,'' Grant argued. ''Surely the Palladiumville Magistrate Division cleaned out this place during the Program of Unification.''

The unification program of the previous century consolidated the continent-spanning network of baronies that arose from the chaos of postnuke America. Although each of the nine villes shared superficial similarities in appearance and government, they were very different from one another, depending upon the whims of the individual ruling baron. The one link they all shared were the Unity Through Action posters stored away like holy texts within the records of all villes. The illustrations were very simple—line drawings of two hands clasping each other, joined at the wrist by a chain.

More than ninety years previous, Unity Through Action was the rallying cry that had spread across the Deathlands by word of mouth and proof of deed. The long-forgotten trust in any form of government had been reawakened, generations after the survivors of the nuclear war had lived through the deadly legacy of politics and the suicidal decisions made by elected officials.

Unity Through Action offered a solution to the constant states of worry and fear—join the unification program and never worry or fear or think again. Humanity was responsible for the arrival of Judgment Day, and it had to accept that responsibility before a truly utopian age could be ushered in. All humankind had to do to earn this utopia was follow the rules, be obedient and be fed and clothed. And accept the new order without question.

For most of the men and women who lived in the villes and the surrounding territories, that was enough, more than enough. Long sought-after dreams of peace and safety had at last been transformed into reality. Of course, fleeting dreams of personal freedom were lost in the exchange, but such aspirations were nothing but childish illusions.

The legions of black-armored Magistrates made doubly certain that everyone realized dreams of liberty were illusions. After skydark the wastelands of America were up for grabs, and as usual, power was the key. Pioneers who tried to rebuild found themselves either shoved off their lands or facing bandits who killed with no pretense of ethical or moral right.

The alternatives were few; one was to live the life of a nomad or join the marauding wolf packs or set up robber baronies. Whatever option was chosen, lives tended to be brutal and short. The blood that had splattered the pages of America's frontier history was a mere sprinkling compared to the crimson tide that flooded postnuke America. It had taken the nine barons and the unified villes to clean it up the only way it could be cleaned up—with an iron-fisted rule.

The Magistrates were formed as a complex police machine that demanded instant obedience to its edicts and to which there was no possible protest. Over the past ninety years, both the oligarchy of barons and the Mags who served them had taken on a fearful, almost legendary aspect. For most of their adult lives, both Kane and Grant had been part of that legend, cogs in a merciless machine. Now, over the past two years, they had done their very best to not just dismantle the machine, but to utterly destroy it and scatter the pieces to the four corners of the world,

Brigid nodded thoughtfully in response to Grant's objection. "That's true enough. Baron Palladium wouldn't allow a cult like the Midnites to survive— providing he knew they existed. A century *is* an awfully long time for a cult like that to survive. They may not have had anything at all to do with that man's condition."

DeFore gently turned the man's head to the left, and metal glinted dully on the side of his neck. A small circular body, gleaming like brushed aluminum, was attached to his mastoid bone. From it stretched ten tiny wires, like spider legs made of jointed alloy, each one tipped with a curving claw. Each of the claws appeared deeply embedded in the man's flesh.

"What the hell is that thing?" the medic demanded of no one in particular.

Kane, Grant and Brigid all leaned forward to get a better look. "I never saw anything like it," Grant murmured. He cast a questioning glance toward Brigid.

"Don't look at me," she declared. "For every one thing I know about, there about twenty things I *don't* know about."

The corners of Kane's mouth quirked in a smile. "I always figured that...I just never figured to hear you admit it."

Brigid matched his smile with a rueful one of her own. "And for every one bit ignorance I'll admit to, there are about a dozen I won't."

Gingerly, DeFore touched the bulbous silver body, then closed a thumb and forefinger around it. She pulled experimentally. The skin at the end of the metal claws stretched upward, but she wasn't able to detach it.

Tension began coiling in the pit of Kane's belly like a length of rope and he said curtly, "Leave it alone. For all we know, it's an explosive. Fooling around with it could get us all killed."

Brigid eyed the contrivance closely. "A tracking device, maybe?"

Grant snorted. "Hell, it could be jewelry, some kind of Chi-town fashion statement."

DeFore lifted her face and gazed at him levelly, trying to tell from his expression if his suggestion was serious or in jest.

Kane opened his mouth to speak when the heart of the storm struck the building broadside like a wrecking ball. Wind-driven sheets of corrosive rain mixed with tiny fragments of hail poured through the open roof. The walls trembled as the wind howled eerily overhead. Flakes of ancient mortar sifted down.

DeFore made the attempt to tug the semiconscious man closer to the wall. He moaned and began to struggle. His eyes flew open and he stared at DeFore without really seeing her.

"Sin!" he shrieked, his voice all but inaudible over the sound of the storm. "I've already confessed! You've excised my sin! Now stay away from me!" He waved blistered, discolored hands, and his fever-bright eyes glared into her own with a fierce blend of hatred and terror.

His mouth convulsed and he screamed, as though he were seeing something too horrible to bear. Flailing the air with his arms, his right elbow struck the medic on the chin and knocked her back on her heels. He lunged to his feet, arms windmilling. Grant reached for him but managed only to latch on to a scrap of sleeve.

It ripped loose in Grant's hand, and the burned man plunged out onto the debris-scattered floor, apparently oblivious to the corrosive touch of the rain on his exposed flesh. He made a shambling dash to the corridor on the opposite side and sprinted into it, swallowed by the shadows.

DeFore rose to her feet and made a motion to follow him, but Brigid thrust out an arm and pressed her back against the wall. "Let him go," she shouted into the medic's ear. "We'll try to find him after the storm passes."

DeFore briefly strained against Brigid, then subsided, nodding in reluctant agreement. Kane pressed up against the wall hard, trying to keep the toes of his boots from being spattered and possibly ruined. The stink of acid wasn't quite as strong now, but he didn't care to find out just how diluted the mixture might be. He was more concerned about the way the walls quivered and how the roar of the wind continued to rise, not abate.

He watched as the swirling dirty water flooded the littered floor, with bits of flotsam bobbing on the rippling surface. As he gazed at the spreading puddle, Kane realized he was tired. The long overland trek from the Montana mountain range that concealed the Cerberus redoubt had been thankfully free of any violent incidents. It had been a bore, in fact. But now the tedium seemed to be over and when situations ended in the Outlands, they ended abruptly and in a big way.

Suddenly he heard a thunderous cataract of noise and felt the wall at his back shudder brutally. Turning, he saw a network of black cracks spreading over the concrete facade. The wall bulged inward, then split open, fragments of concrete and brick bursting from it in a spray. It seemed to totter, then lean inward. Shouting a warning, his words lost in the raging violence of the storm, Kane latched on to Brigid's and DeFore's wrists and pulled them away from the crumbling wall.

They had no choice but to back out into the deluge. Nearly half the wall toppled over and missed burying Grant by a fractional margin. Even as the blocks tumbled down, Kane saw the funneled top of the tornado through the open roof. Spinning and roaring like a great whirlpool, the black funnel cloud looked to be nearly an eighth of a mile across and less than that in proximity to them. As Kane stared at it through the beads of water dancing on the lenses of his sunglasses, he saw a ribbon of bricks being sucked up into the cone and then spit out on all sides. They smashed down all around like artillery shells sending up geysers of tainted water.

"Move!" Kane bellowed at the top of his lungs, but he could hardly hear his own voice and he knew it would was inaudible even to DeFore and Brigid, who stood beside him.

Heeling around, he dashed for the opening of the corridor on the far side of the open piazza. He splashed through the standing water, feeling a slow acidic burn on his hands and cheeks. He glanced quickly over his shoulder and saw his companions following him.

Kane sprinted into the corridor, glancing swiftly from left to right. It wasn't particularly wide, and water leaked through in many places. He rushed deep into the murk, not wasting time to fumble for his Nighthawk microlight. The specially treated lenses of his Mag-issue glasses allowed him to see clearly in deep shadow for approximately ten feet, as long there was any kind of light source. Even so, ancient heaps of garbage formed strange shapes, and he flinched from them more than once.

The howl of the wind became a deafening locomotive roar, so loud he felt the vibration in the marrow of his bones. He looked over his shoulder, past his companions, and saw the twister. It was a solid cone of black, bellowing fury, a screaming explosive force that ripped up, then flung away anything not deeply anchored. Dust, rocks, leaves, vines, small squealing things—all the accumulated violence of the elements landed heavily in the open piazza with the smashing force of a hundred battering rams.

The four people fell flat to the wet corridor floor and clung to one another for several terrifying seconds. Kane gritted his teeth as the air pressure against his eardrums rose and fell sharply. Then the blast of wind and debris passed over them, and it was calm again except for the ominously pelting rain.

Brigid pushed herself to her elbows. "Is everybody all right?"

When she received monosyllabic responses, she crawled forward. "Let's go deeper before the next cyclone gets here."

Kane looked down the dark passageway and hesitated. "I'll take point."

Brigid had lost her cap. Pushing her wet, heavy hair onto her back, she said impatiently, "We'll both do it."

The four people rose to their feet just as the air once more filled with a whistling roar. A giant's hand seemed to snatch at them, wrenching them backward toward the piazza. Bracing their legs, they bent almost double as they fought the powerful suction. The wind was like a giant scoop that tried to drag them from their shelter and into the hungry maw of the twister.

When the drag on their bodies lessened, Kane, Brigid, Grant and DeFore raced deeper into the passageway. Brigid and Kane were several yards ahead of their two companions, and when they heard another respite from the storm, they slowed their pace.

The floor pitched downward, slanting into a dark stairwell. Kane patted his pockets for his flashlight, but before he found it, an amber beam shone from Brigid's hand. Casting the rod of luminescence over the concrete steps, she called over her shoulder to Grant and DeFore, "Let's check this out."

She and Kane carefully descended the stairs, and he repressed a sigh of relief when they ended after only ten feet or so. Another black passageway yawned before them. "I think we've found the way to the basement," she said. "It'll probably be safe enough to ride out the storm down here."

Kane turned to call up to Grant and DeFore when he heard a dull thumping from behind the right-hand wall. The pounding swiftly increased in volume. Little fragments of mortar jumped from the seams.

Grant heard it, too, "What the hell is that noise?" he shouted.

Kane glanced up the short stairway and saw a steady stream of water trickling from a crack in the ceiling at the midway point. Before he could say or do anything, the crack widened and fist-sized pieces of concrete flaked off at the edges and fell to the steps. The trickle became a gush, and Kane stepped backward to avoid being doused. The water didn't smell contaminated, but he didn't care to be splashed.

Then he heard the long, keening blast of the wind again. The air seemed filled with breaking sounds, followed by a long ripping noise that made Kane think the very fabric of reality was being torn to pieces. It stunned his mind and froze him in his tracks.

As the wail rose to a near deafening level, he saw how the gush of water turned into a foaming torrent. A large section of the ceiling collapsed inward. Kane barely managed to push Brigid backward before a slab of concrete crashed down less than six inches from his toes. A solid column of water thundered out of the ceiling, crested over him and smashed him off his feet.

He was only dimly aware of slamming into Brigid and then both of them were carried away by the deluge. Tons of water and rubble poured through the collapsed ceiling, tumbling them head over heels.

Kane tried to hang on to something, sought to grab Brigid, but he was completely submerged by a tidal wave shooting down the dark passageway. Their bodies were buffeted and beaten by the merciless pressure of the water's flow.

Kane forced his body to relax and go limp, a conditioned response from his Mag training. As he was catapulted along, he struck a hard, unyielding object with his right hip and he grunted involuntarily, sucking in a mouthful of foul, muddy water.

Struggling to control the gag reflex, he swallowed the water lest he draw it into his lungs. He flailed out with his arms, fighting the turbulence, trying blindly to check or even slow his headlong plummet.

Kane strained to lift his head above the roiling, rushing surface. "Baptiste!" he shouted, and noted how the echo of his voice was short. The crown of his cap scraped against the roof of the passageway.

A sweeping undertow tangled his legs together and his body dropped vertically. He realized the flood had carried him to a drop-off, perhaps another, deeper stairwell. He didn't have much time to contemplate how far he might plunge.

He struck a wall of smooth stone with his head, and the roar of the torrent faded to a faint burbling.

Chapter 3

Brigid stayed beneath the surface of the floodwaters until the pounding of blood in her temples and the fire in her lungs became intolerable. She kicked upward, dismayed by how much effort it required. Her head broke the surface, and she fought the impulse to suck in great lungfuls of air for fear of inhaling water.

The current carried her around a bend, where the passageway narrowed into a flume. She felt her body whipped forward, hurled faster and faster. Through her water-occluded vision, she glimpsed some sort light, gleaming with a pallid glow ahead of her. Her groping hands slapped around what felt like a length of pipe, anchored firmly in the concrete.

She clung to it for what seemed like a long time, head craned back, inhaling air through her nostrils, lips compressed against the water foaming and splashing against her face. Her muscles ached with the strain of resisting the ferocious, incessant drag of the floodwaters. Her fingers lost all feeling, then the numbness crept into her forearms. Finally, her grip loosened and the current snatched her away from the pipe.

She managed to keep her head above the surface for a few moments. Then, the direction of the torrent went from horizontal to vertical and she fell feetfirst, caught in the midst of a waterfall. Frantically, Brigid twisted her body to one side, kicking with her feet, clawing handfuls of water aside. She flailed, lungs aching as she tried to check her plunge into the roaring cataract.

It seemed that she fell only a few feet before the soles of her boots hit the bottom. Her knees were jacked up into her midriff by the impact, which drove what little air remained in her lungs out through her mouth in a stream of bubbles.

The water was a brownish-green murk. She had no idea where the surface lay, and she felt a fear she had hoped she would never experience again. Months before she had nearly drowned in the Irish Sea and since that day she had developed a morbid terror, almost a phobia, of dying by water.

Before her fear became panic, she became aware that the movement of the floodwaters had eased. They slowed and became more gentle. Brigid kicked hard, hoping she was moving in the right direction. Her lungs felt as if they would burst any second. Then her head rose above the roiling surface, and she gasped in great shuddering mouthfuls of air.

After the cataract, it was like floating in a peaceful

but brackish pond. Brigid was conscious of space around and above her, as is if she were bobbing in a large swimming pool. Blinking hard, she saw a glimmer of light and she stroked toward it. She realized she was outside, in a channel of some sort, with curving concrete walls that sloped upward nearly twenty feet. She felt fairly certain it was a storm sewer. The water was filled with debris. A thick layer of torn foliage and even the bloated bodies of several dead rats floated on the surface.

The water continued rushing around her, apparently pouring into a drain somewhere far ahead. The channel curved sharply a hundred yards ahead her. As the level steadily dropped, Brigid felt solid footing beneath her boots and she stood. The water reached only to her chest and dropped several more inches in the few moments she stood there, filling her oxygen-deprived lungs with air. She waded slowly toward the nearest wall. By the time she reached its base, the water was barely knee-deep. A portion of the bulwark was shattered, with large chunks of concrete tumbling down into the sewer. Reinforcing rods protruded from the broken pile of stone like rusty, gnarled fingers.

Fingering the water from her eyes, Brigid tilted her head back to scan the overcast green-hued sky. The roar of the storm diminished as if a monstrous locomotive were departing. Even the rain squalls were tapering off.

Brigid struggled up the side of the channel, too exhausted to focus on anything other than reaching the top. Her boots slipped a time or two on the muck-slimed slabs, but her single-minded ascent didn't falter. When she reached the top, she half fell, half lay down, her respiration coming in labored pants.

As she lay there, she took stock of herself, gingerly checking her limbs for broken bones or more severe injuries. She realized that either an overfilled river or even a reservoir had caused the storm surge, and she also understood she was more than fortunate to have survived—she was blessed.

After a moment, she pushed herself into a sitting position and glanced up at the dark rectangular outline of a span of concrete stretching above her. She recognized it as a footbridge, probably an old maintenance accessway. Patting herself down, she found her trans-comm unit and rad counter were missing, as well as the Iver Johnson autoblaster in its belt slide holster. Her spectacles were still safe in her breast pocket, and her chron was still strapped around her wrist, but they were no substitute for a gun.

Kane had cautioned her more than once to carry her side arm in a proper holster, but in her opinion he should have been satisfied she agreed to wear a blaster at all. Her antipathy toward guns had been a minor but continuing point of contention between them for almost two years. At least her Sykes-Fairbairn commando dagger was still securely sheathed at the small of her back.

Brigid made herself stand, conscious of an uncomfortable tingling in her extremities. Her legs and arms ached fiercely, and the left side of her rib cage felt sore and bruised. A sharp pain stabbed into the calf of her right leg, letting her know she had strained a tendon. She had gotten off lucky, though. She hadn't struck her head and possibly exacerbated the injury that had put her in a days-long coma a few months before. And at least the floodwaters had rinsed off the acid-rain residue so she didn't have to worry about burns or her clothes rotting off her body.

Wringing out her sodden, mud-clotted hair and raking it away from her face, Brigid studied the bridge ramp arching overhead. Beyond it, to the right, she saw a metal ladder stretching up from the top of the channel to the bottom of the bridge.

Cupping her hands around her mouth, she called, "Kane!" Her voice sounded hoarse and weak, so she cleared her throat, inhaled a deep breath and shouted again, *"Kane!"*

The word echoed hollowly and eerily, but there was no response. She called for DeFore and Grant, but received no answering hail. She hoped they had avoided being swept away by the flood, but since they occupied higher ground than either she or

Kane, she assumed they had. Still, she had no idea how far she had been washed away from them.

Tottering, moving carefully at first to favor her aching leg, Brigid walked toward the ladder, despising the way her boots made squishing sounds with every step. She also despised the way mounting waves of fear over the fates of her friends, particularly Kane, battered at her reason. She reminded herself how Kane had outmaneuvered, ducked and dodged what seemed like certain death many times.

As for Domi, as long as she remained buttoned up inside the Sandcat, she was sure the girl was safe. Although Domi occasionally displayed nitwit tendencies, she had a strong sense of self-preservation to go along with it, so it was doubtful she was traipsing through the ruins when the stormfront arrived. Wryly, Brigid thought it would be wasted effort to end all wasted efforts if they'd traveled so far to find out why Domi hadn't died only to learn she'd been killed by the weather.

A few months ago, during the bloody battle among the forces of three barons to occupy Area 51, Domi had apparently perished, literally vaporized in the detonation of an implode grenade. As heartbreaking as the effort was, Brigid forced herself to come to terms with the girl's death. Even Grant seemed to accept it. Only Kane expressed doubt, but he couldn't explain why.

Kane tried very hard to verbalize why he couldn't

accept the fact Domi was truly dead. Brigid suggested he was in a form of denial, but he pointed out that implode grens didn't usually vaporize targets without leaving some trace—a spattering of blood, a scrap of bone, a hank of hair.

A suspicion lurked at the back of his mind that what he had seen, what all of them had seen, wasn't Domi dying. He was haunted by a subliminal afterimage of an object or movement at the very instant of detonation bobbed at the fringes of his memory, but his conscious mind couldn't analyze it.

On a more visceral level, Domi's death simply *felt* wrong, as if it weren't supposed to have happened. It was an error, a miscalculation like the alternate event horizon that Lakesh postulated had set into motion the events leading to the nukecaust.

It turned out Kane's suspicions and his analogy to the an alternate event horizon both had a foundation in reality. They found out Domi hadn't been killed—she had been time-trawled, apparently by Operation Chronos technology, which focused on the mechanics of time travel.

According to Lakesh, who was the overseer of Project Cerberus, the Totality Concept's research projects were far-flung and involved many nations and just as many secret societies. Although the Totality Concept scientists worked on some remarkable projects, the projects were rarely coordinated. But then, in 1989, Lakesh conducted the first successful long-distance matter transfer of a living subject through the quantum interphase inducers, colloquially known as gateways. That initial success was reproduced many times, and in the process the gateways were improved and modified. Project Cerberus, once it was moved to Redoubt Bravo in Montana's Bitterroot mountain range, began to mass-produce the mat-trans units, designing them in modular form so they could be shipped and assembled elsewhere.

The technicians of Operation Chronos used the mat-trans breakthroughs of Project Cerberus to spin off their own innovations and achieve their own successes. One such Operation Chronos practice was known as "temporal peeping," the ability to peer through a gap in the chronon structure into a future date.

Regardless of the relative truth of Lakesh's story—and Brigid had very little reason to doubt him—it was obvious Domi herself had been "trawled," but by an unknown agency and for a purpose still unrevealed. All they knew was where the action had been engineered.

A few months before, while pursuing another objective entirely, Brigid, Kane and Grant had come across an installation on one of the Western Isles. The facility had apparently housed a major component of Operation Chronos. There was something ominous about all of the Western Isles and this one, named Thunder Isle by its nearest neighbors, the inhabitants of New Edo, was extremely disturbing. According to what they had been told by the ruler of New Edo, Lord Takaun, a cyclical phenomenon occurred on the island. Lightning seemed to strike up, accompanied by sounds like thunder, even if the weather was clear. Takaun had no explanation for it, but he knew that on the heels of the phenomenon often came incursions of what the more impressionable New Edoans claimed were demons. Brigid was shown the corpse of one such demon, and she tentatively identified it as a Dryosaurus, a man-sized dinosaur.

She was able to identify other artifacts found on the shores of Thunder Isle—a helmet from the era of the conquistadors and a stone spearhead that resembled a Folsom point, so named for Folsom, New Mexico, the archaeological site where the first one was found. It was evidence of a prehistoric culture many thousands of years old.

According to Takaun, the phenomena had been very sporadic for the past five years, occurring only a few times. Recently, a new cycle had begun and it was happening with far greater regularity.

When she, Grant and Kane went to Thunder Isle, all of them glimpsed another dinosaur, far larger and more vicious than the Dryosaur. In fact, it killed a group of Magistrates they had been tracking.

Once inside the installation, they found video evidence that Domi had been trawled at the precise instant before she was swallowed by the full lethal fury of the grenade, and then suspended in a noncorporeal matrix. Brigid activated the instruments that retrieved the girl, but she had no recollection whatsoever of what occurred. They themselves saw no one in the installation, but it showed signs of recent habitation.

All of them had pondered the mystery during the intervening months, but they could only speculate. Then, less than ten days ago, the sensor link at the Cerberus redoubt showed activity in the gateway unit in Redoubt Echo, which in itself wasn't unusual. Over the past year the Cerberus network had registered an unprecedented volume of mat-trans traffic. Most of it was due to the concerted search for the renegades from Cobaltville, but there had also been the appearance of anomalous activities, signatures of jump lines that could not be traced back to their origin points.

Certainly, there were any number of unindexed and mass-produced modular gateway units. Years ago, when Lakesh had used Baron Cobalt's trust in him to covertly reactivate the Cerberus redoubt, he had seen to it that the facility was listed as irretrievably unsalvageable on all ville records. He also had altered the modulations of the mat-trans gateway so the transmissions were untraceable, at least by conventional means. However, the gateway in Redoubt

Echo wasn't anomalous. The unit was an indexed part of the Cerberus network, and Lakesh believed the activity was connected to Operation Chronos— primarily because Chronos had been headquartered in a subterranean facility in Chicago, at least for a time.

Brigid reached the ladder and before she began climbing it, she called Kane's name several times. After waiting for a response and not receiving one, she slowly pulled herself up the rust-eaten rungs, wincing at the twinge of pain in her left side, an indication of strained or even ruptured intercostal cartilage in her rib cage. The ladder led to the iron circle of a manhole cover at the underside of the bridge. When she reached it, she hooked her right arm over the top rung and pushed up against the thick metal disk with her left. It didn't budge.

Gritting her teeth, she pressed her shoulder against it, trying not to shove too hard because she couldn't guess what lay on the other side. Rust showered down from the rim, stinging her eyes and coating her wet hair with a fine powder. Finally, the heavy cover shifted and by levering with her legs, she managed to shoulder it aside with a prolonged grinding noise.

Brigid struggled up, panting from the exertion, and crawled out onto the surface of the walkway. To her left, the bridge disappeared into a round tunnel with the number 88 stenciled above it in black paint. To her right, it stretched into an open alley-way. Beyond that, she was able to make out a street.

The wind still gusted intermittently but power-fully, and she had to lean into it. As she climbed to her feet, a blur of movement caught her eye from the mouth of the tunnel and she pivoted toward it, reaching for the dagger at her back. She froze in surprise as a tall figure stepped from the shadows cast by the tunnel overhang.

It was a woman, judging by the billowing cloud of wind-whipped gray hair that swirled around the bony mask of her face. Brigid stared into the ex-pressionless ice-blue eyes of the woman before her. She became aware of her trembling hands, her thumping heart and the sour taste of fear in her sud-denly dry mouth.

The woman was dressed in a billowing black robe, the wind plucking at the frayed hem and the belled sleeves. She didn't speak or even make any motion to leave the tunnel. She merely stared un-blinkingly at Brigid with no apparent emotion in her cold eyes. Brigid checked the movement to draw her knife and returned the stare, wondering briefly if the woman lived in the access tunnels of the city and was afraid to step out even into overcast daylight.

Brigid opened her mouth to voice a greeting, but a preternatural thrill suddenly tickled the buttons of her spine, causing her shoulders to quiver in a shud-der. Biting back a curse, she whirled swiftly. Four dark figures stood at the end of the bridge, blocking her way to the alley.

They were tall, lean men, as gaunt as cadavers. Two of them appeared taller even than Grant. From throat to fingertip to heel they were clad in one-piece black leathery garments that fitted as tightly as doeskin gloves. Even their heads were hooded in tight black cowls. They bore odd devices in their hands, rods of a sleek, gleaming black alloy more than two feet long. They were tipped with spherical knobs of a dull, silvery metal, slightly smaller than fowl's eggs.

It was their faces that struck into her heart a sudden spasm of terror—or rather their lack of faces. Beneath the tight-fitting black cowls, their visages were smooth, featureless ovals.

Chapter 4

Brigid reacted with the speed born of an antipathy to having anything that remotely resembled a weapon pointed at her. She lunged toward the raised side of the ramp, whipping the dagger from its sheath in the same swift motion.

Almost at the same time, a rod in the hand of one of the black, faceless figures emitted small click, as if a piece of wire had broken inside of it. Light glinted dully from the round object that sprang from the end of the rod. Brigid caught a brief glimpse of spindly silver spider legs unfolding as it flashed by her head, missing her by a finger's width.

The little device zipped over the old woman's right shoulder and disappeared into the gloom of the tunnel behind her. No flicker of emotion disturbed her calm, expressionless face. Fisting the Sykes-Fairbairn knife, Brigid bounded toward her, snaking an arm around her wattled neck and positioning the point of her knife over the woman's carotid artery. She felt a little guilty about using an elderly woman as a hostage and a shield, but this was a matter of survival, not a matter of ethics.

One of the black-clad men—Brigid assumed they were men, since she saw no bulges characteristic of femininity—extended his slender rod before him. Brigid moved her dagger so the tapered tip dug into the old woman's flesh but didn't break it. She cried out in an unfamiliar tongue, speaking in a deep, harsh, uninflected voice. The faceless man halted immediately and lowered his baton.

"Thank you," Brigid said quietly into her hostage's ear. "Now tell me who you and your friends are."

The old woman's lips barely moved. Her reply sounded like the rustle of old parchment, and the words were blurred by an unidentifiable accent. "I am Megaera."

The name rang a distant chord of recognition within Brigid's memory, but she didn't want to spare her attention from the men in black and the old woman to flip through her mental index file. "My name is Brigid Baptiste. I mean you no harm."

"I know that. We mean you no harm, either."

"Then why attack me?" When Megaera didn't immediately reply, Brigid added, "You're not one the Midnites, are you?"

Megaera sighed as if bored. "Your words are meaningless."

Brigid gave the gaunt, faceless men a swift visual examination. With a twinge of embarrassment she realized they did indeed have faces, but their features were completely concealed by masks. The masks were delicately shaped to closely fit long-jawed, narrow faces from hairline to chin. But although the masks bore the contours of human faces, they were modeled without any features whatsoever. They only presented blank ovals of some sleek, smooth substance. The effect was very eerie and she wondered how they could possibly see.

"We met a man who had been mutilated," Brigid said, a sharp note entering her tone. "He was castrated and he wore one of those little spiders that your friends shot at me. Do you expect me to believe you know nothing about that?"

"I expect nothing from you," Megaera answered with the same bone-chilling serenity. "But I do know everything about it."

"Then perhaps you'll share what you know."

Megaera's slight shoulders lifted in an attempt at a shrug. "He was a sinner. A fornicator. When he confessed his sins, the appropriate justice was meted out, no more, no less."

Brigid suddenly recalled why the woman's name was familiar and significant. Her flesh crawled at the realization. In ancient Greek mythology, Megaera was a Fury, one of three sisters charged by the gods to pursue sinners on Earth. They were inexorable and relentless in their dispensation of justice. She recalled a bit of verse about them: "Not even the sun will transgress his orbit lest the Furies, the ministers of justice, overtake him."

Eyeing the black, featureless figures, Brigid asked with a forced calm, "Are your sisters Tisiphone and Alecto among them?"

Megaera's response was coldly formal. "They are my Furies, as I said."

"So you did." Brigid slowly removed the point of her blade from the woman's neck. "Tell them to drop their weapons and I'll be on my way."

"They are not weapons."

"What are they, then?"

"The deliverer of the oubolus."

Brigid felt a frown tugging at the corners of her mouth. She found herself very interested despite the circumstances. "As I recall, the oubolus is the collective name for the payment given by souls on their way to the underworld."

"Yes. If payment is not given to Charon, the ferryman for passage across the River Acheron, a soul must wander the riverbank throughout eternity."

"You're really playing mix and match with your myths," Brigid stated. "I think I'm starting to get this—you judge the souls and then provide the payment for their final destination in the afterlife. That's pretty considerate."

"You cannot have one without the other," Megaera said tersely.

"So I've heard. I don't care what you call those sticks, I want them dropped."

"Your wants and your needs are of no importance to me. Only your sins."

"I don't have the time to confess them—" From the tunnel at her back came a faraway click and she felt a weight strike her between the shoulder blades.

Brigid cursed in fear and anger and began to spin. She barely noticed Megaera's right hand dip into the belled sleeve of her left arm. Before Brigid completed her turn, agonizing pain lanced through her torso, impaling her from back to front. It was so sudden and so overwhelming she couldn't even scream. Breath seizing in her lungs, she fell to her hands and knees. She was dimly aware of something crawling up her back, making a path through her hair, over the collar of her shirt and then she felt tiny pinpricks on the left side of her neck.

The pain in her body ebbed. Gasping, she looked up at Megaera standing over her, her face still expressionless. A metal band studded with what appeared to be opals encircled her bony left wrist. The index finger of her right hand hovered over one of the little gems. Brigid instantly knew the wristband controlled the silver spider clinging to her neck. Pressing the buttons on the cuff activated it and sent jolts of voltage to scramble the nervous system.

A black, masked figure stepped close, bending to gather a handful of Brigid's hair. He began dragging her to her feet. The commando dagger was still gripped in her fist and when she achieved a half-standing posture she swung it at the man in a fast backhand slash.

It was a lucky stroke. The blade cut through his long neck just under the right hinge of his jaw, between the rim of the mask and the high collar of his black bodysuit. It laid open his flesh in a clean incision. Amid a jetting of blood, the gaunt figure uttered a gargling groan and staggered backward, clapping his hands over the pulsing wound. The back of his hips struck the raised side of the bridge, and he toppled over it, plunging headfirst into the shallow waters of the channel. Brigid heard a distant splash.

Megaera shrilled angry, incomprehensible words and with a thumb pressed on an opal. Fiery pain scorched its way along Brigid's nervous system like a flood of molten lava. She felt her muscles lock and spasm, and her back arched. The knife dropped from her fingers, chiming dully on the surface of the ramp. She clawed at the air and then fell facedown, a bundle of loose limbs.

Megaera maintained her thumb's pressure on the gem. Brigid didn't lose consciousness, but the agony was so intense she prayed she would. The pain was like nothing she had ever felt before. It seemed to start in an electric field completely outside of her body, then stabbed like a hundred flaming arrows into the muscles, where it burrowed through the tissue and then methodically shredded the nervous system.

Worse than the agony was the sensation of helplessness, of knowing she could do nothing to escape it. She could not twist or turn or even scream.

Then the pain seeped away, but she could do nothing but quiver and twitch. The burning anguish left her, but all her nerve endings crawled and rippled with the tactile memory of what had been inflicted on them. She tried to speak, but the words were garbled, meaningless noises. Above her she heard Megaera speak sharply in the unidentifiable language. She opened her eyes and at first saw nothing.

Brigid felt a surge of panic, wondering if she had been struck blind, but when she shifted her head, she glimpsed the dirty, frayed hem of Megaera's robe. She stirred, and the motion sent a hot bore of pain drilling through her back to her chest. Sweat broke out on her forehead. Her mouth was dirt dry, she felt feverish and nausea was a clawed beast trying to tear its way out of her stomach.

Gritting her teeth, she lay quietly, listening to the slow, steady thud of her heart. Then the old woman stepped into her line of vision, towering over her like a bony vulture. Her deeply creased face was still set in a placid mask, as if she took no delight or even interest in torture. Reaching down, she plucked the dagger from the ground and then negligently tossed it over the side of the bridge.

Anger replaced the fear in Brigid's mind, and she tried to get to her hands and knees but her body reacted in a violent and disjointed spasm. Breathing raggedly, she sprawled on the ramp. Her motor centers seemed to have short circuited, and she prayed the damage wasn't permanent. Shadows shifted around her, and she felt hands close around her arms and legs, lifting her up.

Head lolling limply on her neck, she could do nothing but allow the black-clad men to pull her to her feet. Two of them took an arm and a wrist, clamping down firmly with their strong fingers and hands. They were surprisingly powerful, she felt as if her limbs were in the grip of mighty steel talons. She didn't bother to struggle or prevent the other Fury from swiftly searching her. She conserved her energy, hoping her strength would soon return.

The Furies dragged her along the bridge, the toes of her boots scraping against the concrete. She was a little surprised that they didn't take her into the tunnel. Following a harsh burst of words from Megaera, they manhandled her toward the alley.

Brigid replayed the old woman's vocalizations in her mind, trying to match it to a language or dialect she had heard before. Although she spoke Russian, a smattering of Chinese, German, Japanese and even Lakota, the tongue of the Sioux Indians, she didn't recognize what Megaera spoke as a language. It sounded like gibberish, a succession of noises that had meaning only to her and her Furies.

Control of her limbs returned slowly to Brigid. She tried three times before she finally got her legs under her and made them move, with only a little support from the faceless men. She kept her relief from registering on her face. Megaera trailed along behind them as the Furies lock-stepped Brigid through the rubbish-strewed alley.

She tried to reach up and touch the little silver spider attached her neck, but Megaera uttered a sound between an admonishing cluck and a threatening hiss and the Furies tightened their grips on her arms, wrenching them up behind her back in hammerlocks. The pain was a pinch in comparison to what Megaera had inflicted upon her, and she kept her face composed. During her years as an archivist, Brigid had perfected a poker face and she wore it now.

It wasn't as if she weren't frightened, but over the past two years she had come to accept risk as a part of her way of life, taking chances so that others might find the ground beneath their feet a little more secure. She didn't consider her attitude idealism but simple pragmatism. If she had learned anything from her association with Kane, Grant and Domi, it was to regard death as a part of the challenge of existence, a fact that every man and woman had to face eventually.

She would accept it without humiliating herself if it came as a result of her efforts to remove the yokes of the baronies from the collective necks of humanity. She never spoke of it, certainly not to the cynical Kane, but she had privately vowed to make the future a better, cleaner place than either the past or the present.

Once they were out on the street, the Furies marched her heedlessly through puddles and mud. The mounds of dirt and rubble on either side of the avenue had been leached over the years by the elements, so they had spread, smothering the pavements and sidewalks and making a new, mulchy floor for the dead city. Plants grew almost everywhere, but they looked unhealthy and stunted.

As they marched through the concrete gullies of overgrown and blackened bricks, they passed the remains of several automobiles. The bodywork had long ago been stripped bare of paint and was a mass of flaking rust. Wheelless axles were buried deep in the muck, and raised hoods revealed missing engine blocks. Brigid, who had rarely ventured out of the sheltering walls of Cobaltville, recognized the work of scavengers and felt a twinge of anger. When the survivors of the nukecaust and their descendants tried to build enclaves of civilization around which a new human society could rally, they inevitably failed. There were only so many people in the world, and few of these made either good pioneers or settlers.

It was far easier to wander, to lead the lives of nomads and scavengers, digging out Stockpiles, caches of tools, weapons and technology laid down by the predark government as part of the COG, the predark Continuity of Government program, and building a power base on what was salvaged.

Towering over the street was an elevated train track, but most of its metal rails and treated timbers had been taken, probably a century or more before. Glass seemed to have been ignored by most of the scavengers, probably because it existed only in shattered pieces in darkened windows.

Several buildings seemed to have survived almost intact, and one of them appeared to be a cathedral. At first glance Brigid judged it to be older than most of the blighted surrounding structures but it was still wounded by time and the elements. The roof was in disrepair, but its steepled bell tower still pointed tirelessly at the sky, filling now with regathering rain clouds. The bell could still be seen within the cupola, and it might even be able to ring.

The black-clad Furies passed the church without giving it a glance. They escorted Brigid through an empty lot overgrown with tangles of shrubbery, along a path between scraggly hedgerows that had been beaten down by the passage of many feet over many years. On the far side of the lot rose a collection of flat-roofed brick structures, all built around a low white dome fashioned from thick masonry.

Set in a clearing along a lakefront, the entire compound was half swallowed by creepers and twisting vines. Only the dome looked as if it had tried to put up a fight against the foliage. Apart from a jagged crack arching across one side of it, the dome had remained almost intact. The sign proclaimed it to be the Lake District Central Filtration Plant, even though most of the letters were shrouded by a blanket of greenery.

Brigid sourly but silently noted that if nothing else, the Furies had helped her reach her mission objective, the installation code-named Redoubt Echo. Brigid thought it was an appropriate code name, inasmuch as Redoubt Echo was dedicated to the observation and even the retrieval of echoes from the past.

The men in black pulled Brigid toward the wide stone steps, which led to glass-fronted double doors. Only a few shards of glass remained in the frame, and the metal strips that served as cross braces were rust-eaten. Beyond the doors, light glowed with a flickering, lurid radiance.

Another tall lean man, identically attired, masked and armed with a silver-knobbed rod, pulled open the door as they approached. The Furies escorted

Brigid through a foyer, down a short corridor and then into a huge central rotunda.

Brigid's eyes swept over the dim interior, lit only by a pair of small fires burning in brass, tripod-mounted braziers. White-hot metal pokers rested in the hearts of the braziers. A metal-railed gallery, about twenty feet high, overlooked the area. All of the chamber's furnishings had been removed, so the floor space was vast and hollow. Someone had devoted a great deal of time and trouble to cleaning it of rubbish and rubble. Tilting her head back, she saw a maze of catwalks and beams strung from metal cables and wires, surrounding the bowl-shaped ceiling.

In the shadows cloaking the far walls, she was able to make out a vista of machines with giant fly-wheels, pumps and a complexity of pipes. They no longer worked nor would they ever again, even if anyone had the skills to repair them. They were clogged with the detritus of two centuries' worth of neglect.

Despite the poor illumination, Brigid saw a number of dark figures standing near a slab of concrete elevated almost like a podium. She assumed they were Furies but when she was pulled closer, she realized only a few of them were Megaera's own. They stood among what she first assumed were clusters of statues. Then as she drew nearer, what she saw caused her breath to seize in her lungs, adrenaline to flood her system and her heart rate to increase. She instinctively cringed, digging her heels into the concrete floor, but the Furies continued marching forward, pulling her with them.

The statues were as immobile and as jet-black as the man they had seen earlier. Every fold of cloth, every strand of hair was visible. Scattered here and there with no regard for order, they were all distorted in different postures. The one feature common to all of the figures was the expressions of unendurable terror on their faces.

A couple of statues appeared to be shielding their heads with raised arms, while others rested on their knees with their hands clasped together as if they were begging. Another figure, that of a burly, bearded man, looked as if he had been turned to onyx at the exact instant he reached out for his tormentors with hooked fingers. His charcoal-colored lips were peeled back from his sepia teeth in a silent snarl of dying defiance.

Brigid saw only a few women scattered among the collection of three-dimensional still lifes. She noticed that most of the statues were mutilated or maimed in some way—a missing hand here, a lopped-off ear there or fingers sheared away. One of the female statues had half of her nose missing. As she was dragged past her, Brigid noted absently how beautiful she had to have been in life.

The Furies jerked her to a halt and released her,

stepping back with swift, mechanical motions. Brigid remained standing, surrounded by the black statuary. She tried not to look at the figures, devoting herself to restoring circulation to her arms by vigorously rubbing them. Carefully, she reached up and touched the silver spider clinging to the side of her neck. The metal surface felt faintly warm to the touch, as if it were alive.

Megaera's voice, hollow and ghostly, wafted through the vast chapel. ''The time for judgment has arrived. I have donned my face of judgment.''

Glancing up, Brigid saw the woman standing on the podium. The firelight glinted from the thin mask of what looked like beaten gold lying over her face. The mask was worked in the likeness of a woman of ethereal beauty, but like the visage-concealing coverings worn by the Furies, there were no openings for the eyes or the mouth. The eyes were molded as if closed in sleep.

''Justice is blind,'' Brigid muttered. ''I can't say it's much of an improvement.''

Megaera said nothing, but only bent her golden face toward Brigid, as if the blank eyes saw into the depths of her soul and examined its worth. Silence hung between them for a long tick of time. Brigid broke it by demanding scornfully, ''You're going to kill me, aren't you? So why waste time with this farce of judging me?''

''You have already been judged.'' Megaera's

muffled voice echoed eerily beneath the high ceiling. "I must now determine your most offensive sins in order to mete out the appropriate penalty."

Brigid snorted in derision. "You come to a conclusion first and then you look for facts to support it. Not very scientific and certainly not very fair to the one judged, but I suppose it makes your job easier."

"You have an intrusive tongue." For the first time, a hint of emotion colored Megaera's detached tone.

Encouraged that she'd finally provoked a reaction, Brigid retorted, "And you have an intrusive attitude. How long have you been practicing this form of justice? Not for very long, or you would have run out of sinners quite a while ago."

Megaera cocked her head quizzically. In a genuinely puzzled voice, she asked, "What do you mean?"

"Where are you and your Furies from, Megaera? I don't recognize the language you speak."

"It is the tongue of the gods we serve. Only we, his chosen, are permitted to speak it."

"Who are your gods?" Brigid asked.

"They are our gods, not yours, so you shall not know them. Certainly not the small, smiling god who brought us here."

"The small, smiling god?"

"Of course," the old woman replied, sounding a

bit angry. "He brought us here from our home in the mists and the mountains. We had completed our tasks there, and he gathered the mists around us, drawing us into slumber. When we awoke, we found ourselves in this dark land of depravity and sin. We were fearful at first, then the small, smiling god released us. We understood then he placed us in his realm to seek and cast out the sins that had escaped his notice."

Brigid opened her mouth to ask another question, but she heard a scuff and scutter of feet from behind her and the sound of a struggle. Megaera lifted her masked face to gaze in that direction. Brigid turned to see a pair of the Furies hauling a ragged man through the clusters of black statuary.

Even though the light was poor, she recognized his blistered, terror-etched features. He was the castrated man who had staggered into their shelter. His eyes darted frantically from Brigid to Megaera to the statues and back to Brigid again.

A torrent of hissed syllables issued from beneath Megaera's mask. The Furies obediently forced the man to his knees before the podium and stepped back. He hung his head, making wheezing, strangulated noises like a dog trying to cough up a bone. Pink foam drooled from his lips.

"Do you have something to say before the sentence is carried out?" Megaera asked quietly.

After a few seconds of trying, the man managed

to choke out, "Why are you doing this to me? To my people? Haven't I been punished enough?"

Megaera lifted her left hand, and the sleeve of her robe slipped down to reveal the metal band encircling her thin wrist.

In a surprisingly gentle, almost sympathetic tone, she said, "We must cast out the sin, exorcise it utterly. You fled before this could be done. You can't escape because you have nowhere to escape to. You cannot flee your sin and you cannot escape justice. I have the power to remove your sin. It's like cutting out a cancer—a surgical technique performed with precision. It will save your soul."

"The cancer is in you," Brigid snapped. "The disease of self-righteous delusions."

"That is arrogance talking," Megaera stated matter-of-factly, "combined with ignorance. Always a deadly combination for the advancement of the spirit."

Brigid stopped short of spitting at the podium but she said angrily, "Look who's talking."

Megaera returned her attention to the kneeling man. "You are not being punished. Once you've paid your penalty, your sin is cleansed and your soul is purified. Then it will move on, leaving the husk of your physical body behind." She nodded to the statuary scattered about the chapel.

The man didn't respond. His shoulders quaked with barely repressed sobs. The bony fingers of Megaera's left hand brushed two of the opals on the wristband. Brigid made a reflexive motion to lunge at the woman. A pair of hands that felt like tempered steel closed around her upper arms, immobilizing her and almost instantly cutting off circulation. Sweat collected at her hairline and trickled down her forehead as fear arose in her. Megaera lovingly caressed the gems on the wristband, then pressed down hard.

The kneeling man jerked convulsively, straightening so quickly Brigid heard his vertebrae pop. He clawed at the silver spider on the side of his neck. A halo of pale blue light sprang up and shimmered around it.

The air in the chamber seemed to shiver. The man's body swayed, the sway became a tremble and the tremble turned into a spasm. His eyes remained open, but they did not see. His mouth gaped open, but no words came out. He croaked a sound of pain and terror and agony.

With a faint crackling sound similar to that of burning wood, a gray pallor suddenly swept over the man's body, spreading out from the device attached to his neck. Before Brigid's horrified eyes, his flesh and clothes were transmuted to an ash-gray substance. It swiftly darkened, becoming like a layer of anthracite between one eye blink and another.

The man's back arched violently, as if he had received a heavy blow between the shoulders. His arms contorted and drew up like the gnarled branches of a leafless tree as the blanket of dark gray petrification crept over his torso and down his legs.

A ghastly dry gargling came from his mouth, then the gray tide covered his lips, smothering his voice. Within another a pair of eye blinks, a coal-black calcified statue knelt before the podium. The silver spider seemed to have dissolved, absorbed by the same process that turned flesh to carbon.

Nausea roiled in the pit of Brigid's stomach, and she swallowed a column of burning bile working its way up her throat. The little spider clinging to her own flesh suddenly seemed to weigh a ton. Her heart pounded frantically in terror, but she forced herself to raise defiant eyes to Megaera's blank, golden face. Reflected firelight cast red highlights across its dully gleaming surface, lending it an expression of cold, superior mockery.

The woman was not just a Fury, Brigid told herself, trying to control her scattered, stumbling thoughts. She was a Gorgon; she was Medusa herself.

Megaera tilted her head in Brigid's direction and her sibilant voice announced, "Arrogance and hubris are products of the mind. And the way to the mind is through the eyes."

Two Furies seemed to materialize out of the shadows and slammed into Brigid simultaneously, pressing her between them. They secured painfully tight grips on her arms and held her suspended, with only the toes of her boots touching the floor. Shoulder blades grinding into each other, Brigid was made to stand straddle-legged to support her own weight without having her shoulders dislocated.

Another Fury ghosted into view, holding a poker like a white-hot rapier. He approached slowly and even with several feet separating them, Brigid felt the heat radiating from the glowing tip of the metal rod.

"Through the right eye, I should think," Megaera said calmly. "A swift, straight puncture should suffice."

Brigid stared in horrified fascination as the sharp end of the poker filled her field of vision. The tip shimmered like a sunburst. She started to struggle, but the Furies cinched down their grips and she bit back a cry of pain.

Then she heard the distant tolling of a bell.

Chapter 5

Domi had slept for a time but she dreamed and the dreams were full of sadness, of dying babies that were blendings of human and nonhuman but babies just the same.

She awakened with a jerk at the sound of thunder, her hand reflexively streaking for the Detonics Combat Master snugged in a shoulder holster. Born and honed in the Outlands, her senses were not mazed by slumber and she instantly knew where she was and what was happening.

Sitting in the pilot's chair of the Sandcat, she listened to the first faint patter of raindrops against the armaglass-and-ceramic-coated hull of the vehicle. The rain was sporadic at first, an on-and-off drizzle. Then it swiftly became a hammering downpour.

Domi carefully opened the port-side ob slit a crack and looked outside.

The sky was a canopy of billowing clouds, completely blotting out the sunlight. Discolored and livid, streaked with green, the sky looked as if it had been bruised. Incandescent flares of lightning seared her sensitive eyes. A gale-force wind howled around the ruins, swirling curtains of loose debris mixed in with hail.

A flash of lightning, dazzlingly close, burned its afterimage into her retinas, followed by a peal of thunder so violent it made the Sandcat quiver. Hastily, Domi closed the ob port, her nose wrinkling at the chemical stink. She wasn't concerned about the acid rain penetrating the skin of the Cat. Built two centuries ago to take part in a ground war that was never fought, the Sandcat's low-slung, blocky chassis was supported by a pair of flat, retractable tracks.

The gun turret, concealed within an armored bubble topside, held a pair of USMG-73 heavy machine guns. The vehicle's armor not only served as protection from projectiles, but also went opaque when exposed to energy-based weapons, such as particle-beam emitters. It was also too tough to be adversely affected by corrosives.

The interior was the perfect size to comfortably hold four people. At the front of the compartment were the pilot's and copilot's chairs; the rear storage module housed the computer links for the electronic systems. A double row of three jump seats faced one another. The seats could be folded down to make serviceable, narrow bunks.

Another thunderclap, sounding like an artillery shell exploding at point-blank range, caused the floor plates under Domi's feet to vibrate for a second. She didn't react, even though the loud noise made her bite back a startled curse. An albino by birth, her skin was normally as white as milk so she couldn't turn pale no matter how frightened she was.

She was every inch of five feet tall and barely weighed a hundred pounds. On either side of her thin-bridged nose, her eyes glittered grimly like drops of blood. Her disarrayed, short-cropped hair was the color of bone.

The storm increased in intensity, and within a moment Domi had the impression she was trapped in a bubble at the center of a maelstrom of shrieking violence. She remained outwardly calm as the Sandcat rocked on its tracks. During her upbringing in the Outland settlement of Hells Canyon, she had survived any number of natural and unnatural threats, from mutie animals to mutie weather.

Domi had lived most of her young life in the wild places, far from the cushioned tyranny of the baronies. She had spent years cautiously treading the ragged edge of death, and her inner fiber had been forged into an iron strength and an implacable stoicism. She didn't react when pieces of wind-tossed rubble banged loudly on the exterior of the Sandcat, most of it sounding like stone, but some of it was metal, judging by the gonglike chimes.

Although she felt a pang of anxiety about Kane and Brigid, a particularly sharp one in regard to Grant, she didn't bother trying to raise them on the Sandcat's comm equipment. She wasn't technologically adept, but she knew the storm would make a hash out of radio waves.

To pass the time she checked the action of her handgun. Since the stainless-steel blaster weighed only a pound and a half, it was perfectly suited for a girl of her petite build. Grant had expressed doubt she could handle the recoil when she selected it from Cerberus redoubt's exceptionally well-equipped armory nearly a year and half ago. She had never experienced problems with it, except during the period when she recovered from a bullet wound that shattered the coracoid bone of her right shoulder.

Ejecting the 7-round magazine from within the pistol's checkered walnut grip, she inspected the spring mechanism, then slid the clip back in place. Reaching down, she patted the knife with its nine-inch, wickedly serrated blade sheathed to her right calf. It was her only memento of the six months she'd spent as Guana Teague's sex slave in the Tartarus Pits of Cobaltville. She'd sold herself into slavery in an effort to get a piece of the good life available to ville dwellers. She ended the term of slavery by cutting the monstrous Teague's throat with the blade, and saved Grant's life with the same impulsive act.

Thinking about Grant caused her full lips to twitch unconsciously in a half frown, half smile. Whenever she thought about the big man with his lion's growl of a voice, she felt a mingling of love, anger and disappointment.

She loved the man for his courage and compassion, but she experienced anger and disappointment that he never allowed that compassion to turn into passion—at least not toward her. Domi was too practical, too pragmatic to expend much energy on girlish daydreams that had already proved to be lost causes.

Grant, like Kane, had been through the dehumanizing cruelty of Magistrate training yet they had somehow, almost miraculously, managed to retain their humanity. But vestiges of their Mag years still lurked close to the surface, particularly in Grant. He presented a dour, closed and private persona, rarely showing emotion. He was taciturn and slow to genuine anger, but when he was provoked, his destructive ruthlessness could be frightening. With him, slights were never forgotten, and she knew he still stung from the whip of angry words she had lashed him with months ago: "Big man, big chest, big shoulders, legs like trees. Guess they don't tell the story, huh?"

Domi regretted speaking those words almost as soon as they left her lips, but she had never apologized. When Grant rejected her love again on that day, she swore it was for the last time. Then, a month or so later, when she came across Grant and Shizuka, the female samurai from New Edo, locked in a fierce embrace, she also swore she would never forgive him.

Shaking her head, Domi tried to drive the memories of that night from her mind. There were a lot of memories swimming around within the walls of her skull she would just as soon have excised, and that brief glimpse of Grant showering the Japanese woman's face with passionate kisses topped the list.

Another memory she wished could be removed from her brain was one that had recently invaded her dreams. Like Kane, she had spent two weeks in captivity within the vast subterranean installation known as Area 51. Both of them had been shown the end result of their war against the barons—dying hybrid infants.

She didn't know why the sight of the dying hybrid babies horrified her so profoundly, filling her with guilt and remorse. After all, she had gone to the installation in the Nevada desert to kill hybrids. The very concept of the hybrids triggered a xenophobic madness in her, the overwhelming urge to kill them as she had killed venomous snakes that slithered into her Outland settlement. But upon visiting the nursery turned morgue, she felt only shame, as if the guilt of the entire human race were laid on her small shoulders.

She knew what everyone knew about the formation of ville society. In the century following sky-dark, self-proclaimed barons had warred against one another, each struggling for control and absolute power over territory. Then they realized that greater rewards were possible if unity in command, purpose and organization was achieved.

The nine most powerful baronies that survived the long wars over territorial expansion and resources divided control of the continent among themselves. A hierarchical ruling system was put into place, and the city-states adopted the name of the titular heads of state.

But it wasn't until she arrived in Cerberus that she learned the true nature of the ville rulers. The baronial oligarchy ruling the nine villes was more than the governing body of postnukecaust America—they were a living expression of the ancient god-king system. Their semidivine status derived from the means of their birth. They were hybrids of human and nonhuman, a blending of genetic material with the sole purpose of creating new humans to inherit the Earth. The barons served as a bridge between predark and postdark, the plenipotentiaries of the alien Archon Directorate itself.

According to what Kane, Brigid, Domi and Grant had been told by Lakesh upon their arrival at the Cerberus redoubt nearly two years before, the entirety of human history was intertwined with the entities called Archons, who conspired with willing human pawns to control humankind through political chaos, staged wars, famines, plagues and natural

disasters. Their goal was always the unification of
the world under their control, with all nonessential
and nonproductive humans eliminated.

But over the past few months, Brigid, Kane, Domi
and Grant had learned that the elaborate backstory
was all a ruse, bits of truth mixed in with outrageous
fiction. The Archon Directorate did not exist, except
as a vast cover story, created in the twentieth century
and grown larger with each succeeding generation.
The only so-called Archon on Earth was Balam, the
last of an extinct race that had once shared the planet
with humankind.

Balam claimed that the Archon Directorate was
an appellation and a myth created by the predark
government agencies as a control mechanism. Lakesh referred to it as the Oz Effect, wherein a single
vulnerable entity created the illusion of being the
representative of an all-powerful body.

Once they learned that, then they realized victory
over hybrid tyranny was an achievable goal. In fur-
therance of that goal, Domi and her companions inadvertently destroyed the medical facility beneath
the Archuleta Mesa in New Mexico. The barons de-
pended on the facility to bolster their immune systems. Once a year the oligarchy traveled to the installation for medical treatments. They received
fresh transfusions of blood, and a regimen of bio-
chemical genetic therapy designed to strengthen
their autoimmune systems, thus granting them an-

other year of life and power. The six-leveled facility
in New Mexico had originally been constructed to
house two main divisions of the Totality Concept—
Overproject Whisper and Overproject Excalibur.
Whisper dealt with finding new pathways across
space and time, and Excalibur was exclusively involved in creating new forms of life. According to
Lakesh, after the institution of the unification program, only Excalibur's biological section was revived to maintain the lives of the barons and to grow
new hybrids.

The destruction of the Archuleta Mesa had done
more than smash the barons' ability to sustain their
lives. It had also taken away their future by destroying the incubation chambers. Less than two dozen
infants remained out of two thousand.

When Domi was finally reunited with Kane, he
expressed deep skepticism of her sea-change of beliefs, even after seeing the babies for himself. He
reminded her how devoted she was to the war
against the hybrid barons, and she recalled with
crystal clarity the furious, accusatory words she
flung at him: "War isn't against babies, not even
against hybrids. It's against the barons and against
men like you and Grant! Men like you used to be.
I wasn't afraid of hybrids in the Outlands. Didn't
even know such as them existed. But I was sure as
shit scared of the baron's sec men—the Mags.
That's who was my enemy."

When Kane darkly observed that the words she spoke didn't sound in character, she retorted angrily, "You and Grant didn't stay what you were. I don't have to stay what I am. If it means working with the hybrids against the barons, against the Mags, then I will. I'll forgive 'em for being born."

He seemed to understand her point of view. She hoped he did, but it didn't really matter. They hadn't spoken of what they witnessed or what they went through during their captivity. Kane was reticent to talk about it, particularly to Brigid. Domi didn't blame him, but she kept her own knowledge of his experiences to herself.

Brigid and Grant treated her differently now, but not necessarily with the kind of respect they would accord an equal. Instead, they were extremely solicitous of her, as if she had miraculously recovered from a terminal illness.

Domi knew it had something to do with her impulsive actions during the final violent moments of the battle to occupy the Area 51 installation. She remembered snatching up the implode gren Kane dropped, but she had no recollection of its detonation. Her very next conscious memory was of being on her hands and knees throwing up.

A momentous event had occurred, she knew, but she couldn't recall what it entailed. But sometimes, in her slumber, when her consciousness teetered between sleep and waking, fragmented images flashed through her mind, so fleeting and brief they were like impressionistic sketches, not memories. Over the past couple of months Domi had mentally compiled a number of images and tried to arrange them in some kind of coherent form. So far, she hadn't been successful.

She became aware that the keening of the wind and the drumming on the Sandcat's hull was tapering off, but Domi waited, not opening any of the ob ports until she was sure the heart of the storm had passed over or blown itself out.

After several minutes passed with no renewal of the elements' fury, she touched a switch on the instrument console and lowered the thin metal shutters that covered the forward windshield. Peering out through the double-glazed thickness of bulletproof polymers, she looked at the ruins spread out all around.

The rubble glistened with moisture, and the characteristic reek of the chem storm was faint. Another cloudburst had followed hard on the heels of the acid-rain downpour and diluted the most potent of the toxins. In the distance she could easily see the black charring of countless ancient fires on the facades of surviving buildings.

Debris was heaped so high in so many places, the decision had been made not to risk damaging the Sandcat by pushing through it, around or over it.

None of them relished the idea of being stranded so many miles from Cerberus.

Checking the chron on the instrument panel, Domi uneasily noted two hours had elapsed since she had last heard from her companions. Putting on a headset, she punched in Brigid's trans-comm channel and received only the hissing and popping of static. She got the same result when she tried raising Kane, so she reluctantly opened Grant's frequency.

His response, when it finally filtered into her ear, was so shot through with buzzes and electronic snaps he was barely comprehensible. "—lost Kane and Br— Stay where...are until I...you. We'll be—"

His voice dissolved in a mushy stream of hisses. Domi tried to reestablish contact but gave up after a minute. She knew the local atmosphere was still too ionized by the recent passage of the storm to allow for clear communications.

She thought about trying the satellite uplink to Cerberus, which Bry was so fond of, but decided not to waste her time. Even if she managed to get through, she doubted the advice Lakesh might offer would be of any use.

If Kane and Brigid were dead, Grant wouldn't have employed the euphemism "lost." He was blunt and straightforward, and if he said lost, that's what he meant. After sitting and thinking for another few minutes, she came to a decision. Domi popped open the passenger-side gull-wing door and climbed out, surveying her surroundings. The skies were still overcast, almost smoky. The air held the stench of sulfur. She looked in the direction her companions had taken, lifting her gaze to the distant stem of the building Brigid referred to as the Sears Tower. Fixing the landmark in relation to her present position, she made up her mind to follow them on foot.

Domi closed and locked the Sandcat's door, made sure her trans-comm and own pair of microbinoculars were clipped to her belt and started walking. Everywhere she looked there seemed to be nothing but piles of blackened stone and half-slagged metal, some of them heaped as high as fifty feet.

She followed the same trail she'd seen her companions take, but once they were out of her field of vision, she had to take her best guess. What little track they might've left was completely obliterated by the scouring of the wind and rain.

Some of the avenues were so completely blocked by fallen buildings, Domi detoured around them rather than try to climb them. Always she kept the looming tower in her line of sight. When she came to a knitted mass of wreckage that appeared to be several buildings that had fallen together, she paused to study it, looking for a way through it or over it rather than around.

A series of concrete slabs formed something of a crude staircase over the top of the rubble, and she began clambering up them. She froze in midstep when she heard the tramp of running feet—and the screams. Her hand leaped to the butt of her Combat Master as she pivoted on the ball of her right foot, tracking for the source of the commotion. Far in the distance she heard the brazen peal of a bell.

Chapter 6

Kane's body crashed into a bend, and the relentless current washed him around it, the cornerstones flaying his clothes and the skin beneath. His arms were outstretched in a semblance of a dive, and his head sunk between his shoulders as the floodwaters launched him down the shaft like a projectile.

He felt himself falling headfirst, surrounded by the thundering torrent. He was all but unconscious, and by the time his sluggish thought processes understood he was floating, not rocketing along a chute, water had filled his mouth and he swallowed it rather than inhale. He had no idea of where he was. Struggling, he twisted and lifted his head, instinctively trying to force his body upright. Above him he saw a faint gray radiance, and he managed to stroke for it.

Kane's head and shoulders broke the surface and his strangulated inhalation echoed hollowly all around him. Feebly, he paddled through the water, sneezing water from his sinus passages. His vision blurry, he saw he floated in a narrow inlet at the base of a towering, smooth-faced cliff. It required a moment or two of squinting and focusing for him to recognize the cliff as a building looming high above him.

The inlet was bisected by a stout wire fence. Leaves, bits of wood and pieces of flotsam less identifiable bobbed against the links. Kane swam laboriously to the fence, hooking his fingers into the diamond-shaped openings, and heaved himself half out of the muddy water swirling around his legs.

Kane hung on to it spread-eagled, racked by vomiting, his stomach and lungs emptying themselves of the foul water he had inhaled and swallowed. He was oblivious to the lessening of the wind's strength and the distant rumbling of thunder as the storm center moved away. Finally, he felt strong enough to move. He turned his head and squinted blearily at his surroundings. The concrete-walled channel cut between two towering buildings, casting it into deep shadow. He realized after a few seconds of careful study that the buildings weren't actually all that tall or massive. The channel was just sunk deep below them, and they were positioned on high bulwarks of stone. The brickwork and concrete blocks were coated by damp green moss. From the direction he had come, he saw how the man-made canal bent around a thirty-degree curve and disappeared.

Clinging to the wire by his right hand, Kane performed a careful inventory. His clothes were torn in places, the skin underneath abraded, but no bones seemed broken. He probed carefully at the swelling on the side of his head, but his fingertips didn't come away bloody. Still, he wasn't overly relieved. He could be suffering from a serious closed-skull injury, and he knew head traumas were always tricky. He could have sustained a skull fracture and be suffering from a subdural leakage of blood.

His trans-comm unit was gone, as well as his wrist chron. His Copperhead subgun no longer dangled from his shoulder. His Sin Eater was still snugly holstered to his forearm, but he hoped he had the time to inspect it before he was forced to use it. His web belt with his fourteen-inch combat knife was still in place, too, so he wasn't helpless despite how he felt.

Drawing in a deep breath, he started to call Brigid's name, but his throat was constricted due to the water he swallowed and raw from his stomach's efforts to eject it. His voice was a raspy croak, and even the attempt to shout her name triggered a spasm of shuddering and dry heaving.

After he recovered, he deliberately forced himself not to think about Brigid, Grant or DeFore. Grim determination replaced the anxiety in his mind. Slowly, Kane began to inch his way along the fence toward the left wall of the channel, holding on to the interlocked wire strands with his hands, his feet still in the water. He noted absently how the water level was slowly but steadily dropping. It was difficult to move at first. His muscles were stiff and aching, but as he made more progress the pain receded somewhat.

He had crept sideways less than a yard when an impact against his legs nearly jarred him from his perch. Kane twisted his body, his mouth uttering a harshly whispered obscenity. He gazed down and saw a black shape pressing against the backs of his legs, washed there by the current. His body tautened as he tried to identify the nature of the shape. With the electric shock of surprise, energy flooded back into him, driving away the lethargy.

After a few seconds of slit-eyed study, Kane finally recognized a human figure bobbing lifelessly against the fence. In the dim light, he at first thought it was a man dipped in black ink, then he wondered fleeting if it were another man turned to an obsidian statue. Regardless, he had seen and made enough corpses in his life to recognize one when it floated at his feet. He reached down to grasp a wrist. The fabric clinging to the limb felt like leather.

Kane continued edging sideways, pulling the body with him. By the time he reached the curved wall of the inlet and the left the fence, the water level had dropped so much that the corpse's legs dragged on the silt-covered bottom.

Kane wrestled him up onto the concrete and dropped him facedown. After catching his breath, he turned him over. The man was nearly seven feet tall and gaunt to the point of emaciation. A blank, featureless face was turned to the sky, and Kane eyed it warily. Although he knew it was a mask of some sort, he didn't like the looks of it. Tentatively, he touched it, noting how it felt like spun glass beneath his fingertips.

Running the fingers of both hands around the edges of the mask, then inserting them beneath the rim, he pulled up slowly. With a faint click, the covering lifted away. The face that stared up at him wasn't much of an improvement over the mask. His skin was pallid and white, but not due to the type of albinism Domi was born with. It was the kind of grub white that came of never being exposed to sunlight. A strand of hair escaping from beneath the tight cowl was faintly golden, too, like silky flax.

Kane looked the corpse over, studying its long jaw, narrow chin and high cheekbones. Dead and lusterless black eyes stared up from beneath eyebrows that resembled tufts of white thread. His stomach turned a cold flip-flop. He recognized the facial type—he had seen it often enough over the past year or so, particularly during his captivity in Area 51.

The man was a hybrid. If not a full-fledged one, then certainly some traces of Archon genetic material were buried in his familial woodpile. Certainly none of the barons or the other hybrids in Kane's experience had ever attained such a height. Nor did the eyes possess the prominent supraorbital ridges. They were of normal human size and shape, as well, not overly large or back-slanted. However, the eyes were so pale a gray as to be almost the color of water.

He inspected the mask, surprised by how thin and lightweight it was. He assumed it was made of a material like one-way glass, but to his consternation it was just as opaque on the inside as the outside. It was of exquisite workmanship, but Kane saw no manner by which the man could have seen through it, relying just on his vision. He turned it over in his hands several times. A thread-thin black line formed a complete border around the inner rim, and Kane guessed it was a magnetic strip.

Setting the face covering down, Kane turned the man's head to one side, searching for a seal on the cowl. Although he looked as if he had been dead for some time, his unnaturally smooth skin still retained warmth. There was a dry crunching of fractured cervical vertebrae and when Kane withdrew his hands, his fingers came away bloody.

Leaning closer, he saw how the long column of the throat had been slashed, right at the jaw hinge. The wound however looked superficial, more unsightly than truly life-threatening. He decided it was more likely the man had died of a broken neck, not of a cut one, the injury probably sustained in a fall.

At the back of the pale man's head, his groping

fingers found a seal, an almost invisible and imperceptible seam. It opened when he exerted pressure on it, tracing a finger along its length. He peeled it off, seeing that the corpse's hair was little more than a finely textured golden down, like the fine fur on the underbelly of a mouse. The headpiece felt like lightweight leather, almost as soft and flexible as doeskin.

When Kane turned it inside out, light gleamed from an inlay of delicate microcircuitry, a webwork no more substantial in appearance than gossamer. He frowned at it, perplexed by its purpose, touching it, scratching at it with a fingernail. On the outer edges of the headpiece was a very narrow double fold, so narrow he couldn't see between the two pieces of fabric.

Moving on a sudden impulse, Kane tugged the cowl over his head, seriously doubting it would fit at all, much less snugly. To his surprise the fit was perfect, and he received the distinct impression the material automatically adjusted and adhered to the contours of his skull.

Picking up the mask, he cautiously raised it, placing it over his own face. He pressed the rim against the edges of the cowl. When he brought his hands away, the mask remained in place, affixed to the cowl by the magnetic strip. Then, to his surprise, he sensed rather than felt a weak electrical field juicing through the face shield. For an instant, he saw nothing, then the inside of the mask shimmered with an effect like water sluicing away dust on a pane of glass. The mask seemed to turn transparent.

Slowly, Kane turned his head, to the left and right, looking at his surroundings through the visor. Everything seemed to have a slightly more luminous sheen, all the hard edges and sharp corners blunted by a faint amber haze as of late-autumn sunlight filtered through golden-and-orange leaves.

Craning his neck, he studied the wall of the building looming above him. He focused on a decorative, scrolled cornice that jutted a foot or more from the roof. It abruptly swelled in his vision, rushing forward so fast, he almost stumbled backward into the channel.

Seeming to float in the air between his eyes and the interior of the mask, a column of numbers appeared, glowing red against the amber. The outthrusting piece of masonry looked close enough to touch. After a few seconds of confusion, Kane realized that when he focused on a distant object, the visor magnified it and provided a readout as to distance and dimension.

He swore in astonishment. He hadn't come across any predark tech with such abilities in all of the places he had visited over the past year and a half. For the next minute, he experimented with the visor, his fascination pushing away his aches, pains and worries. In conjunction with the microcircuitry in the headpiece, the mask functioned as a very efficient range finder. He also discovered the visor possessed a thermal-viewing capability.

When he looked at the body of the black-clad man, what little body heat radiated by his head registered as a yellowish shimmer. The skintight suit he wore apparently blocked his thermal signature, much like the uncomfortable and unreliable Stealth cloaks available in the Cerberus armory. With the face shield in place, a person in the suit would become a living shadow.

Although Kane experienced a pang of disgust, he ran his hands over the bodysuit, searching for zippers or buttons. On the right side, he found a magnetic seal and he opened it the same way he had done with the cowl. He peeled the coverall off the corpse, a little dismayed to see that the garment was one continuous piece, from the hard-soled boots to the gloves. Fortunately, rigor hadn't settled in the corpse's limbs, so removing the suit wasn't as difficult or as time-consuming as it could have been otherwise. Still, his flesh crawled whenever he touched the marble-white, clammy flesh.

The man was naked beneath the shadowsuit—as Kane found himself referring to it—and he was completely dry. Amazingly, no water had seeped in. Unlike the other male hybrids he had encountered, the man's genitals appeared to be of normal development.

Glancing inside the shadowsuit, Kane saw a similar pattern of microcircuitry spread out in a webwork pattern as in the cowl. He could only guess at its purpose, and he decided he had already spent enough time with the corpse and his clothes.

Removing the cowl and face shield, Kane rolled both up within the black bodysuit. Tucking them beneath an arm, he began scaling the wall of the channel, careful of his footing, but with all possible haste. Although the storm front was gone, the sky was still deeply overcast, the thick clouds blurring the sun to little more than a weak, grayish-yellow disk.

Kane figured only two or three hours of ineffectual daylight remained. Dusk would arrive quickly, with almost no demarcation between day and night. He had no intention of being caught out in the open, particularly if the dead man had living friends who might find him with his clothes under his arm and jump to the wrong conclusions. Of course, he told himself wryly, he would jump to the very same wrong conclusions himself.

The climb was strenuous, and the various pains in his body returned with a vengeance. The concrete was smooth and footholds were hard to come by. Most of the handholds were mere slits between slabs of the concrete, but he wedged his fingers in and pulled himself along. Twice, he nearly lost his grip and slid back down the rain-wet wall. Finally, Kane reached a flat shelf of crumbling concrete, and, panting heavily, he clambered on top of it.

He massaged his cramped fingers and forearms and looked around. Behind him were the rusting remains of a high fence topped with broken coils of razor wire. The building on the other side of it was part of a compound of single-story, windowless structures. Doing his best to soften the harshness of his breathing, he listened for sounds of human habitation or, considering Brigid's tales of Midnites, inhuman habitation.

Other than the faint drone of swarms of tiny winged gnats flying around, he heard nothing. Kane tested the sensitive spring-and-cable mechanism of his Sin Eater's holster, making sure it wasn't fouled by mud. He flexed his wrist tendons and the weapon slapped into his waiting hand, but a bit slower than was normal.

Kane repeated the motion several times, more to find something to occupy his attention than worrying about Brigid Baptiste. Most of the time he shied away from scrutinizing his feelings for the woman. They were as deep as they were complicated, and the unspoken bond between them was an issue neither one discussed.

From the very first time he had met her, he was affected by the energy Brigid radiated, a force intangible, yet one that triggered a melancholy longing in his soul. That strange, sad longing only deepened after a bout of jump sickness both of them suffered during mat-trans jump to Russia. The main symptoms of jump sickness were vivid, almost-real hallucinations.

He and Brigid had shared the same hallucination, but both knew on a visceral, primal level it hadn't been triggered by the gateway delirium. It was a revelation that they were joined by chains of fate, their destinies linked. Lakesh had postulated the so-called jump dreams might not be hallucinations at all, but inchoate glimpses into other lives and other realities triggered by the quantum channels opened by the gateway units. At the time, Kane had refused to consider that possibility, but now he wasn't so certain. At any rate, he and Brigid never spoke of their shared vision, although Kane often wondered if that spiritual bond was the primary reason he had sacrificed everything he had attained as a Magistrate to save her from execution.

The possibility confused him, made him feel defensive and insecure. That insecurity was one reason he always addressed her as Baptiste, almost never by her first name, so as to maintain a certain formal distance between them. But that distance had been shrinking every day, particularly after the head injury she had sustained in the Antarctic.

Sighing wearily, he returned the Sin Eater to the holster and levered himself to his feet. Wet boots squishing, he began picking his way carefully along the narrow concrete track atop the channel wall, looking for an opening in the fence. He walked less than twenty yards when he came to a gap, a rent where the galvanized metal links had separated. It was a tight squeeze, and the jagged ends of the wire caught at his clothes, but he managed to struggle through it.

The ground beneath his feet was brown mud, liberally splashed with pools and puddles of water. There was a great deal of deep grass, and in the shallow depressions floated a soup of slime and decomposing vegetable matter. Flying insects like dragonflies darted low over the grass, preying on the gnats.

Circling one of the brick-and-concrete-block buildings, he paused at a corner and took a comprehensive look at the compound. Many of the roofs of the buildings had collapsed, and the ravages of time had completed the job begun by the nukecaust and the skydark. The only structure that appeared more or less intact was the largest, with a white domed roof. He had no idea what the complex had been. It could have been the ruins of a school or even a penitentiary.

Kane didn't approach the dome boldly. One never knew what kind of menace lurked in predark ruins or what devices were on alert for intruders such as himself. As far as he knew, he was already being watched, although his sixth sense had yet to signal an alarm. He scanned the blind windows and tangles of undergrowth, but nothing moved. Turning, he went to the building's rear, looking for an open window or doorway. He found a metal-sheathed door equipped with a push bar. A stenciled legend in faded black paint proclaimed it an emergency exit. Gingerly, he applied pressure to the bar and shouldered the door open gradually.

The hinges squeaked in faint protest, but he heard nothing else. Before he entered, he tossed the shadowsuit and visor into a clump of grass sprouting from the base of the building. He didn't want his hands encumbered when he crossed into dark territory. Holding the door open so as to admit light, he carefully stepped inside.

The floor was slippery with moss and algae, and puddles of stagnant water had accumulated in corners. The interior had been totally gutted of anything useful, probably within the first few weeks of the onset of skydark.

Looking down, Kane saw a shard of brick on the floor and he toed it over to the door, jamming it beneath the bottom edge to keep it propped open. The light filtering into the interior was feeble, but since he had lost his dark-vision glasses, it was better than nothing. He took a few steps forward, unconsciously walking heel to toe as he always did when entering a potential killzone.

His ears registered a sudden slight noise somewhere to his left. From the gloom he heard a woman's voice, vibrating with barely leashed terror, say, "Don't move or I'll blow your fuckin' head off."

Before Kane could even begin to respond, either in words or actions, he heard the tolling of a bell.

Chapter 7

A tsunami of foaming water poured into the passageway with a rumbling roar like that of a great-wheeled machine. Bits and pieces of masonry pelted down from overhead, and Grant pushed DeFore backward with a sweep of his left arm. Chunks of stone and debris rained from the ceiling with splintering cracks and crashes. The entire roof seemed to be in downward motion.

Grant grabbed DeFore by the sleeve and wrestled her down the shaft in the direction they had come. She shouted something, but he couldn't hear what she said. The walls trembled around them, riven with ugly, spreading cracks that spewed brown water.

The life of a medic hadn't trained DeFore as a sprinter. Within a few yards, she was reeling in her gait as behind them the rumbling gave way to crashing, and the entire length of the corridor began collapsing in on itself. Grant's arm around DeFore's waist half lifted her from the floor. She resisted Grant's help when she realized he intended to run outside, back into the storm.

With a ferocious scowl, Grant pushed her a few feet ahead of him, bent over and heaved her onto the broad yoke of his shoulders without breaking stride. She cried out in alarmed anger at the indignity of the forced fireman's carry, but she could do nothing about it. The flat medical kit hanging from her shoulder bounced against his lower back as he ran.

As they reached the door, Grant heard an earsplitting roar behind him. He didn't need to look to know ceiling had fallen in. He sprang out into the open piazza, staggering a little under DeFore's weight. She wasn't a particularly large woman, but she was solid.

Grant's boots slipped on the layer of sludge coating the floor tiles. As he staggered, he tried but failed to put down DeFore. Both of them hit the piazza floor with great splashes and bone-jarring impacts. They stayed where they had fallen for a moment, though DeFore struggled into a sitting position, sputtering curses and looking fearfully skyward.

Although the black maelstrom of the funnel cloud had been sucked back into the massed thunderheads, the wind was still strong and rain fell in sheets. However, when it struck their exposed flesh they didn't feel an acidic sting.

The braids in her hair had come undone, and she raked the wet strands out of her face with sharp, impatient gestures. "I don't appreciate being lugged around like a sack of goddamn potatoes!"

Grant climbed quickly to his feet. "Then you shouldn't have moved like one."

He extended a hand to her, but the medic ignored it. She stood, wincing at the twinge of pain in her hip. Even as she regained her feet, the downpour ebbed to a steady drizzle. The roar of the wind all but died. Although the sky remained the color of verdigris-eaten pewter, the sudden cessation of the storm's fury made it seem as if they had entered a vacuum.

Grant glanced into the rubble-choked corridor and made a wordless utterance of disgust. "No point to looking for them that way."

Despite the fact she was already soaked to the skin with her shirt plastered to her ample bosom, DeFore placed the flat case on top of her head as a makeshift umbrella. "You're assuming they're still alive?"

Grant cast a swift glower in her direction. "Why the hell wouldn't I?"

DeFore rolled her eyes in exasperation. "I don't know. Maybe because half of Lake Michigan broke its banks and washed them away?"

Grant strode purposefully across the piazza, his boots sending up splashes of foul water. "It washed them somewhere, but it didn't necessarily drown them. As far as I'm concerned, until I see their bodies they're still alive. If you don't feel the same way, you can either stay here or go back to the Cat. Domi would probably be glad of the company.''

DeFore didn't respond, but she glared at his retreating back. After a few seconds of standing uncertainly in ankle-deep water holding the medical kit on top of her head, she hurried to catch up with the big man. ''I didn't say I thought they were dead.''

Grant only grunted.

''And if they're not,'' DeFore continued, ''how do you figure we'll be able to find them?''

Grant stopped at the collapsed wall and fished around in his pants pocket, withdrawing his trans-comm unit. He thumbed up the cover and keyed in the broad-band frequency to connect to both Brigid and Kane's radiophones at the same time. His face showed no emotion when all he received was static. He tried the Sandcat's channel with the same result.

He exchanged the trans-comm for a small compass. Holding it in the palm of his hand, he frowned, moving slowly a few paces to the left, then to the right and then half turning. Finally, he gestured to the northeast. ''The filtration plant is over there, about two klicks. We went off course only a little, but we were still headed in roughly the right direction before we came in here.''

DeFore removed the case from her head. ''So you think if they're still alive, both of them would go there?'' she ventured.

Grant shrugged. "Since it's our destination, yes, I do. Both Brigid and Kane would head there to rendezvous with us rather than wandering around Chicago hoping we'd all bump into each other by chance."

DeFore nodded in reluctant agreement. "That makes sense. I guess."

Grant gusted out a sigh. "I know you're not a veteran of field missions. I'm glad you volunteered for this one. But you've got to learn to leave the tactics and strategy to the more experienced members of the team. In this instance, that's me. Understand?"

DeFore's full lips pursed in disapproval at the mild rebuke, but she said only, "Understood."

By the time they reached the street, the rain had tapered off completely, leaving behind pools of standing water and mud-clogged gutters, all of which smelled faintly sulfurous. The two of them tramped side by side. Grant couldn't in good conscience really blame Reba DeFore for covering her nervousness with asperity.

He sympathized with her apprehension and appreciated her decision to accompany them on the journey. During her nearly five years as an exile, DeFore had only twice ventured from the safety of the Cerberus redoubt. The first time was part of a rescue party to retrieve an imprisoned Lakesh from Cobaltville. The second mission was months later, and it was a truly nightmarish experience to the dark bayous of Louisiana. Since then, she didn't even like to walk outside the sheltering vanadium walls of the installation on the mountain plateau. From what he had heard of her sufferings down South, Grant was surprised she hadn't fused out completely.

As for himself, he had never enjoyed strolling through the ruins of predark settlements. In fact, he hated the oppressive sensation of walking through a desecrated graveyard. He always suspected he was being watched, and the feeling ate away at his nerve ends like acid. As he led the way through the ugly landscape of rubble, he felt a cold fear and even some anger.

Here was a city that had to have vied with all the great metropolises of humanity. The network of streets was still visible, though the buildings that had lined them were leveled by the double team of concussive shock and time. He could see the avenues, roadways and squares, and here and there was the single tower of some surviving structure. Now and then they saw the sagging framework of an elevated transportation system and occasionally a charred, high-ridged bomb crater.

After about twenty minutes, Grant and DeFore followed a trail up the deeply furrowed outer wall of a crater. Since it was the diameter of a city block, it was easier to walk up the slope, then around the rim, rather than find a way to avoid it altogether.

The ridge top, which reared about twenty-five feet above street level, ran all the way around the puncture wound in the earth. It was uneven with numerous broken-off pinnacles.

Below it, in a shallow declivity, a group of squat structures was arranged in a semicircle. They were small, little more than huts or shacks, and they had about them an indefinable aura of desolation and abandonment. The crater floor was barren except for the litter of trash and decayed bits of wood and fabric that once could have been anything. Grant and DeFore crept around the perimeter of the settlement, alert for any movement or sound. All they heard was the eerie hum of the wind.

The stillness was uncanny. Grant repressed a shiver, feeling the hairs on his arms and neck stir uneasily. It seemed to him that a silent host of invisible watchers regarded them curiously.

DeFore fingered her nose and made a face of disgust. Grant cast a quizzical glance toward her. "What?"

"Don't you smell that?" she demanded.

Grant didn't answer immediately. His sense of smell had been impaired for years. His nose had been broken three times in the past and always poorly reset. A running joke during his Magistrate days was that he could eat a hearty dinner with a dead skunk lying next to his plate.

Inhaling deeply through his nostrils, he caught

first an unpleasant whiff, then the cloying stench of something dead, something a long time dead. The bottom of the crater seemed saturated by the charnel-house reek. Queasiness settled in his stomach, and his mouth filled with sour saliva.

"Dead bodies down there," he murmured. "Animal or human or otherwise, they're most thoroughly dead."

DeFore nodded uneasily. "Should we investigate?"

Grant shook his head. "I don't see why we should."

"Because someone might need help."

"That looks like the camp of scavengers," he replied, forcing a reasonable note into his voice. "Roamers, Farers, maybe even Dregs. If anybody *is* still alive down there, they would just as soon kill us as accept help from us."

After a moment of thoughtful silence, DeFore retorted a little bitterly, "I guess you're the expert on outlanders."

"That's right," he declared flatly. "I am."

Outlanders, or anyone who chose to live outside ville society, or had that fate chosen for them, were of a different breed. Born into a raw, wild world, they were accustomed to living on the edge of death. Grim necessity had taught them the skills to survive, even thrive, in the postnuke environment. They may have been the great-great-great-grandchildren of civilized men and women, but they had no choice but to embrace lives of semibarbarism.

In the Outlands, people were divided into small, regional units, communications were stifled, rivalries bred, education impeded. The people who lived outside the direct influence of the villes, who worked the farms, toiled in the field, or simply roamed from place to place were reviled and hated. No one worried about an outlander, or even cared. They were the outcasts of the new feudalism, the cheap, expendable labor forces, even the cannon fodder when circumstances warranted. Generations of Americans were born into serfdom, slavery in everything but name. Whatever their parents or grandparents had been before skydark, they were now only commodities and they cursed the suicidal foolishness of their forebears who had brought on the nightmare.

Grant had come to realize that the outlanders, sneered at by the elite of the villes, were possibly the last real human beings on the planet, and they were an endangered species. As a Magistrate, he had killed dozens of outlanders in the performance of his duty, but he had murdered more than their bodies. He had destroyed their spirits, as well.

"You're right," DeFore said softly. "As far as we know, they died of a communicable disease. There's no point in endangering ourselves just so I can play doctor."

"You're not playing doctor," Grant told her matter-of-factly. "You are one. I understand how your first impulse is to help those who may be in need. I admire you for it. I always have. But in a place like this, helping is sometimes nothing more than prolonging some poor bastard's agony."

She raised her deep brown eyes to his. "You sound like you're speaking from experience."

He started walking along the ridgeline again. "I'm afraid I am."

When they reached the mouth of a path that twisted down into the ruins again, Grant paused to remove the compact set of microbinoculars from a clip on his web belt. He brought them to his eyes, peering through the ruby-coated lenses. As he swept them over the rubble-strewn terrain, the binoculars' magnifying power brought into sharp relief the broken buildings jutting from the overgrown streets.

Far in the distance, he glimpsed a city block with a cluster of buildings that appeared to be intact, and he tightened the focus. They were ugly structures of brick and concrete block, completely utilitarian. Rising from the center of them, like the cap of a mushroom, he made out a white dome. Behind the complex, ribbons of water gleamed dully, either a river or a canal.

Slowly, he shifted his focus away from the complex, scanning several other buildings. He barely made out the steeple of an old church. Just as he slid the binoculars away, a blur of movement caught his gaze. He tried to find it again and was on the verge of deciding he had glimpsed only a trick of light and shadows when a clot of blackness appeared in an alley between two structures.

He squinted through the eyepieces, and the clot resolved itself into a number of black-clad figures marching along the narrow passageway in the general direction of the church. Grant studied them only for a couple of seconds before they were hidden from view, but he was positive he saw a head topped with matted red-gold hair among the shadow-shapes.

DeFore noticed his back stiffen and his posture turn tense. "What is it?" she asked.

Grant didn't answer for such a long moment, DeFore almost repeated the question, but he lowered the binoculars and announced grimly, "I think I found Brigid."

DeFore's eyebrows crawled up toward her hairline. She opened her mouth to voice another question, but before she could speak Grant's trans-comm trilled. The sound was so unexpected, so startling Grant jerked in reaction and nearly lost his balance.

Grunting an embarrassed curse, Grant snatched the unit from his belt. "Grant here."

For a second only fuzzy crackles filtered from the receiver, then Domi's faint, childlike voice said, "This is Domi. I'm still with the Cat. What's going on?"

The reception was poor, but if she hadn't been using the Sandcat's more powerful transmitter, a connection could not have been established at all. The handheld comms only had a range of a mile, perhaps two miles on flat terrain and in exceptionally clear weather. Although the storm had moved on, the weather was anything but clear and the landscape certainly wasn't level.

"We've lost Kane and Brigid," he said, raising his voice. "Stay where you are until I tell you otherwise. We'll be trying to find them, so stand by."

No response came from the trans-comm. If Domi replied, her words were completely smothered by a jumble of squeals, snaps and hisses. Growling in wordless frustration, he closed the unit's cover and returned it to his belt.

A faint line of consternation appeared at the bridge of DeFore's nose. "Do you think she heard you?"

Grant shook his head. "I don't know. Even if she did, that's no guarantee she'll follow my orders."

DeFore forced a smile. "She's been a little on the disobedient side lately, hasn't she?"

Grant glared at her. "What's that supposed to mean?"

The woman wasn't intimidated. "It means what I said. She's not exactly toeing the mark you set for her. Kind of like a child defying parental authority."

Grant snorted in derision. "Save the sandbox psy-choanalysis. Let's go."

As they climbed down the face of the crater, the medic's observations circled within the walls of Grant's skull, stirring up unwanted and confusing emotions in their wake. Almost since the day they met, Domi had claimed to be in love with him, viewing him as a gallant black knight who rescued her from the shackles of Guana Teague's slavery. In reality, quite the reverse was true. Teague was crushing the life out of Grant beneath his three-hundred-plus pounds of flab when Domi expertly slit his throat.

Regardless of the facts, Domi had attached herself to him and made it fiercely clear to everyone that Grant was hers and hers alone. She had even evinced jealousy of DeFore, suspecting the woman of having designs on Grant. He was fairly certain the medic had no such intent, but he made sure there was nothing between them but a guarded friendship.

Of course, he reflected, he had fought hard to make sure there was nothing but friendship between him and Domi, too. He had no idea of Domi's true age, and neither did she. She could be as young as sixteen or as old as twenty-six, but either way, he was pushing forty and felt twice as old.

Always before he had tried to make the gap in their ages the reason he didn't want to get sexually involved with her. He knew how lame the excuse was, since Domi was certainly no stranger to sex, not after spending six months servicing the gross lusts of Guana Teague.

In truth, she represented a simple kind of innocence, a waiflike winsomeness he didn't want to complicate. And hovering always at the back of his mind and emotions was the memory of Olivia, the only woman who'd truly claimed his heart.

Although he hadn't seen her in many years, the image of her light brown, café-au-lait complexion, black plaited hair and big eyes was always with him. Her eyes were her most memorable and haunting feature—wise eyes, yet innocent, deep and brown. He still remembered with a painful clarity the last time he had looked into those eyes, more than six years ago.

They had submitted a formal mating contract application. It was summarily reviewed and rejected and once that happened, he and Olivia had drawn attention to themselves. Their relationship became officially unsanctioned and could not continue lawfully. Although matrimony and child producing were considered the supreme social responsibility by the baronial government, it was also considered only a temporary arrangement.

Children were a necessity for the continuation of society, but only those passing stringent tests were allowed to bear them. Genetics, moral values and social standing were the most important criteria.

Generally, a man and a woman were bound together for a term of time stipulated in a contract.

Once the child entered a training regimen of one of the ville divisions, the parents were required to separate, particularly in the case of male children recruited by the Magistrates. Certainly, babies still needed to be born, but only the right kinds of babies. A faceless council had determined that he and Olivia could not produce the type of offspring which made desirable ville citizens.

Grant remembered how, after breaking the spirit-rending news to her, he prowled the promenades of all four levels of the residential Enclaves, seeking a way to escape his own grief. He had considered barging in on Kane, but then he would have been obliged to explain his presence at 0300, and he simply didn't have the words.

Years later, he still didn't have the words. He had only spoken of the incident to one person, confiding his heartbreak only to Shizuka. Although the pain hadn't completely left him, she had helped it become a little less sharp, blunting some of the jagged edges. And now, when he thought of Olivia, more often than not, Shizuka's eyes superimposed themselves over the image of her face.

Her eyes were just as dark, just as wise, but they held a proud glint like that of a fierce young eagle. He would have never admitted to anyone, certainly not within earshot of Domi, that he missed her very much.

He'd never really given much thought to kids after Olivia, at least, not to having any of his own. But lately, since meeting Shizuka, he'd started thinking about it a bit more seriously. He wondered if creating a new life might not be a way to balance out the lives he had taken over the years.

Grant and DeFore crossed the face of the crater with little difficulty, and made for the nearest thoroughfare. Weeds sprouted from cracks in the pavement and footpaths, sickly greenish-black growth with ropy stems that twined around streetlight poles like serpents.

At an intersection, Grant stopped to consult the compass and get his bearings, then he turned right. A narrow lane between two burned-out buildings stretched before him, shadowed by the late-afternoon sunlight. A rectangular stone block, nearly five feet tall, rose above the sidewalk. Letters were painted on it, and though they were faded to near illegibility he was able to read Pedestrians Only.

Some seventy feet away, the lane terminated in an arched entranceway cut into the facade of the building, like an oval with a squared-off bottom. Grant strode toward it purposefully. As he drew closer, he saw it was tunnel. On the far side, light gleamed feebly.

He suddenly realized DeFore was hanging back

several yards. Glancing over his shoulder, he snapped gruffly, "Close it up."

Reba DeFore's temperament was quick and volatile. Her dark eyes flashing in anger, she retorted curtly, "Whoever castrated that man we saw earlier could be in there."

"I know," Grant agreed. "If so, their eunuch-making days will be over."

To punctuate his declaration, his Sin Eater sprang from the holster on his forearm and slapped into his right hand.

The tunnel wasn't very long, barely a hundred feet. Brackets that had once held fluorescent lights were arranged at regular intervals on the arched ceiling. It opened onto a narrow ramp, a footbridge spanning a drainage canal. On the opposite side was another lane running between two buildings. A partially dislodged manhole cover lay on the ground.

Grant stopped to study the layout, but DeFore's quiet voice intruded upon his concentration. "Look at this."

He turned around and saw her kneeling over a spattering of crimson liquid on the ground. More scarlet droplets speckled the waist-high barrier that ran the length of the bridge.

"Blood," Grant stated unnecessarily.

"Blood," DeFore repeated, touching her index finger to one of the largest drops, smearing it over the concrete. "Fresh blood at that. It hasn't had the time to dry out."

Tension knotted at the base of Grant's spine as if a fist closed around his vertebrae. He glanced over the side into the canal but saw nothing but a sluggish stream of muddy water.

"Let's keep moving," he said, marching across the bridge. This time DeFore followed him closely, drawing her small pistol. They strode through the debris-clogged lane and out into a very broad avenue.

The street, though rutted and deeply furrowed, was wide enough for them to avoid the heaps of rubble that had fallen from the ramparts of the taller buildings. Grant led the way past the rusted out husks of automobiles, noting how they had been stripped of anything salvageable years, if not decades ago. Although bushes sprouted in profusion, all of them were blighted.

Among a collection of buildings that seemed more or less intact, Grant saw a church. The shape of a bell could still be identified hanging from a cross bar in the steeple. He eyed the bell tower closely as they approached it, then came to a sudden halt.

DeFore nearly trod on his heels. "What is it?" she demanded in an annoyed tone.

"An idea," he responded absently, then he

swiftly headed toward the wide steps that led up to the big door.

"Where are you going?"

"To call Kane and Brigid," he replied. "Or at least, let them know we're around."

She followed him up the crumbling steps. "How do you figure to do that?"

Grant shouldered open the church door. The wood was only partially rotted, the planks still held together by rust-streaked bands of black iron. He entered the central chapel area. All the pews had long ago been removed by scavengers. Only pegs jutting from the floor showed where they had once been anchored. Feeble shafts of sunlight streamed in through the broken stained-glass windows. Dead leaves covered the floor in an ankle-deep layer. Moldering rubbish was heaped in the corners.

An ornately balustraded gallery, about twenty feet above, encircled the chapel. He saw a flight of stairs leading up to it and on the far side, a black, wrought-iron spiral staircase corkscrewing up into the darkness among the roof beams.

"Are you going to answer me?" DeFore's tone held an edge of impatience.

Grant pointed toward the shadow-shrouded roof. "Morse code. If that bell still works, I'll ring it in code. If they're anywhere within earshot, they'll hear it and come a-running."

He didn't need to add, "If they're still alive, that is."

At first DeFore's expression remained a skeptical mask, then an admiring smile tugged at the corners of her lips. "That's actually a pretty good idea."

"I have them occasionally. Stay here."

Grant crossed the chapel and went up the steps to the gallery. At the foot of the spiral staircase, he paused long enough to take his Nighthawk microlight from a pouch on his web belt. He attached it to his left index finger by its tiny Velcro strap, wearing it like a ring.

Grant scaled the first few treads of the stairs, testing them, noting how the risers and handrails were flecked and flaking with rust. The steps creaked a bit under his weight, and he heard little showers of rust sifting down from the undersides, but the staircase seemed solid enough.

He began climbing, casting the Nighthawk's 5,000 minicandlepower beam ahead of him. The staircase squeaked and groaned alarmingly during his upward progress, and he couldn't repress a sigh of relief when he reached the trapdoor.

Throwing it aside and ripping out the hinges in the process, Grant climbed up into the little cupola, sweeping his gaze over the terrain below him. On the far side of an area overgrown with tangled shrubbery, he saw the white domed building. It rested inside a fenced compound, reminding him of the ruins of a prison he had seen during his Mag days on a foray into the Arizona Outlands.

He quickly examined the bell. No rope dangled from the pivot, and the outer shell was rust-eaten, as was the iron clapper, but neither one was in danger of falling apart. The tone of the bell would be ruined by rust, but he wasn't interested in making music.

Grasping the bell, he swung it back and forth. The resulting gong was not melodic, but it was certainly loud and that was all he hoped for.

Chapter 8

The tolling of the bell meant nothing to Brigid Baptiste. It was just a noise completely unconnected to her present circumstances. The clangor only dimly penetrated the fog of panic clouding her mind.

The Furies either didn't hear the brazen peal or they decided to ignore it. The white-hot tip of the poker didn't falter or slow on its inexorable way to her eye. Brigid strained against the hands holding her, continuing to cringe.

Megaera stiffened at the sound, her masked face swiveling sharply toward the door. From beneath the thin layer of gold burst an incomprehensible garble of surprise.

The Fury wielding the poker hesitated. Brigid let her body go limp in the hands of the black-clad faceless men. She allowed her knees to bend, as if she were losing consciousness, and the Furies shifted position to keep her body upright. They hadn't expected her to sag within their grips.

Before they could cinch up on her arms, Brigid managed to plant both feet flat on the floor. When they jerked her upright, she straightened her legs like springs, kicking herself off the concrete, using the faceless men as braces.

With a whiplash motion of her body, Brigid turned in midair, her feet slamming against the poker-wielding Fury's torso, literally walking up his body horizontally.

The toe of her right boot knocked the poker aside, and her left foot connected hard against the underside of the Fury's jaw, lifting him up on his toes and sending him staggering backward. The poker described a smoking eddy as it fell from his hand and clanged loudly on the floor. Arms windmilling as he tried to regain his balance, the man fell against a black statue. The impact caused the body to topple to the floor. The limbs splintered and fragmented, and a cloud of black oily smoke poured from the cracks in the petrified flesh.

Brigid's body continued turning. A year ago, the very suggestion she could have performed such a stunt without a serious physical consequence would have made her laugh. Now she performed the back flip like a veteran acrobat, somersaulting between the two Furies and wriggling out of their grasps in the same motion.

She landed a little clumsily, but she turned her misstep into a forward lunge, tucking and rolling, shouldering aside the faceless men. Her path was blocked by the Fury whose bodysuit bore the muddy imprints of her boot treads from lower belly to clavicle. Stooping, he tried to snatch up the smoldering poker before she dodged around him.

Brigid came out of her roll and her right arm scythed down, the edge of her hand striking the neural center where the back of the Fury's neck joined his shoulders. The blow hammered him to the floor, and Brigid continued her forward bound toward the elevated platform.

Megaera stepped back, but not quickly enough. Brigid grabbed her by the hem of her robe and yanked. With a crowlike squawk of alarm, the old woman fell from the platform into Brigid's arms. Her golden mask clattered to the floor. Brigid swung the old woman around with enough violence to lift her from her feet and placed her between the approaching Furies and herself. They continued moving.

Grasping Megaera by the right wrist, her hand completely encircling it, Brigid forced her brittle left arm behind her back. She said, "Tell them to stop, you demented old bitch, or I'll break every bone in your body."

Megaera writhed like an animated skeleton in her grasp, and Brigid tightened her hold. "Monster! Blasphemer!" Megaera hissed.

"Send your Furies away or I'll show you how much of a monster I am." Brigid's tone was hard with conviction. "I'll start with breaking your fingers, one at a time. At your age, it takes a long time for bones to knit.''

Megaera spit out a clucking, nasal stream of vituperation. When she was done, the Furies lurched to a halt. Brigid's fingers briefly explored the woman's wristband, careful not to exert too much pressure on the opals.

''Why didn't you carbonize me when you had the chance?'' she asked quietly.

Megaera didn't answer, and Brigid squeezed her pipe-stem arm. The old woman cried out in angry pain. ''The sentence for your sin had yet to be meted out. It was still inside you. I would be guilty of murdering a soul had I done as you say.''

Despite the situation, Brigid couldn't help but smile sourly. Mad the old witch might be, but she was just as bound by protocol and procedure as the most officious archivists Brigid had known in the Historical Division.

''Which one of these buttons removes the spider?'' she demanded.

''Spider?'' the woman echoed.

''The oubolus.''

Megaera shook her head. ''That I will not say. Do not expect to escape my justice.''

''Yeah, and nobody expected the Spanish Inquisition, either. Answer my question.''

Lifting her chin at a prideful angle, Megaera declared pompously, ''That I will not do.''

Gritting her teeth in frustrated anger, Brigid wrenched the woman's right arm backward and found the catch on the wristband. She opened it and pulled it off, evoking another spitting snarl of "Blasphemer!" from Megaera.

Brigid started to retort, then suddenly realized the brazen tones of the bell she had almost tuned out were not a series of random clangs. Megaera shifted position and said petulantly, "There is no escape—"

"Shut the hell up," Brigid commanded. She listened intently for a moment, then relief washed through her, so intense her knees went momentarily weak. The chiming of the bell sounded more like a smith banging on an anvil, but when she recognized the dot and dashes of Morse code, it was the sweetest music she had ever heard. The message was simple but profoundly comforting: "Grant is here. Come to the church. Grant is here."

Brigid began slowly backing toward the double doors, dragging Megaera with her. She resisted and shrilled, "I cannot leave here with you!"

"And why is that?" Brigid asked distractedly, her eyes darting from the Furies to the statues.

"Your sin is still with you. If I accompany you, I will be judged for allowing a sinner to escape justice."

Brigid knew the old woman was terrified by the concept of sharing a sinner's fate. Three Furies were circling warily, sliding among the statues, their oubolus rods in plain sight, their masked faces opaque.

"Tell them to back off," Brigid snapped.

"I cannot, for they will not," Megaera stammered in a high, wild voice. "They will fulfill their duty."

Brigid jerked the old woman to a stop. The Furies froze almost at the same instant. Glancing to her left, she saw the statue of the woman whose nose had been cut off. Although it caused her a pang of guilt, as if she were desecrating the dead, she launched a stab-kick at it. The body shattered into fragments and acrid plumes of thick, sulfurous smoke boiled out.

Brigid took quick advantage of the distraction. She thrust Megaera into the arms of the nearest Fury and heeled around in the direction opposite the exit. She was certain at least two of the black-clad faceless men had skulked behind her to cut off her retreat.

With the furious shrieks of the old woman ringing in her ears, Brigid dodged among the petrified people, zagging one way and then zigging the other. Knowing that Megaera couldn't trigger the spider on her neck made her feel a little more confident, but not so much she became careless.

She sprinted into a long corridor and reached a flight of steps that slanted downward into complete, impenetrable blackness. Brigid paused, heart racing, staring into the well of darkness and listening to the scuff of running feet behind her. From somewhere outside the building came the sharp report of an explosion.

THE DARK-HAIRED WOMAN who aimed the blaster at Kane's head reminded him of an undernourished monkey with a serious nervous affliction. Her thin brown hands never ceased their disconcerting jerky movements along the barrel of the muzzle loader.

It appeared to be a musket, but in the dim light he couldn't be sure if it wasn't just a piece of narrow-gauge pipe. Her small, intense face was a mass of tics and spasms, and her large, dark-ringed eyes appeared incapable of focusing on one spot for more than a second at a time.

Kane didn't move. "I mean you no harm."

The woman ran her tongue over her chapped lips. "Heard that before, mister."

"I'm sure you have," Kane replied as calmly as he could. "I won't bother repeating it, then. But let me point out that your blaster is a one-shot piece of shit. You could miss with it or it could misfire." He paused and added, "Or it might not fire at all."

The woman's back stiffened, and her tongue returned to her mouth. Kane saw a sudden relief register on her face, and her eyes darted to a point behind him. Before he could turn, a hand grasped his shoulder and spun him deftly, slamming him against the wall. The cold tip of a gun barrel touched the back of his neck and a knee slid between his thighs, positioned uncomfortably against his testicles.

Kane felt hot, rancid breath on the side of his face, and a deep voice growled, "Don't move, sec man."

The woman exclaimed happily, "You did good, Hub!"

"Thanks, Zit," he replied. "I was taught by the best."

Kane said in a slow, deliberate tone, "Like I said to her, I mean you no harm."

Hub snarled out a derisive laugh and grabbed Kane's right forearm. Kane saw with dismay that the beefy paw nearly closed completely around his arm and holstered Sin Eater. "Fuckin' Mag come in here and tell us he mean no harm."

"You think I'm a Mag?"

Zit demanded, "Who else carries a blaster like that...in a holster like that?"

Kane forced himself to relax. *Sec man* was an obsolete term dating back to preunification days when self-styled barons formed their own private armies to safeguard their territories. It was still applied to Magistrates in hinterlands beyond the villes, so Kane figured Zit and Hub were either Roamers or Farers. Roamers were basically marauders, undisciplined bandit gangs who paid lip service to defying the ville governments as a justification for their depredations.

Farers, on the other hand, were nomads, a loosely

knit conglomeration of wanderers, scavengers and self-styled salvage experts and traders. Their territory was the Midwest, so Farer presence in and around Chicago would not have been unusual. Regardless, Magistrates were feared and despised all over the Outlands by Roamer and Farer alike.

Impatiently, Kane asked, "Lady, if I was a Mag, wouldn't I have killed you as soon as you opened your mouth?"

Hub voiced a sneering chuckle. "She got the drop on you, sec man...you didn't have no time to do nothin'."

Very quietly but very firmly, Kane said, "You know that's not true, Zit."

The woman didn't respond, but Kane guessed the kind of thoughts wheeling through her mind as she considered the implications of granting him a limited benefit of the doubt. He couldn't blame her for distrusting him. His own work with the Cerberus exiles kept him in a shadow world of danger and eternal suspicion, of sudden crisis and alarm, where human beings died in a covert war that ranged from the sands of the Black Gobi to the utter remoteness of a forgotten colony on Mars.

"How about letting me turn around," Kane suggested, "so I can explain?"

A moment of uncomfortable silence stretched between Zit and Hub before the woman said, "Do it slow."

Hub started to utter a protest, keeping Kane pinned against the wall, but Zit snapped sternly, "Let him go."

The woman was obviously the dominant one of the pair, but Kane wasn't sure if that was good or bad for him. Hub released him and stepped back. Kane pushed himself away from the wall, making sure to keep his hands visible.

Hub was a brawny man with tousled brown hair, wearing a gray zippered coverall. His heavy-jowled face was dark with beard stubble. What appeared to be a gun barrel protruded from the crook his left elbow, as if he were trying to give the impression he held a shotgun and his right hand supported the stock.

Like Hub, Zit wore a ragged one-piece garment. She was as skinny as a piece of cordwood and appeared to be in her forties, which probably made her closer to thirty. Life was short and hard in the Outlands. She nodded to his forearm. "If you ain't a Mag, where'd you get a Mag blaster?"

"Took it off one I killed," he replied casually. "Out Montana way. A triple-coldheart bastard named Kane."

"Bullshit," Hub grated. "Never heard of him."

Kane ignored the comment. "What are you two doing here?"

"We live here," Zit replied. "Leastways, we tried to live here afore the night-gaunts showed up."

"Night-gaunts?"

Zit inhaled a shuddery breath. "Black monsters with no faces led by a demon queen. They been huntin' and chillin' us for the last month."

"Us?" Kane inquired. On the fringes of his awareness, he became aware that the distant tolling of the bell had established a rhythm, one that sounded vaguely familiar. He couldn't afford to have his attention diverted, so he ignored the sound.

The woman indicated Hub with a jerk of her head. "We're Farers...we staked out this ville about a year ago and been workin' it."

"No sign of muties?"

Hub answered flatly, "No sign of nobody...until the night-gaunts showed up."

"Where'd they come from?" Kane asked.

Hub started to gesture with one arm but contented himself with a backward tilt of his head. "From the dome, we think. We don't know for sure. Too busy hidin'."

"You're hiding pretty close," Kane pointed out.

Zit forced a laugh, but it had no real humor in it. "Figured they wouldn't look for us in their own backyard."

The woman's face suddenly hardened. "Now what are you doin' here? I can tell you ain't a Farer nor a Roamer, neither."

"Yeah," Hub muttered suspiciously. "You know anything about that fuckin' bell?"

Kane started to voice a denial, but when Hub mentioned the bell, he listened to its rhythm. After a few seconds, he recognized the dot-dash pattern as spelling out: "Grant is here. Come to the church. Grant is here." He couldn't suppress the grin that spread across his face.

"What's so fuckin' funny?" Hub demanded.

"As a matter of fact, I do know something about the bell. Is there a church anywhere around?"

"Yeah," Zit answered. "Just across the lot."

"A friend of mine is ringing the bell. If we can get over there and hook up with him, we may be able to do something about these night-gaunts of yours."

"No!" Hub's harsh voice punched against Kane's eardrums. "We're not goin' anywhere. I think we should chill you and take your blaster."

Kane favored him with an icy stare. In an uninflected tone, he said, "I'd prefer you think that course of action over."

An ugly grin of superiority curled Hub's lips. "Two of us. You're outgunned."

"There may be two of you, but I'm betting I'm not outgunned."

Hub snarled wordlessly and took a menacing step forward, poking the barrel of his blaster hard into the pit of Kane's stomach. "You want to bet your life on that, asshole?"

Kane back fisted the barrel away with his right

144 JAMES AXLER

hand, and sprang forward to head butt the man in the face. Zit's voice rose in a frightened shout as Hub staggered against the wall. A length of dark pipe clattered to the floor as he lifted both hands to staunch the flow of blood from his nose and split lips. Pivoting on his right foot, Kane kicked his left leg up so the toe of his boot caught the underside of the long barrel in Zit's hand, sending the weapon spinning upward.

Kane flexed his wrist tendons and the electric motor droned, but the Sin Eater didn't pop into his hand. The big man shambled erect. Baring blood-filmed teeth, Hub roared in rage and started toward him, reaching for his throat.

As Kane stepped back, the holster's actuator's finally slapped his Sin Eater into his hand. Rather than shooting Hub, he chopped at his left hand with the flat of the frame. He heard the crunching of knuckles, but the man was already in so much pain from a broken nose and split lips that the blow was hardly more than a twinge. He pounded a right into Kane's body, just below the heart.

Kane swallowed a grunt of pain and staggered against the edge of the propped-open door. Hub rushed for him, and Kane rolled aside, grabbing a handful of coveralls and using his momentum to pitch him out the door. The man's hands flew instinctively out to catch himself, but Kane kicked his feet out from under him.

He fell facefirst to the ground and before he could rise, Kane crashed the barrel of his Sin Eater against the back of skull with an ugly crack of bone colliding with metal. Hub's body seemed to turn to rubber and collapsed bonelessly on the wet ground.

Kane whirled as Zit charged out of the building. Unlike Hub, she wasn't running a bluff with a piece of pipe. Her blaster was real, even if it was home forged. She shrieked, "You chilled my sweet Hub!"

He wanted to point out to her that it would require a hell of a lot more than a blow on the head to chill her sweet Hub, but she didn't give him the opportunity. The explosion that erupted from the muzzle of the gun wasn't quite as loud as a bomb going off, but it didn't miss by much. Kane felt his eardrums compressed by the concussion and his body shook to the jolt. A tongue of flame and a blinding ball of smoke gouted from the bore.

DOMI AUTOMATICALLY DROPPED into a crouch atop the slab of concrete as the cries of fear grew louder. She ignored the bell, focusing on the closer sounds. Her Combat Master came out of its holster in a smooth practiced motion and she held it in a double-handed grip, her left hand cupping her right.

Several voices shouted at once, men, women, children or a combination. It was hard to say. Within seconds a group of figures came into view from around a heap of vine-covered bricks. Panting and stumbling along was a quartet of outlanders. She was able to see one woman, a girl really, among them. She kept looking fearfully over her shoulder, and the weak sunlight reflected off something on the side of her neck. The distance was too great for Domi to ascertain what it was.

It was instantly obvious that the ragged people were terrified and in the last stages of exhaustion. They were followed around the pile of bricks by two more figures. Domi's heart skipped a beat and then began to thud frantically. At first glance, it appeared the outlanders were prodded along by thin black shadows with no faces.

She realized a moment later the pursuers were attired in one-piece uniforms of such a deep black it almost looked as if they wore shadows. But it was their faces, or rather their lack of faces, that caught her eye. In their hands were rods with little silver knobs that flashed at the tips.

The woman tripped over a piece of stone and dropped to her hands and knees, her head bowed and her shoulders quaking as if she were trying to be sick.

One of the shadow men poked with her with the silver-tipped baton. The woman didn't move. She didn't make any attempt to struggle as she was heaved upright, standing between the two faceless men who each held her by an arm.

Moving on impulse, almost without thought,

Domi leveled her handblaster and swiftly brought the shadow man on the woman's left into target acquisition. Fifty yards was long range for a handblaster, but she had made more difficult shots. When the ebony figure was framed within the Combat Master's sights, she adjusted for elevation and windage, then she squeezed the trigger three times.

The big automatic blaster bucked in her hands, sending out booming shock waves of ear-shattering sound. The first .45-caliber bullet hit the man directly in the center of his featureless face. He catapulted backward, releasing the woman, who dived to safety.

The second round struck the other shadow man in the torso, tearing through the black skin amid a spouting of blood. He went over backward. The third shot ricocheted off the pile of bricks with a keening whine and a spray of red dust.

The outlanders scattered, running in all directions. Only the girl remained, gazing in Domi's direction, her eyes big and shocked in her hollow-cheeked face. Domi felt a pang of pity for her, knowing she'd spend her young life in a struggle just to exist or, if she went to one of the villes, in sexual servitude to a Pit boss. Once she was worn out or lost her appeal, she'd be killed or thrown out with the rest of the refuse. It didn't happen to Domi, but only because she'd struck first.

The girl climbed to her feet, gathering a ratty

blanket around her shoulders. Domi watched her
scuttle away into the ruins. She had no inclination
to run after the girl to try to convince her she was
a friend. Nor was she inclined to climb down from
her perch and examine the faceless corpses. Although she knew they were men in suits, they awakened in her a superstitious dread, rekindling old folk
tales told around campfires about soul-stealing demons, gibbering ghosts and night-gaunts. As she recalled, those were the worst. They never spoke or
laughed and never smiled, because they had no faces
at all to smile with.

"Stupe," Domi muttered, embarrassed by her re-
gression to childish fears. She returned her attention
and energy to climbing the pile of rubble. She dug
her fingers into narrow niches and pulled herself
nimbly upward, bracing herself with footholds. She
climbed recklessly, clawing and kicking her way up.

When Domi reached the summit, she chinned herself up to stretch out on the three-foot-wide slab and
catch her breath. Her fingers were sore and she massaged them. From her vantage point, she surveyed
the ruins. The fields of devastation stretched almost
out of sight. The few structures still recognizable as
buildings rose at the skyline, then collapsed with
ragged abruptness. She slowly became aware that
the tolling of the bell sounded strange, as if it were
sounding a signal. Shading her sensitive eyes with

her hands, she looked around, trying to pinpoint its source.

Far in the distance the steeple of a church pointed like a finger above the roofs of buildings that still stood. Domi unhooked her binoculars from her belt and brought them to her eyes, focusing on the structure. She saw the outline of a man inside the cupola, vigorously pulling and pushing the bell back and forth, but he did so in a jerky, mannered way. When the outline shifted position, she recognized his broad shoulders.

Domi had no idea why Grant was ringing a church bell, but she knew it wasn't a whim on his part. He was about as whimsical as an incend grenade. She was fairly certain it had to do with an attempt to find Kane and Brigid. Lowering her binoculars, Domi removed the trans-comm from her belt, knowing in advance he would try to upbraid her for leaving the Sandcat when he'd ordered her to stay put. Silently, she rehearsed her response. It wasn't a difficult speech to memorize since it consisted of only two words.

Chapter 9

Because of the racket of the bell, Grant didn't immediately hear the trilling of the trans-comm. If he hadn't paused to rest his arms after swinging the heavy metal shell back and forth for the past five minutes, he wouldn't have heard it at all.

His eardrums still vibrating with the echoes of the gonging, he barely recognized Domi's voice when he opened the comm channel. As it was, he didn't catch most of what she said. "Repeat," he growled into the transceiver. "I didn't hear you."

"I said," she replied a touch impatiently, "what are you doing with that damn bell?"

Grant's hearing recovered sufficiently so he noticed the lack of static over the frequency. "I'm signaling in Morse code. If Brigid and Kane are anywhere near, they'll hear it."

A sudden notion occurred to him and he demanded, "How did you know I was ringing the bell? Where are you?"

Her response was silky with amused triumph. "Look to your right."

Grant did so and saw nothing but acres of debris. "I don't see anything," he said darkly.

"You'll have to use your binoculars. I should've mentioned that."

Unclipping them from his belt, he put them to his eyes and scanned the ruins. "Up a little," she suggested. "You're getting warmer."

He did as she said and glimpsed a slight, distant figure standing atop a hillock of rubble, waving an arm. For a moment Grant experienced a surge of rage that the girl had disobeyed his order to stay with the Sandcat. After he reassessed his initial reaction, the anger didn't last long. The more active players in the field increased the odds of finding the two missing members of their party.

"Good enough," he declared flatly. "You think you can make your way over here?"

In a slightly surprised, vaguely troubled tone, Domi answered, "Sure. I guess so."

"Do it as fast as you can."

"Sure—if that's what you want."

"It's what I want. Double-time it, but be careful."

He watched Domi stow her comm and the binoculars and begin picking her nimble way down the face of the heap. When she made a misstep, his breath caught in his throat. Domi quickly recovered her balance and kept moving, adopting a studiedly diffident attitude as if to say "I meant to do that."

Grant lowered the binoculars and turned away,

reminding himself of Domi's almost supernatural agility. He had often compared her acrobatic abilities to those of a scalded monkey's. He also recalled Domi's offer to show him interesting variations on how her gymnastic skills could be applied to their mutual benefit. She hadn't made an offer like that in several months now, and he wasn't quite sure how he felt about it.

Repressing a sigh, Grant massaged the aching tendons in his forearms and placed his hands on the pitted surface of the bell. Although it was rusted through to paper thinness in some spots, the bell was still heavy and ponderous to swing on its unlubricated pivots. The squealing it made was almost as loud as the tolling.

He took a deep breath, pulled the bell toward him in preparation for another swing—then he heard a sharp, door-banging report, like that of a gren detonating. Releasing the bell, Grant fumbled for his binoculars, stepping to the edge of the bell tower and ignoring how the floorboards creaked and sagged alarmingly beneath his 230-odd pounds.

Although he couldn't be positive, he was fairly certain the explosion came from the direction of the fenced-in compound. He swept the ruby-coated lenses back and forth over the flat roofs of the buildings. A gray umbrella of smoke rose lazily from an alley between two of the brick structures. It didn't hold the mushroom configuration indicative of a

high-explosive charge. In fact, it looked more like
smoke exuded by black powder.

He continued to squint into the eyepieces, cursing
beneath his breath at the buildings that obstructed
his view. Then, rolling through the air came a booming crack like the breaking of a distant branch.
Grant's stomach muscles tensed in an adrenaline-
fueled spasm. "Shit!" he hissed. He tensed his wrist
tendons and unleathered his blaster as he recognized
the unmistakable report of a Sin Eater.

Pointing the weapon at the sky, Grant squeezed
off a single round, listening to the echoes of the shot
rolling over the fields of rubble. Within a few seconds, he heard an answering crack from the vicinity
of the compound. He whirled toward the trapdoor,
heedless of the bell in his way. It gave out with a
feeble chime when his shoulder struck it, but he
couldn't care less now.

As THE CONCUSSION jarred him to the marrow of his
bones, Kane shoulder rolled away from the fiery
flare and burst of smoke. He fetched up against the
side of the building and heard the metallic rattle of
objects striking the brickwork over his head.

Index finger hovering over the trigger stud of his
Sin Eater, Kane cautiously lifted his head. The hot,
sharp reek of black powder cut into his nostrils. Flat
planes of gray-white smoke floated in the air like a
dirty fog bank.

Rising slowly, Kane fanned the thick vapor away from his face, trying not to inhale any of it. He took a tentative step forward, and saw more or less what he expected to see. The shotgun lay on the ground, the barrel split open and peeled back like a banana skin. The wooden stock was nestled within a red, wet mess that Kane had difficulty identifying as Zit's maimed hand.

The woman's face was far worse, flesh flayed open to the bone as if a flensing knife had been applied to it. Her jugular vein, severed by a razor-edged shard of metal, pumped out ropes of blood that oozed over the grass and turned the mud into a crimson-tinged sludge.

Kane coughed and shook his head, either in pity or disgust, he wasn't sure which. Home-forged blasters were notoriously untrustworthy. Although one of the first priorities of the Program of Unification was the disarmament of the people, books and diagrams survived the sweeps. Self-styled gunsmiths continued to forge weapons, though blasters more complicated than black-powder muzzle loaders were beyond their capacities.

Making gunpowder wasn't an easy process, either. Usually, outlanders practiced a great deal of thrift with their powder. Zit apparently decided to go to the other end of the spectrum, and in doing so turned her shotgun into a pipe bomb.

A rustle of cloth caused Kane to whirl. Hub, his

eyes slightly glassy, hiked himself up to a sitting position. He blinked in dumbfounded wonderment at Zit's mutilated corpse, then glared in unregenerate hatred at Kane. He made a move to push himself to his feet.

Kane tapped the firing stud of the Sin Eater and it boomed. A 9 mm round kicked up dirt between the man's thighs, barely a quarter of an inch from the crotch of his trousers. "Stay there or you'll have a lovely soprano singing voice."

Hub subsided, but his lips worked as if he were contemplating spitting at him. He contented himself with snarling, "Fuckin' Mag!"

"I'm not a Mag and I didn't kill her. It was an accident." Kane's tone was curt and matter-of-fact.

Tears glimmered in Hub's eyes, and he wiped them away with angry swipes of his callused hands. Bitterly he said, "Might as well chill me, too."

Before Kane could reply, he jumped at the sound of the shot. It wasn't close but it wasn't far away, either. A grin tugged at the corners of his mouth when he recognized the report of a Sin Eater. Raising his pistol he squeezed off two rounds into the sky. Hub misinterpreted the meaning of the grin and the shots.

He levered himself up by his arms, but he achieved only a half crouch before Kane kicked him in the chest. He sat down hard on the ground. Kane aimed his pistol at his broad forehead. "Give me some information and you can go on your way."

"What kind of information?" Hub demanded.

Kane jerked his head toward the rolled-up shadowsuit and opaque face mask he had left on the ground beside the outbuilding. "Information about the people who wear clothes like that. You call them night-gaunts?"

Hub nodded.

"I saw a man earlier with a little metal bug attached to him." Kane tapped the side of his neck. "Right about here. You know anything about that?"

Hub nodded again, but this time he spoke. "Yeah. The night-gaunts shoot 'em out of little sticks."

"What do they do to you?"

Hub's expression twisted in a rictus of horror and fury. "Go into the dome, sec man, and you'll find out for yourself."

"I'm not a—" Kane caught himself and cut off his automatic denial. He saw no reason to continue hammering home the point he wasn't a Magistrate. Hub's mind, what there was of it, had already been made.

Keeping the bore of the Sin Eater trained on the man's broad forehead, he retreated a few paces and picked up the shadowsuit and mask. He circled around Hub, getting behind him.

"All right," he announced. "You and I are done. Take your woman's body and get out of here. If you come after me, I'll make sure you join her. Understand?''

Hub didn't expend any effort in turning his head toward him. He only husked out, "Yeah. Fuck off, maggot."

Kane felt a hot flush of anger, and he briefly considered trimming one of the man's earlobes with a well-placed bullet. It would be an adequate penalty for his impudence. Of course, if he'd still been a Magistrate, he would have planted the bullet in the back of Hub's head.

He decided Grant would misunderstand the meaning of the shot, and there had been enough communication problems already today. Kane turned and set off quickly in the direction of the dome.

BRIGID HESITATED at the mouth of the stairwell. The notion of rushing headlong into impenetrable darkness pimpled her flesh with an almost superstitious chill. She knew she couldn't hope to fight off the Furies, as lanky as they were. They possessed muscles with the tensile strength of steel.

She looked down the corridor and saw a shadow-shape approaching her at an almost casual gait, as if he had decided to let her wear herself out in flight before he recaptured her. Clenching her teeth and fists in frustrated fury, Brigid plunged down the stairwell, holding on to the banister with one hand and taking two steps at a time.

The flight of stairs ended after only a dozen or so feet, but when she sprinted down the passageway what little light peeped from above was completely swallowed by the darkness.

She retained a vivid recollection of the fear that had nearly consumed her when she and Kane groped blindly through the lightless caverns of Agartha, and she wasn't too eager to repeat the experience. Fright increased with every step Brigid took into the chute of darkness. She became aware less by sight and hearing than a shuddery sensation of the Fury descending the stairwell behind her.

Brigid cast a quick glance over her shoulder, and was startled to see an oval shimmering a pale amber against the deep dark. She was reminded of a cyclopean eye, and for an instant doubts rose in her mind as to the relative humanity of the Furies. She told herself the masks were probably a night-vision system of some sort. The possibility she could be tracked by her body-heat signature didn't make her feel any better, but at least she contended with technology, not magic.

With her right hand on the wall, she trotted down the corridor. It made several turnings until she felt she was lost in a maze of black passages. Even the sense of direction in which she took so much pride was confused. Mentally, she swore at herself for allowing herself to be run like a deer into a labyrinth, but it was too late to turn back now.

Brigid's hand suddenly slipped from the wall, encountering nothing but slightly stale air. Coming to an unsteady halt, she stretched out both arms and stood baffled for a long moment. She had reached a T junction where the corridor split in three branches. She recalled reading how when rats were tested by being run through a maze, they habitually chose a right-hand path.

On a sudden venture, she chose the left-hand corridor. The smooth floor slanted slightly downward, like a ramp, and she touched the cold metal tubing of a handrail. The floor continued to decline steadily. She fancied she could feel the pressure of tons of bedrock over her head. She knew that the Totality Concept projects were usually hidden in subterranean annexes. All of the redoubts she had visited always seemed haunted by the ghosts of a hopeless, despairing past age. The walls seemed to exude the terror, the utter despondency of souls trapped here when the first mushroom cloud erupted from Washington on that chill January noon.

Suddenly, her ears caught a faint clicking and she grabbed the rail to pull herself to a stop. She listened intently as the clicking was repeated, but more distant now. The sound was definitely mechanical in nature, like switches being thrown.

On the ceiling, crescent-shaped light fixtures wavered, then shed a watery illumination. Brigid blinked up at them as, in a staggered sequence, lights flashed on along the length of the corridor's ceiling. The dim, suffuse illumination produced by the crescents wasn't bright enough to dazzle her, but she could at least see what lay ahead of her and to either side. The view was unimpressive and certainly unsurprising—a long expanse of featureless corridor made of smooth concrete blocks. Since the layout of so many redoubts was standardized, she experienced a brief sensation of déjà vu.

A large illuminated map was set at the center of an intersection. Three other passages, slightly narrower, forked off in different directions, dark directions. She stepped up to the map, but when she heard a stealthy footfall behind her, she broke into a sprint, wondering if she had inadvertently tripped a photoelectric beam that activated the lighting system. As she ran, she passed several sealed doors on both sides of the corridor, but each one bore a keypad instead of a knob or handle. She reached another stairwell and ran down it, barely touching the risers, bounding from one landing to the other.

The corridor doglegged to the left. Painted on the right wall in huge smeared letters were the words GOODI WINDI CITI. She didn't comprehend the reference at first, then recalled in predark days, Chicago had been nicknamed the Windy City. A few more yards down the passage, she passed another legend painted on the wall: SO LONG CHI-TOWN.

A wide arched doorway led into an adjoining an-

techamber. Artifacts of glistening metal and crystal
were arrayed on shelves. As much as she wanted to,
Brigid didn't pause to examine them. Chamber followed chamber in a straight line.

At the terminus, she entered a large vault-walled
room. She saw a single, simplified master-control
console running the length of one wall, and recognized a few of the basic command panels from the
Cerberus installation. In one corner she saw a functioning vid sec cam. A red indicator light shone like
a pinprick of blood on the casing.

The far wall consisted only of a thick metal door
upon which was imprinted a warning—Entry To
Chron-Temp Section Strictly Forbidden To All Personnel Below B-12 Clearance. Emblazoned below
was a symbol she had seen once before, that of a
stylized hourglass, the top half of it colored black,
the bottom red.

She saw no keypad, knob or lever. Throat muscles
constricting, Brigid ran her hands over the door and
its rivet-studded frame, fingers seeking a hidden
latch. When she found nothing, she turned her attention to the console and the built-in CPUs. She
stroked a few keys, thumbed a couple of buttons,
but the two monitor screens remained dark. With a
sinking sensation in the pit of her stomach, she realized that even if she could get a comp on-line, she
could spend the next week searching for the right

commands to raise the door. She doubted she had a full minute.

When Brigid heard a footfall, she amended her time limit to a few seconds or less. Whirling, she saw the black-clad Fury approaching her with a measured tread. She pressed her back against the door, and her eyes darted wildly around the chamber, searching for anything that either resembled a weapon or a loose object that could be used as one.

The Fury halted ten feet away from her and raised his oubolos rod, pointing it at her upper body. "That won't do you any good," she said, startled by the hollow, echoing quality of her voice in the room. She patted a pants pocket. "I have the controls for your little spiders."

It was impossible to tell if her declaration registered at all with the Fury. He didn't react in any way, as if he hadn't heard her or considered her statement so irrelevant it wasn't worth a response. She made a sliding sideways motion. The rod followed her, silver winking dully from the tip. The man spoke from beneath the mask, but not in the heavily accented English Megaera employed. The tone of his voice was almost wheedling.

Brigid listened to him closely, the realization slowly dawning on her that although it sounded like gibberish, it was due to the fact the language he spoke was mainly monosyllabic. The vowels were not clearly articulated, and the enunciation of the consonants was slurred. Still, Brigid heard one word repeated several times. It sounded like *"Di-ku."*

When the man in black paused, Brigid interjected, "If you're trying to convince me to give up and stop making your job difficult, you can forget it."

Loudly, the Fury exclaimed, *"Di-ku!"*

"Di-ku you, too," Brigid retorted.

The Fury took a slow, ominous step toward her. Brigid set herself to spring to one side.

"Touch her and you die."

The voice bursting from a speaker on the console held a hard note of utter conviction. Brigid jumped, heart pounding. The Fury's featureless head swiveled to and fro on his neck as he cast about for the source of the voice.

"Don't bother looking for me. I can see you— you can't see me. That's usually the way of gods, isn't it?" Despite its electronic timbre, the voice was well modulated, with a sonorous tenor quality. It was also blood-chillingly familiar, and caused Brigid's belly to turn a cold flip-flop of nausea. She set her teeth on a groan of both anger and disbelief.

The Fury continued to stand motionless in the room, although the rod in his hand shook ever so slightly.

"Your god commands you to depart," the voice said imperiously. "This woman is not to be harmed. Her sins are too great to be dealt with by the likes of you."

A vibration shivered through the portal at Brigid's back. With a hum and a mechanical clanking, the slab of metal rose, slid between a pair of baffled slots and locked into place with two loud snaps. Looking over her shoulder, Brigid saw only a dark room. The Fury took a hesitant step back and then halted. Despite his lack of features, he was obviously confused and not a little frightened.

"Go!" the voice roared. "Go now, or I shall consign your soul to the perdition where the disobedient are given eternal enemas of jalapeno juice and rock salt!"

The Fury's nerve broke. Heeling around, he sprinted out of the chamber. Watching him go, Brigid did not feel relief. Trying to minimize the tremor in her voice, she demanded, "You can see and hear me?"

"Very clearly. You apparently could do with a hot shower and dry clothes."

Brigid heaved a weary sigh and ran her hands through her still damp hair. "Are you making me an offer?"

"Not quite. At the moment, I don't feel any qualms about seeing you suffer a little bit." The voice acquired a cold, hard edge. "As I recall, the last time we saw each other, you left me to die. I'm still trying to make up my mind what to do about that. It's a problem that has vexed me for some time."

"Something will occur to you," she countered with icy irony. "I'm sure you've been scheming and brooding about it for the past six months. Whatever you come up with will be very clever, very diabolical and a colossal waste of your ingenuity. But diverting your resources so you can indulge an egotistical whim always takes precedence over any other consideration, doesn't it?"

"You think you know me so well." This time the voice was not filtered over a comm channel but emanated from the room behind her. She turned, doing her best to appear calm and composed.

The man who walked out was extraordinarily small, but his proportions were extraordinarily perfect. There was much about him that was perfect. If he had been three feet taller, a hundred or more pounds heavier, he would have been one of the most beautiful men Brigid had ever seen.

His thick, dark blond hair was swept back from a high forehead, tied in a foxtail at his nape. Under level brows, big eyes of the clearest, cleanest blue, like the high sky on a cloudless summer's day, regarded her sympathetically. Beneath his finely chiseled nose, a wide, beautifully shaped mouth stretched in an engaging grin, displaying white, even teeth.

He was attired in a duplicate of the skin-tight black bodysuits worn by the Furies, but without the cowl. In his right hand, he carried a miniature black

walking stick, with a hammered-silver knob and fer-
rule. In the left he gripped a very utilitarian short-
barreled revolver. He gestured with it negligently,
and just as negligently, Brigid raised her hands.

"The small, smiling god I presume," she said
flatly. "I should have guessed."

Upon seeing the grave expression on her face, the
small god laughed with genuine amusement. "I'm
so glad you're here, Miss Brigid. It'll be the cap-
stone of my life to prove all your preconceived notions about me wrong."

Chapter 10

The tangles of thorny undergrowth snagged Grant's clothes and scratched DeFore's hands, but neither person uttered a complaint. Grant bulled through the dense thicket until they reached a deeply furrowed avenue. On the other side was a sprawling complex of buildings. The domed structure was overgrown with vines and creepers, masking the facade and almost blanketing the sign that identified the compound as the Lake District Central Filtration Plant.

Grant paused, studying the shadows beyond the double doors of the central building. He could see the lurid glow of firelight.

"What are we waiting for?" DeFore whispered anxiously. "If it was Brigid you saw before, more than likely she's in there."

Not answering, Grant unclipped his trans-comm and keyed in Domi's channel. She responded after a moment, sounding slightly winded. "I'm here."

"Forget the church," Grant said in a low tone. "There's a park on the other side of the street from it. Go through there. You can probably find the path me and DeFore made."

"Then what?"

"Then you'll see a bunch of buildings, one with a dome. That's the filtration plant."

"Will you be waiting for me?" she asked.

"I don't know. That depends."

"On what?"

"I don't know," he repeated. "Grant out." He closed the cover of the comm unit and returned it to his belt.

Sounding more than a little peeved, DeFore demanded, "What's the plan? What are we going to do?"

By way of a response, Grant's body tensed and he bent his knees, dropping into a half crouch, his Sin Eater snapping up. Mystified, DeFore imitated him, following his intent gaze. Both people exhaled noisy sighs of relief when they saw Kane sidling around the dome-roofed building.

"We're going over there," Grant announced, stepping onto the avenue. "That's the plan."

Before they had crossed the street, Kane caught sight of them and waited for the two people to make their way up the cracked sidewalk to his position. DeFore noted that neither man seemed overly surprised to see the other. She figured their faith in each other's survival skills was so strong, they always proceeded from the assumption that even during long periods of separation, Kane knew Grant could more than fend for himself, and vice versa.

Speaking in terse sentences, they brought each other up to date. When Grant stated he believed he'd glimpsed Brigid, and she was inside the main building of the filtration plant, Kane's eyes narrowed momentarily,

"I'm sure she's all right," DeFore said reassuringly.

Kane acknowledged her comment with a short nod. "Let's hope she's *not* inside. According to a couple Farers I questioned, that's where the night-gaunts hang their laundry."

"The night-gaunts?" Grant echoed.

Turning, Kane reached into a clump of brush and brought out the shadowsuit. He rolled it with a snap of his wrist and repeated what Hub and Zit had told him.

"They apparently have something to do with those little metal bugs we found on the man's neck." Kane's tone was flat and neutral. "I'm not sure what."

Grant eyed the wide steps leading to the double doors of the dome-roofed building. "The only way to be sure is to go in there. That's our only option."

"Since when have we had more than one?" Kane snapped.

Both DeFore and Grant assumed his query was rhetorical, so they didn't answer. Glancing uneasily across the avenue, Grant murmured, "I'll feel a lot better about going in there with Domi to cover our backs. She should have been here by now."

He unclipped his trans-comm from his belt and thumbed up the cover. Domi's slight figure appeared at the edge of the park, her white face and hair contrasting starkly with the greenery. Sighting the three people, she trotted across the thoroughfare. When she reached them, she asked, "Why are you hanging around out here?" She had unconsciously lowered her voice.

Grant and Kane took turns briefing her. Her lips pursed at the mention of the night-gaunts. "Chilled me a couple of the bastards about half an hour ago. They'd captured some outlanders."

"Farers," Kane corrected. He moved toward the foot of the steps. "The answer to where the night-gaunts came from and why they're here is in there. Let's go."

Taking the point, Kane went up the stairs at an oblique angle from the doors. Motioning the people behind him to stop, Kane went to one knee, taking a slow visual recce of the structure and the murky area beyond the doors. He considered circling the building, approaching it from the rear. However, he saw no signs of movement anywhere. Standing, he gestured for his companions to come forward.

"Standard deployment," he said to them quietly. "We're going in by the front door. Triple red."

The four people fanned out in a wedge as they

moved toward the front of the building. Domi's
crimson eyes blazed in anticipation of combat. She
held her Combat Master in a two-fisted grip, the
barrel as steady as stone. Next to her, DeFore
crouched to make herself a smaller target, the Titan
FIE braced at her hip, finger on the trigger. Grant,
standing behind Kane, held his Sin Eater in both
hands, barrel pointing up.

When he shouldered open the door, the sunlight
peeping in from outside showed Kane that a foyer-
like room and short corridor beyond were deserted.
He moved in fast, shifting the barrel of his Sin Eater
back and forth. The others came in behind him.

Stealthily, the four people crept into a vast circular chamber. It was windowless, but there was sufficient daylight shafting in through a crack in the
domed roof so they could see the second level. By
the firelight flickering from a pair of braziers, it appeared at first glance the rotunda was full of people.
But their lack of movement was so pronounced, they
knew it was unnatural. Hanging in the air was the
nostril-abrading stench of hot sulfur mixed with ammonia. Kane had smelled the same odor when the
calcified man turned into smoke.

Grant growled deep in his throat, sweeping the
barrel of his pistol back and forth in short left-to-
right arcs. Kane sensed the big man's angry tension.
Target acquisition would be exceptionally difficult
under the circumstances. Trying to differentiate a

live, black-clad enemy hiding among the dead black statues strained even his point man's senses.

"What the hell is this place?" DeFore asked, hoarsely.

"Don't know if I want to know," Domi whispered.

Grit crunched beneath Kane's boots, and the sulfurous stench wafted up. He spared a quick downward glance at the thick layer of black ash on the floor. Fingering his nose, he said over his shoulder, "Watch your step."

A faint metallic click reached his ears, and he froze in place, wondering if he'd stepped on one of the silver bugs. He wasn't sure if the sound came from underfoot because of the acoustics in the cavernous chamber. At the periphery of his vision, silver flashed dully.

Heeling around, Kane's eyes registered only the most disjointed glimpse of a small round gleaming object lancing toward his head, following a steep downward trajectory. Almost as soon as his brain recognized the image fed to it by the optic nerves, the silver oval disintegrated in midair. Shards of metal and circuitry flew in all directions. Kane felt the thundering shock wave and the bullet splash of hot air across his cheek.

Grant raised his aim a trifle and squeezed off another round. On the gallery, a black-garbed figure clutched at his belly, folded over the rail and pitched over it. His plummeting body disappeared into the gloom, but they all heard the thud of impact.

Grant grimaced, but didn't lower his pistol. "I meant to wing him so he could be questioned."

During his many years as a Magistrate, Grant had often dumbfounded his colleagues with his snap shots, as accurate as they were uncannily swift. He had won a number of contests, competing with his fellow Mags and always outshooting any self-styled marksmen the academy produced.

Kane always placed his bets on him, and he always won. He had won this time, too. He threw Grant a fleeting, appreciative grin. "Too bad I didn't have any jack riding on you making that shot."

DeFore knelt and plucked a fragment of silver casing from the floor. Holding it gingerly between thumb and forefinger, she turned toward the light. "Some type of lightweight alloy, like aluminum. A little heavier, though."

A shadow shifted as a body moved between DeFore and the light. She reflexively dodged to one side, bumping into Domi. In a shaved splinter of a second, all of the organization of the four people and the situation changed. All around them was a blur of bodies and mad movement.

A faceless night-gaunt pointed a short rod on a direct line with Domi's head. Kane had no idea of the rod's purpose, but since he saw silver glinting at the tip, he assumed it fired the little metal bugs.

Kane clamped his left hand around the end of the wand and jerked backward, at the same time driving the barrel of his Sin Eater into the black-clad man's right kidney—or where a human male's kidney should be. A hoarse, gargling cry burst from beneath the opaque material of the mask.

He staggered to one side, and as he sagged to the floor, Kane wrested the rod from his slack fingers. He had no time to examine it. A night-gaunt closed in on him. Dropping the rod and stepping away, Kane bumped into a statue and it shattered. Thick, blinding smoke boiled up. The concentration of stenches was overpowering.

As Kane recoiled, tears streaming from his eyes, he heard a raucous female voice screeching incomprehensible words. He recognized the tone, however—she was exhorting the men in black to kill them.

Clearing his vision with the heel of one hand, he saw the night-gaunt materializing out of the vapor. He caught only a glimpse of the silver-knobbed baton in the figure's hand before he depressed the Sin Eater's trigger stud. The weapon responded with a stutter, as six 9 mm rounds easily flipped the man backward. Hunched in a tight posture, Kane narrowed his eyes, trying to see through the stinking haze.

He had about half a second of warning before he felt an agonizing viselike grip close on his upper arms from behind. He felt his muscles grinding against bone as the night-gaunt yanked him up from the floor. The night-gaunt tossed him ten feet, and he slapped the concrete floor chest first. All the air went out of his lungs in an agonized bellow.

He elbowed himself onto his back, snapping at air, rising to his feet just as the night-gaunt closed in on him. Feinting to the right, then swinging over the left, he delivered a spinning crescent kick to the right side of the black-clad man's head. The night-gaunt crashed into another statue, and the odor of sulfur exploded in the air.

Kane reeled backward as he was showered with foul-smelling ash and blinded by the black mushroom of smoke billowing up. He inhaled a mouthful of vapor and succumbed to a coughing fit. His watering eyes registered a flash of light, like an errant reflection of the sun. He felt a dull impact on the center of his chest and he barely made out the chrome spider clinging to his shirtfront. Then a terrible stunning shock lifted him, flung him back and bowled him over. He fell as limp and cold as a corpse to the floor.

Before his body had fully settled, the air shivered with a shriek of rage from Domi, followed a fraction of an instant later by the ear-knocking report of her handblaster. The .45-caliber round struck the night-gaunt in the center of his back. The faceless man flailed forward, as if he had just received a kick.

The bullet exited just above his pelvis in a splattering welter of scarlet liquid ribbons and blue-pink intestinal tissue. The silver-knobbed baton went skittering out of his hand.

Domi rolled back up on the balls of her feet and turned to see night-gaunts crowding in around Grant's body, thrusting at him with the rods. Her first two shots struck a night-gaunt full in his featureless face. The next one caught a smaller black-clad man in the right side of the head. The fourth shot was a little low, blowing a piece out of the thigh of a man. Domi instantly corrected for aim and put another round through his forehead. The back of the headpiece puffed out momentarily as a red mist squirted out around the edges of the mask.

The voice of the woman continued to shriek exhortations.

The rods in the hands of the night-gaunts on the gallery flicked back and forth between Grant and DeFore, spitting little silver eggs. Grant twisted his body in a painful contortion as a metal object passed very close by him. It struck the floor and bounced.

Grant raised his pistol at a shadowy shape on the second level and squeezed the trigger stud of his Sin Eater. A 245-grain hollowpoint round pounded into the abdomen of a night-gaunt. The masked man went over backward, bent double around his belly wound and voicing a very human howl of agony.

The silver-tipped rod spun from his hand, falling and clattering across the floor.

DeFore shoulder rolled over piles of foul-smelling ash, snatching up the fallen rod. She raised it hastily, surprised by its light weight. Her finger found a small trigger lever. Sighting down it, framing a night-gaunt before it, she pressed the lever. Nothing happened. Cursing beneath her breath, DeFore triggered a shot at the nearest night-gaunt. The .25-caliber round smashed into the back of his right hand. Although she saw no blood, the man cried out and the rod dropped from suddenly nerve-dead fingers.

Grant raced toward the staircase that led to the gallery. Holding the Sin Eater high, he started firing and kept the trigger down. The subsonic 9 mm rounds ripped through the air, ricocheting off the handrails with flares of blue sparks and keening whines.

He sprinted up the stairs, two steps at a time. Beyond the head of the stairs loomed stainless-steel vats, like vast caldrons. A grille-floored iron catwalk ran alongside them. On the far end he saw three of the night-gaunts. They saw him at the same time, and a trio of silver eggs flashed toward him.

Grant fell flat, banging his elbows painfully. He heard the little devices clanging into the sides of the vats. One fell down right between his outstretched arms, and he glimpsed nasty little double prongs extending from both ends of it. A thread-thin skein of electricity arced between the prongs with a faint sizzle.

With a muttered "Fuck this," Grant extended both arms, holding his pistol steady, and depressed the trigger stud. The autopistol hammered in a staccato roar. He exercised no mercy, burning down the night-gaunts, not stopping until the clip cycled dry. The three corpses lay in bloody, limb-twisted heaps.

Grant quickly changed magazines, outfitting the Sin Eater with another clip. It clicked solidly into place, then he shot the bolt and chambered the top round. He climbed to his feet and went back toward the stairway. He didn't look at the dead shadow men any longer than he had to. A faceless man wielding a rod rose up from beneath the catwalk. He pointed the silver-knobbed tip straight at Grant's head.

Having no choice, Grant lined up the Sin Eater's muzzle automatically and fired six rounds. The stream of 9 mm bullets caught the man in the center of his stomach and rapidly tracked upward, punching him backward, then splitting his mask in two. Grant continued down the stairs, back onto the rotunda's floor.

The woman's voice cried out again, and the night-gaunts scattered into the murk. Then as suddenly as it began, the pandemonium of the attack ended. Several black-clad corpses lay amid black ash, leaking fluids that turned it into a scarlet-tinged muck.

Grant squinted through the haze, seeking a moving target. It was like trying to see through a sediment-clouded pond. Although he couldn't fully smell the cess-pit stink from the destroyed statues, the foul tang of sulfur was sharp on his tongue. He turned his head and spit.

"Watch it." Grant saw Kane straining to hike himself up on his elbows. His voice was a croak, his face covered by a sheen of perspiration. He struggled to rise, but only managed to shamble to one knee. He labored for breath.

DeFore leaned down, putting a hand under his crooked left arm. His hand was cupped almost protectively over the left side of his neck. Between clenched teeth, she groaned, "Don't tell me—"

"Yeah," Kane rasped, staggering erect. He lowered his hand and revealed the gleam of the metal spider on his neck, the hooks tipping its spindly legs embedded in the flesh. "I felt it crawling up there, but I couldn't do a damn thing about it." He rubbed his chest and winced. "Goddamn thing shocked me."

"Shocked you?" Grant echoed in a challenging tone.

Kane nodded dourly. "I guess when the thing first hits you, it delivers a jolt of current. While you're incapacitated, it attaches itself more or less permanently. Pretty clever, actually."

"I know I'm impressed," Grant rumbled sardonically. "I'm sure you will be, too, if you end up as part of this statuary collection."

Kane said nothing, knowing as all of them did that Grant was hiding his genuine concern under a veil of sarcasm.

DeFore examined the rod, peering into it. "This is just a hollow tube, except for a spring mechanism. That's how the spiders are fired—just a spring. Nothing too complicated."

"That makes me feel a whole lot better," Kane said dryly, tentatively touching the device on his neck.

DeFore eyed it keenly. "Does it hurt?"

"Not really. Not yet, anyhow."

Domi leaned down to touch the handle of her knife in its boot sheath. "We can mebbe pry it off."

Kane glared at her. "And you can mebbe leave it alone. For all we know, fooling around with it is what turns you to stone."

DeFore gestured to the motionless figures scattered around the chamber. "They're not made of stone. I don't know what causes the effect, but it's like their skeletal structures and internal organs are dissolved, leaving only an empty husk in the shape of the person."

She did a poor job of repressing a shudder of loathing.

Grant surveyed the area and growled, "Where the hell did those night-gaunts get to?"

Domi pointed across the rotunda to the shadowed mouth of a corridor. "Saw 'em run in there."

Grant started striding toward it. "Let's find them and persuade them to take that goddamn thing off your neck."

Domi's eyes glittered like blood-drenched rubies in her white face. She whipped out her knife. She thumbed the serrated edge and showed her teeth in a savage grin. "When we catch 'em, let me be the one to start."

Chapter 11

They followed the corridor along two turns, first to the left, then to the right, down a stairwell and a ramp. When they reached a T junction, the left-hand branch wasn't lit, but the right-side passageway glowed with ceiling lights.

"That's some kind of sign," Grant observed dourly.

"Yeah," agreed Kane. "God knows what, though."

The four people strode down the corridor for approximately fifty yards before it led them past a small control room and then through an open door. The room beyond was dark, and the four people hesitated before entering.

"If the gaunts are in there," Kane said in a low voice, "they'll be able to track us by our body-heat signatures."

Grant regarded him suspiciously. "How do you know that?"

Kane lifted a shoulder in a dismissive shrug. "I checked out one of their masks. I forgot to mention that."

"Wonderful," Grant snapped. "As if I wasn't nervous enough already."

"We don't have much choice," DeFore interjected. "If Brigid is here, she's probably through the door."

"I know," Kane said uneasily. "I just wish there was some light."

As if on cue, a neon strip on the ceiling flickered on and cast a white light. The corridor beyond the door was broad, a flat gray in color and it exuded a cold impersonality.

Grant exchanged a quizzical glance with Kane. "Maybe you can wish us a rocket launcher the next time."

"Next time," Kane replied absently, stepping into the hall and assuming the point man position.

The four people made their way carefully along the hall, Grant and Kane unconsciously walking heel-to-toe as they always did when entering a potential killzone. Kane noted there didn't seem to be any doors along the walls.

They traversed a vestibule that both Kane and Grant knew once served as a security checkpoint. The opposite wall bore a barred door. The bars were made of high-grade vanadium steel and were as thick as an index finger. The cross bars were three inches apart. The top, the sides and bottom of the gate were set flush in a concrete frame. The barrier was secured by a keypad electronic lock. Having encountered similar barriers before, he knew not even a high-ex gren could breach it.

Kane scowled and fetched the door a frustrated kick. To his surprise, it swung open on oiled hinges. He gave the electronic lock a swift examination. It had been disabled. He inhaled a deep, slow breath. The unlocked barrier didn't make him feel any better. He supposed the fleeing night-gaunts could have been too panicky to close and lock doors behind them, but he doubted it. He doubted the night-gaunts were even in this section of the facility.

They couldn't see the exact size of the place. It was certainly immense, nearly three times the breadth and length of the Cerberus operations center. It was trileveled, with banks of glass-covered consoles spanning all three tiers. The central area was enclosed by towering crystal-fronted panels that rose to a high vault, like floor-to-ceiling windows. Light danced across the surface of the panels, but Kane wasn't sure if it was reflected light or generated from within.

Most of the chamber was in semidarkness except for a pool of white light shining over three isolated man-sized canisters hanging above a free-standing console. The console faced a black glass panel twelve feet high, which looked like an optics test board. It was covered with winking lights in all colors, sliding illuminated bars, concentric circles twirling in dimly glowing dials, tiny LCD windows with numbers flashing behind them, bright columns with indicators moving up and down and blips passing across grilled screens. Everything still functioned, all the circuitry still drawing on the nearly eternal power provided by nuclear engines.

As they moved deeper into the enormous chamber, they passed an open door. Beyond it they saw the familiar arrangement of armaglass slabs enclosing a mat-trans jump chamber. The semitranslucent armaglass was tinted a ruddy red, the hue of glowing embers.

Kane gestured to it. "At least we've got another way out of here other than overland."

Before any of his companions responded, a cavernous voice boomed, "Good evening."

The voice caused Kane to skip around, raising his Sin Eater, trying to find who had spoken. A wild, searching gaze showed him nothing but the huge chamber. Domi, lips peeled back from her teeth in a silent snarl, swung the barrel of her Combat Master in short arcs. DeFore stared around with wide eyes, lights reflecting in little specks from her irises. She swallowed hard. Grant's only reaction was a frown, casting his deep-set eyes into little pools of shadow.

The voice continued, "Miss Brigid's compliments to you. She trusts you are well, and she's sorry not to be here to greet you. However, if you follow my instructions you will be reunited with her very soon.''

The voice was electronically altered, sounding like a basso profundo orator proclaiming from the bottom of a well, while gargling at the same time. Still, something about it struck a chord of unwelcome familiarity within Kane. He couldn't pin it down, but he was positive the familiarity didn't derive from a pleasant memory. Suspicion swelled in his mind.

''Who are you?'' Grant demanded, his eyes flicking around the chamber. He saw no vid spy-eye or speaker.

''No, you won't see anything. At this moment I am an invisible power. If you do as I say, I will make myself visible.''

Domi uttered a wordless scoffing hiss, swinging the barrel of her blaster back and forth. She marched toward the nearest computer console. ''Mebbe if I start shooting things, you'll show yourself.''

''I was afraid you'd ask that,'' the voice declared with a note of sadness.

DeFore's eyebrows knitted at the bridge of her nose. ''We didn't ask anything—''

Domi had gone only four paces before she cried out and went into a series of dancing convulsions. All of them heard the faint crackle of electric current as she writhed, trying to free her feet from the floor. Within a second, they came free and she staggered

back, cursing. She sat down hard on the floor.
DeFore knelt beside her as the little albino lifted first
one leg then the other, rubbing them vigorously.
"Shocked. Hurts."

DeFore observed, "You can move your legs, so
the damage wasn't severe."

Domi nodded grimly, massaging her calves, her
lips compressed in a tight line. "Get yourself
shocked like this and tell me it's not severe."

The pneumatic hissing of compressed air, the
squeak of gears and a pair heavy, floor-jarring thuds
resounded through the chamber. Kane knew instantly what had happened even before the voice
stated, "You are now imprisoned. All exits have
been sealed. You really have no choice but to do as
I say unless you choose to remain here and perish
of thirst or hunger. And there's not even a toilet for
you ladies."

Kane declared, "The voice is taped. There's nobody here." He glanced around and saw a monitor
screen on a computer console suddenly flicker with
an image.

"However," the altered voice went on, "I anticipated your reluctance to trust me, so I'm providing
something of an inducement and also reminding you
of a debt that has yet to be paid."

The eyebrows of Grant and Kane lifted. Warily,
the two men approached the monitor. They regarded
the image, and despite the high aerial perspective,

they recognized the scene instantly. They had seen the tape before.

They saw the vast hangar at Area 51 during the last desperate seconds of the battle when Ramirez and his Mags turned on Grant and Brigid. Kane watched himself preparing to throw the implode gren with bullets kicking up sand and dust all around him.

A stray slug caught him in the arm, and despite his black body armor, the impact sent him staggering. The gren dropped from his hand and rolled across the concrete pad toward the elevator cupola.

Suddenly, Domi darted out from the cupola, scooped the gren up in one hand and cocked her arm back to throw it at the vehicle. Grant saw himself rushing toward her, and though there was no sound, he saw his mouth working as he bellowed at her to drop the gren.

Then her diminutive form was completely engulfed by a brilliant incandescent blaze of white light. Frozen in place, Kane and Grant watched as the tremendous suction created by the implosion yanked their bodies forward in headlong, clumsy somersaults. Then the scene broke up in jagged lines and pixels and faded from the screen.

Both men continued to stare at the blank monitor, their throats constricted, their mouths dirt dry. Kane was first to speak. "That's the same tape we saw on Thunder Isle...in the Chronos facility."

Grant nodded shortly. "And whoever has us trapped in here is the same one who snatched Domi out of the implosion."

One corner of Kane's mouth quirked in a mirthless smile. "Who do we know who could do that?"

Grant's response was a husky whisper. "The same pissant who can tinker around with the Cerberus mat-trans network?"

"And the only pissant who calls Baptiste 'Miss Brigid.'"

The amplified voice interrupted them with a chuckle. "You see? Now, at the risk of making a rather obvious pun, we must not waste any more time. The gateway unit's destination codes are already locked in and ready to engage. All you have to do is close the door and you're on your way to me."

The sec door blocking the entrance to the mat-trans section slid upward. Grant eyed the armaglass jump chamber, gnawed his lower lip for a thoughtful moment, then cast a penetrating look in Domi's direction. She still sat on the floor, rubbing her legs.

He announced curtly, "Me and Kane will make the jump. Reba, you and Domi will jump back to Cerberus once we're gone. You know the destination code."

Both women favored him with incredulous stares, although relief shone briefly in DeFore's eyes. Domi

staggered to her feet, blurting angrily, "No fuckin'
way! I'm going with you—"

"*No!*" Grant's voice hit a deep pitch of fury and
anguish. Kane was so startled by the violence of his
reaction, all he could do was stare in nonplussed
silence, listening to the reverberations of the one-
word response echoing throughout the chamber.

DeFore stared at him, too. She had never seen the
normally phlegmatic and taciturn Grant display
more than mild annoyance, even when attacked. He
took a step toward Domi, and DeFore hastily regained her feet, moving out of his way.

Between clenched teeth, Grant stated, "You're
jumping back to Cerberus with DeFore. That's all
there is to it." His tone brooked no hope of debate.

Domi glared at him, her eyes snapping red sparks
of rage. "I don't take orders from you, Grant. Not
anymore I don't."

Grant continued walking toward her, his gait
menacing and ominous. Domi's pistol came up, the
bore on a direct line with his chest. He hesitated,
examined the hollow, cyclopean eye of the muzzle
and continued walking toward her.

"Stay back!" Domi shrilled, fear and anger vibrating through her voice in equal measure. "Touch
me and I'll shoot you, I swear I will!"

Kane and DeFore watched in wide-eyed, breath-
less anxiety. Kane stared at the automatic blaster in
the girl's hands, feeling cold nausea leap-frog in his

belly, chill fingers tapping out a ditty of dread up and down the buttons of his spine. He knew full well the reason behind Domi's current resentment of Grant. Although he had never treated her badly, certainly never abused her physically or emotionally, she felt she had never earned his respect—or his love. Since hoping to one day gain his love was no longer a mitigating influence on her behavior, Domi had pretty much discarded the little self-restraint she had practiced in the past. Grant was not an authority figure in her mind any longer.

But Kane also knew the depth of Grant's love for the girl, and the guilt he felt about treating her as less than a fully developed human being and more as an empty-headed stereotype. In many ways, guilt was the whole foundation of the ville society.

For the past ninety years, it was beaten into the descendants of the survivors of the nukecaust that when Judgment Day arrived, humanity was rightly punished. Therefore, people were encouraged to tolerate, even welcome, a world of unremitting ordeals, conflict and death; because humanity had ruined the world, punishment was therefore deserved. Love among humans was the hardest bond to break, so people were conditioned to believe that since all humans were intrinsically evil, to love another one was to love evil. That way, all human beings forever remained strangers to one another.

Both Kane and Grant had been conditioned to believe that, as they had so many other spurious beliefs. But he recalled what Domi had said to him in Area 51: "You and Grant didn't stay what you were. I don't have to stay what I am."

Domi had never spoken truer words, Kane reflected. A few months before, a stern word or stern look from Grant would have cowed any outburst. Now she refused to give ground to Grant. Nor did she lower her Combat Master, not even when he pressed his chest against the muzzle.

He kept his dark gaze fastened on her face, his expression as immobile as if it had been carved out of teak. By degrees, the twin flames of rage glittering in Domi's eyes guttered out. In a remarkably gentle, almost affectionate tone, he said, "You couldn't hurt a hair on my head," and he lightly pushed the barrel of the pistol away with a forefinger.

Placing both big hands on her shoulders, he told her quietly, "I have my reasons for asking you to go back to Cerberus. Please accept them."

Domi titled her head back, unshed tears glimmering in her eyes. "Can take care of myself. Always have."

Under stress she reverted to her abbreviated mode of outlander speech.

"I know that," Grant replied. "My reasons have nothing to do with whether you can or can't take care of yourself. Please—do this one thing for me without an argument.''

Domi's shoulder's sagged and she bowed her head in resignation. Her whispered ''Okay'' was barely audible.

Grant turned away from her. Both Kane and DeFore released their pent-up breaths in noisy exhalations of relief. They and Domi followed him through the doorway to where the gateway chamber stood.

The mat-trans unit, like most of the others they had seen, was a six-sided chamber whose floor and ceiling consisted of an interlocking pattern of raised metal disks. Although all of them were superficially familiar with the fundamental working principles behind the matter transmitters, they sometimes still seemed like magic.

Kane understood, in theory, that the mat-trans units required a dizzying number of maddeningly intricate electronic procedures, all occurring within milliseconds of one another, to minimize the margins for error. The actual conversion process was automated for this reason, sequenced by an array of computers and microprocessors. Sometimes he wondered if Lakesh, despite his former position as Project Cerberus overseer, knew as much as he claimed about the devices.

As one of the major components of the Totality Concept's Overproject Whisper, the quantum interphase mat-trans inducers opened a rift in the hyperdimensional quantum stream, a wormhole between a relativistic here and there. That much of the theory and concept Kane understood, even though it seemed fiendishly complicated. He knew the pathways always had to lead to an active destination gateway, whether it was across the country or on the other side of the world. If a destination lock was not achieved, or a transit line not opened, then jumpers could conceivably materialize at completely random points in linear space—or worse, endlessly speed through Cerberus's global mat-trans network, going for eternity absolutely nowhere, with no chance of reconstitution.

Although he accepted at face value that the machines worked, he had never grown accustomed to the concept that minds that created such stupendously complicated devices could not have found a way to prevent the nukecaust.

Kane pointed to the electronic keypad at the side of the jump chamber's door. The LCD glowed with a string of numerals. In a low voice, he asked DeFore, "You remember the two-digit encrypted ID you'll have to enter after you program the Cerberus destination code, right? If not, you won't be going anywhere."

The extra pair of numbers was a security precaution concocted by Lakesh and his apprentice, Bry, to make doubly certain no one could jump unannounced into the Cerberus redoubt.

DeFore did her best to hide her nervousness when she nodded. "I remember."

Kane stepped into the chamber and waited for Grant to join him. With a wry smile, Domi lifted her right index finger to her nose and snapped it away in the sharp "one percent" salute. It was a gesture Kane and Grant had developed during their Mag days, symbolizing undertakings with very small ratios of success. Domi had seen the two men exchange the salute often enough to imitate it perfectly.

Grant returned the salute gravely. He started to step into the chamber, but Domi latched on to his arm and threw her arms around him. She stood on her tiptoes, pulled his head down and kissed him with a fierce possessiveness. She released him and stepped back.

By the metal handle affixed to the armaglass, Grant sealed the door. The lock clicked, circuitry engaged and the automatic transit process began. He leaned against the wall, pushing his Sin Eater back into its holster. Kane followed suit. Inasmuch as the Sin Eaters were not equipped with safety switches, a reflexive jerk of the finger while reviving from the transit process could result in fatal consequences for the rest of the jump team.

As the hexagonal disks above and below them

exuded a silvery glow, Kane wondered briefly if Domi had any idea why Grant was so violently opposed to her accompanying them on the jump. He decided it really didn't matter.

Plasma wave forms resembling white, early-morning mist began wafting from the emitter array above and below. Kane closed his eyes, waiting to be swept up in the nanosecond of nonexistence.

Chapter 12

Kane came to wakefulness with a faint electronic hum in his ears. He blinked, and the world swam mistily back into reality. He swayed on unsteady legs, a bit surprised to see he had ended the mat-trans jump in the same standing posture in which he had begun it.

Usually, no matter how jumpers arranged themselves before a transit, they arrived at their destinations flat on their backs. This time he remained upright, but he faced away from the door, staring at the smoke-gray armaglass. He felt remarkably clear-headed, a small bonus for which he breathed a sigh of relief. Sometimes, even the cleanest of jumps had debilitating effects.

Grant, however, lay on the hexagonal floor plates, his prone body wreathed by fading wisps of vapor, a byproduct of what Lakesh referred to as the "quincunx effect."

With a snorting exhalation of breath, Grant pushed himself into a sitting position, staring around anxiously. He climbed to his feet, stumbling slightly from a brief surge of vertigo. "Not too bad," he commented. "How do you feel?"

"No jump sickness, if that's what you mean."

"I could see that," Grant said impatiently. "For one thing, we're not puking our guts out. For another, I knew we weren't jumping to a Russian unit."

Kane repressed a smile. Grant always held up their jump to Russia as the standard for bad transits. The Cerberus gateway link had been unable to establish a link with the Russian unit's autosequence initiators. The matter-stream carrier-wave modulations couldn't be synchronized, which resulted in a severe bout of jump sickness, symptoms of which included vomiting, excruciating head pain, weakness and hallucinations.

Grant grasped the door handle. His Sin Eater popped into his waiting palm. Kane unleathered his own side arm. "You ready?" Grant asked.

Kane only nodded, dropping into a crouch.

Heaving up on the handle, Grant shouldered the door open. The heavy armaglass portal swung outward on counterbalanced hinges. Grant ducked back inside the chamber and both men waited for a tense tick of time. Nothing happened, so they cautiously eased through the doorway. Kane wasn't particularly surprised by what he saw.

They were in a very long room, at least twenty yards. The wall on their left was completely covered

by armaglass, running the entire length of the room.
On the far side of it they saw a catwalk leading to
a central control complex. Instrument consoles with
glass-covered gauges and computer terminals lined
the walls. Even at this distance they could hear the
purposeful hum of drive units and banks of computers chittering like a flock of startled birds.

"This place look the slightest bit familiar?"
Grant inquired in a husky whisper.

"Only the slightest bit," Kane answered in the
same subdued tone. "We're on Thunder Isle...
pretty much within spitting distance of New Edo and
Shizuka."

Grant swiveled his head on his neck, anger glittering briefly in his dark eyes. Kane met his gaze
with no particular expression on his face. "That
couldn't be the reason you forbade Domi to come
with us, could it?"

In a threatening rumble, Grant retorted, "You
know better than that."

Kane didn't respond. In fact, he didn't know better than that, but it wasn't the time or place to in-
terrogate Grant as to his motives for insisting Domi
stay behind. His own concern for Brigid rose with
every passing second, considering the company she
was no doubt being forced to keep.

They walked onto the railed catwalk, listening to
a low hum ahead of them, almost like the vibrations
of a gong that had been struck. The hum gradually

became a whine, and the air all around them seemed to shiver with the sound.

The catwalk overlooked a vast chamber shaped like a hexagon, and was far larger than looked possible from the outside. A dim glow shone down from the high, flat ceiling. Two faint columns of light beamed from twin fixtures, both the size of wag tires. Massive wedge-shaped ribs of metal supported the roof.

The shafts of luminescence fell upon a huge forked pylon made of some burnished metal that projected up from a sunken concave area in the center of the chamber. The two horns of the pylon curved up and around, facing each other. Mounted on the tips of each prong were spheres that looked as if they had been sculpted from multifaceted quartz crystals. The pylon was at least twenty feet tall, with ten feet separating the forked branches. Extending outward from the base of the pylon at ever decreasing angles into the low shadows was a taut network of fiber-optic filaments. They disappeared into sleeve sockets that perforated the plates of dully gleaming alloy sheathing the floor. Many of them were buckled here and there, bulging but not showing splits. The faint odor of scorched rose blossoms tickled their nostrils.

They paused to look down at the pylon, recalling the last time they had seen it. It had been encapsulated chaos, a cosmic madness. Sparks sizzled through the facets of the prisms, crackling fingers of energy darted from one sphere to the other and back again.

They remembered how the crystals spit arcs of energy in random, corkscrewing patterns, and how the floor supporting the pylon suddenly heaved beneath their feet, the metal plates squealing, rivets popping loose with the sound of gunshots. Plasma had lanced from the prongs of the pylon, two coruscating fountains of fiery sparks that shed glowing droplets of molten silver.

"I would have figured this place would have blown itself to hell within minutes after we jumped out of here," Grant muttered.

"Me, too," Kane agreed. "But look around—most of the damage has been repaired."

Shiny new floor plates had been riveted down, replacing those that had buckled. Even scorch marks left by the wild energy overspills were gone, apparently scrubbed away.

"One thing you have to say about him," Kane commented, turning away from the pylon, "he's neat."

As they strode down the catwalk, Grant inquired lowly, "So you're sure he's behind this?"

"Who else has the technical expertise—and the sheer gall—to experiment with Operation Chronos technology?"

"You said he was dead," Grant pointed out glumly.

"No, I said I *assumed* he was. I also said I never saw his body."

The catwalk terminated in a room packed with module after module, console upon console of advanced computer equipment. Electronic instruments and machinery rose from plinths and podia from all around. Overhead lights gleamed on alloys, glass coverings, the CPUs. Ten chairs rose from the floor before each console. Covering four walls were crystal-fronted vid screens. Two of the screens were blank, while another showed only whorls of color. Images slid across the fourth screen, attracting Grant's and Kane's attention.

In grim silence they watched the vid record of the last few minutes of their previous visit to the installation. The camera had apparently been focused on the pylon. They had no problem remembering how the crackling display of energy between the forks of the pylon increased until a virtual ribbon of blue current seemed to stretch from one to the other.

The air between the prongs had wavered with a blurry shimmer like heat waves rising off sunbaked asphalt, and tiny glittering specks, like motes of diamond dust, swirled within the area of distortion. They spun, then whirled faster and faster, turning into a funnel cloud, like a tornado made of gold-and-silver confetti.

The funnel cloud seemed to peel back on itself, turning inside out amid vivid bursts of color. The recording didn't have a sound track, but both men remembered the deafening, cannonading blast that accompanied the pyrotechnics.

Waves of dazzling white flame and variegated lightning bolts streaked and blazed. From the curving prongs spit sharp bolts of lightning, which whipped and hissed along the network of wires like serpents made of blue plasma.

Crooked fingers of energy continued to stab between the prongs, forming a cat's cradle of red lightning. They watched, feeling the same awe and dread as they had on that day a few months previous, when thousands of crackling threads of light coalesced in the center of the forks.

Gushing lines of energy formed a luminous cloud between the prongs, and almost faster than the eye could perceive, the cloud grew more dense and definite of outline. The shimmer built to a blinding borealis.

Then a star seemed to go nova, bringing a millisecond of eye-searing brilliance. The funnel cloud burst apart in fragments, as if a giant mirror shattered, and the shards flew out in all directions.

Amid the flying, glittering splinters, a small body plummeted out of the heart of darkness and fell heavily to the platform. The body wore a black, bulky combat vest, which contrasted sharply with her porcelain-hued skin and bone-white hair.

The two men watched the image of Domi pushing herself to all fours by trembling arms, then hanging her head and vomiting.

Grant swung away from the screen, moisture gleaming in his eyes, his face contorted into an indefinable expression. Inhaling a lungful of air, he shouted, "*Sindri!* Show yourself!"

The echoes of his bellow chased one another through the room. Grant roared again, "Sindri! You went to a lot of trouble to lure us here, so stop playing hide-and-seek!"

A lilting voice said mildly, "It wasn't all that much trouble, Mr. Grant."

Kane shifted position so Grant didn't block his view of the very small man stepping out from an alcove between a pair of free-standing consoles. Sindri was walking hand in hand with a very tall woman. She looked taller than she actually was, because of her hip-to-head proximity with the little man. Although his head went light with relief that she was alive and apparently unharmed, he said nothing. When facing Sindri, he knew it was best to put on the facade of being unsurprised by anything and everything.

Both Brigid and Sindri appeared to have been dipped in jet-black dye from the necks down. After a second, Grant and Kane realized they wore the same formfitting bodysuits as the night-gaunts. Although they weren't wearing the cowls or masks, the big Casull revolver pointed at Brigid more than made up for it.

"Mr. Kane. Mr. Grant." Sindri nodded in turn to both men. "Nice to see you again. You're looking well."

Kane ignored him. To Brigid he inquired, "You're all right?"

She gave him a wan, jittery smile. "Except for being held hostage again, I'm fine."

Although Kane pretended Sindri wasn't present, Grant addressed him in a loud, snarling tone. "What the fuck are you up to here, pissant?"

Anger glittered briefly in Sindri's blue eyes. "That you will find out for yourselves. And might I ask you to lower your voice a trifle? It disturbs the *feng shui* of this place."

Kane rolled his eyes ceilingward.

KANE RARELY DEVOTED much thought to his enemies, primarily due to the fact that most of them were dead. They either had died at his or Grant's hands, or through their own machinations. Sindri was one of the exceptions, an enemy who had apparently perished twice before. Despite the fact he had returned from the dead after their first collision, Kane didn't figure it was reasonable to think they'd ever contend with him again. But Sindri delighted in unpredictability. The fact he existed at all was due to unpredictability and the often cruel whims of nature.

Nearly a year before, while exploring an anomaly in the Cerberus network of functioning gateway units, Lakesh, Brigid and Kane visited Redoubt Papa near Washington Hole. They found the body of a strange, stunted, troll-like man and returned with it to Cerberus. After a postmortem, the troll was found not to be a mutant or a hybrid but a human being modified to live in an environment with a rarefied atmosphere and low gravity.

After a bit of investigation and a process of elimination, Lakesh traced the quantum conduit used by the transadapt to jump into Redoubt Papa, to a point in outer space—a predark space station on the far side of the Moon known as *Parallax Red*.

Kane, Grant and Brigid jumped to the station, which was functional, if not exactly comfortable. It was populated by a group of stunted people known as transadapts, and led by an ingenious gnome of a man calling himself Sindri, after the master forger of the troll race in Norse mythology.

Sindri impressed them all with his wit, his charm, his probing intellect and his affected manner. They were particularly impressed by the startling story he told about *Parallax Red* and its connection to a human colony on Mars.

However, dreams of empire consumed him. After

living his entire life under the heel of a minority human ruling committee, Sindri was fixated on establishing his own kingdom regardless of the cost. To that end, he planned a double strike that would not only unseat the barons, but literally destroy Mars, his birthplace and the world he despised.

That was only one element of Sindri's plan. Even if he and his transadapts migrated to Earth, the males were sterile, the women barren and utter extinction was less than thirty years away. He realized their only chance for survival was to successfully hybridize their genetic structure with those of native Terrans, so the women at least could reproduce. When Kane, Grant and Brigid arrived on *Parallax Red* via the gateway, Sindri saw them as both fonts of information about Earth and the salvation of the transadapts.

Though his plans were foiled, and Kane, Brigid and Grant escaped from the space station, it wasn't the last they heard from Sindri.

The day following their return to Cerberus, the ingenious dwarf had sent them, via the mat-trans unit, his signature walking stick. The theatrical gesture told them he was still alive and could overcome their security locks. Although the Cerberus mat-trans computers analyzed and committed to their memory matrixes the modulation frequency of Sindri's carrier wave, and set up a digital block, it stood to reason if he could overcome one security lock, he could overcome another.

A few months later, he proved he could do so. Sindri set into motion a set of circumstances to draw Lakesh, Brigid and Kane to the Anthill, the primary Continuity of Government installation built within Mount Rushmore.

Sindri forced them all into taking a flight on the Aurora stealth plane, and announced his intention to use the nuclear weapons on board to force the barons into line, even if it meant destroying one or two. Lakesh managed to distract Sindri and his party of transadapts, but in the process the little man's gun went off and disabled the controls. Brigid, Kane and Lakesh ejected from the Aurora and watched it crash.

In the months that followed the incident, Kane had never spoken of his suspicions Sindri might have survived. The episode had been traumatic on a number of counts, so he had kept quiet.

There certainly seemed to be no reason to mention it now, with the little man himself smirking up at him over the sights of a revolver.

Chapter 13

Kane composed his face into a mask of placid non-interest. Sindri cocked his head quizzically at him, then he cocked back the hammer of the huge revolver. The double clicks sounded frighteningly loud. In direct counterpoint, Sindri's voice was little more than a croon. "Lower your weapons, both of you."

Kane met Brigid's eyes and she nodded shortly. He dropped his arm to his side, and after a moment's hesitation, Grant did the same.

"Nothing to say, Mr. Kane?" Sindri asked. "No gasps of astonishment, no exclamations of 'You! You're supposed to be dead!'?"

Coldly, Kane said, "This was all a very nice piece of subterfuge. You shouldn't have signed it."

Sindri's eyebrows angled up his high forehead toward his hairline. He assumed an expression of mock hurt. "Are you implying that you knew all along you'd find your old pal Sindri working his magic behind the scenes?"

"Magic?" Kane repeated disdainfully.

He noticed Brigid surreptitiously edging away

from the little man, seeking to reach a position where Sindri would be forced to take his eyes off Grant and Kane in order to keep her within his range of vision.

"Picking over old predark tech isn't the act of a magician," Kane continued. "It's the practice of a scavenger, a grubber with delusions."

Sindri's lips compressed in a tight line, and rage glittered in his eyes. The barrel of the revolver trembled slightly, whether from its weight or Sindri's struggle to tamp down in his fury, Kane had no way of knowing. His lips stretched in a hard, stitched-on smile. "You're trying to provoke me, Mr. Kane, and doing a rather execrable job of it...just as Miss Brigid is doing an execrable job of skulking way from me. Please stop. I'd truly hate to shoot one of your legs out from under you."

Kane's Sin Eater came up, the bore on a direct line with Sindri's forehead. The barrel of Sindri's pistol didn't waver from Kane's own head. "Or," the little man continued, not missing a beat, "I could blow out the undercooked gruel that passes for Mr. Kane's brains."

Brigid came to a halt and the look she directed toward him was so full of barely suppressed fury and loathing, Kane was surprised Sindri didn't shudder. Instead, the little man said in a calm, reasonable tone, "Let's not spoil our reunion with a display of bad temper. I mean none of you harm."

"And why is that?" Grant demanded skeptically.

"Don't try to convince us you've changed your ways," Kane remarked. "We didn't fall for that the last time."

Sindri sneered. "The hell you didn't. Unbuckle those damn power holsters and drop them."

Kane and Grant didn't move.

"I wasn't making a request, gentlemen."

"No," Kane said flatly. "We won't do it. I'm sick and fed the fuck up of dealing with you, Sindri. We've done this dance before, and it's past time to come up with a new tune."

"Mr. Kane—" Sindri began in a tone sibilant with warning.

"You're outgunned two to one," Kane broke in impatiently. "You may manage to shoot both of us, but you damn well know you won't be able to kill both of us before you're shot full of holes."

"Especially," Grant put in, "not with that gun you've got."

Sindri frowned. "What's wrong with it?"

Grant shrugged. "Nothing, if you're an antique collector. It's a Smith & Wesson Army revolver, Model 1869. Also known as model number three. It's a .44 cal, and I doubt someone your size would be able to handle its kick. Since it's single action, you'd only get off one shot before either me or Kane or both of us burned you down."

Sindri's frown deepened as Grant spoke, and he eyed the long barrel of the pistol critically.

"I don't know where the hell you got the damn thing," Grant went on, "or whether it's the genuine article or a repro, but it's an awfully chancy blaster to bet your life on."

Sindri made a "hmm" of contemplation, and a line of worry creased his high forehead. Then, with a laugh he lowered the big revolver. "As a mere novice in the mysteries of firearms, I bow to your master's knowledge, Mr. Grant."

Reversing his grip on the pistol, he presented it to Grant butt first. He grinned up at the two men who stared at him numbly, struck speechless by astonishment. Slowly and carefully, as if he were reaching for a venomous serpent, Grant took the proffered revolver.

"Don't look so shocked, gentlemen," Sindri admonished. "I've been trying to convince Miss Brigid that I mean you no harm." He glanced toward her. "I trust I've proved my point?"

Brigid shook her head. "Hardly. What was all that talk of shooting out legs and brains?"

Sindri fluttered a dismissive hand through the air. "Theater. Psycho-drama. If you believed my intentions were hurtful—or in your case, vengeful—then making myself helpless before you should alleviate any lingering doubts."

Brigid smiled scornfully. "You're never helpless,

Sindri. It's in your nature to always have an ace on the line."

Sindri scowled at her. "The meaning of your vernacular is very often obscure. What are you talking about?"

Tossing back her hair, Brigid touched the left side of her neck. With a sinking sensation in the pit of his stomach, Kane saw the glint of silver beneath her mane. She wore a mate to his own chrome spider.

"When you confiscated the control mechanism," she intoned, "you claimed you knew how to get this thing off me. You have yet to do it. Kane has the very same new addition. You'd go a long way toward persuading us you were sincere if you kept your word."

"My apologies," Sindri replied earnestly. "I felt you would be more apt to behave yourself if I held something over you."

He turned toward a desk and opened a deep drawer. The barrels of the Sin Eaters came up, training on his back.

"So you ran into the night-gaunts, too?" Kane asked, trying to force a casual, conversational note into his voice, as if he were inquiring simply to be polite.

Brigid replied noncommittally, "Something like that." She indicated Sindri with a nod of her head.

"You might want to ask him about them. Apparently, he's their god."

Rummaging through the drawer, Sindri said distractedly, "It was an accidental identification. But once it was made, I went along with the masquerade in order to learn."

"Learn what?" Grant rumbled. "How to exploit people's faith in you? That's not a subject you need a refresher course in."

Sindri turned, affecting not to notice the two pistols aimed at him. A little defensively he said, "That is true enough, Mr. Grant. But at least I learned how to remove the oubolus." He held up a circlet of metal, its surface studded with small gemstones.

Kane squinted toward it. "The what?"

Tersely and briefly, Brigid explained what she had learned about Megaera and her Furies. She touched the metal spider on her neck. "I don't know how these things do what they do. It's beyond any science I know."

Kane quirked a challenging eyebrow at Sindri. "And what about the science you know?"

Sindri tossed the wristband from hand to hand, shrugging dismissively. Brigid tensed, breathing in sharply through her nostrils. The little man glanced toward her, then with a sly smile ran his fingers lightly over the gems. He murmured, "Let's see... which one is it...which one..."

Kane took a step toward him, growling, "That's enough, you little—"

With a triumphant "Ah!" Sindri's thumb pressed down on a white stone. Kane heard a faint buzz emanate from the spider on his neck, a noise echoed by the object clinging to Brigid. He barely felt the leg filaments withdrawing from his flesh. Then a silver egg clinked against the floor and rolled, bumping gently against the one that had fallen from Brigid.

Both of them heaved sighs of relief and rubbed the places on their necks where the devices had been attached. Except for a slight itchy tenderness, Kane felt no puncture wounds or lacerations.

Sindri's blue eyes flicked from Kane to Brigid expectantly. "No words of thanks?" he asked ingenuously.

"Since you're somehow responsible for Megaera and her Furies being in here in the first place," Brigid retorted darkly, "no."

Stepping warily away from the bulbous objects on the floor, Kane commented, "I figured as much, since he's adopted their fashions."

Sindri brushed his fingers over the front of his bodysuit. "This old thing? Actually, Mr. Kane, I adopted this regalia for purely functional reasons."

"Like what?" Grant demanded, a hint of menace underscoring his tone. "Exactly what have you been up to here and in Chicago?"

Sindri beamed up at him, laugh lines deepening

around his azure eyes. "I thought that would be obvious. A little bit of this and little bit of that."

"Explain a bit of this and that," Kane suggested.

Sindri's smile broadened into an engaging, boyish grin. "The usual, as you'd expect from me. Becoming the master of space and time, that sort of thing."

RATHER THAN RESPOND to Sindri's melodramatic boast, Kane asked in a tone bordering on complete disinterest, "Since you raised the subject earlier, just how *did* you live through the crash of the Aurora?"

Sindri shrugged as if the matter were of only minor importance. "I could say I simply reversed an old law of physics to suit myself—whatever goes down must come up, but I doubt you'd be satisfied with that explanation."

Grant made a spitting sound of derision. "You got that pegged."

Sindri shrugged. "The actual explanation is exceptionally mundane. I bailed out of the Aurora before it crashed into the side of Mount Rushmore. It was a very near thing, though, if that makes any difference."

"Not to me it doesn't," Brigid snapped.

He looked at her reproachfully. "You're still angry at me about what happened with the commander?"

"No," she answered. "Not angry."

Grant and Kane knew Brigid was fast, but even

they were taken aback by how swiftly she shot out her left leg. The sole of her foot impacted with a meaty thud directly in the center of Sindri's midsection, doubling him up and sending him reeling backward. He fell unceremoniously on his right side, hugging his belly and sucking in great lungfuls of air.

Kane knew Brigid hadn't used her full strength in the stab-kick and even if she had, Sindri was far tougher and more resilient than he looked. Brigid glared down at him, rage seething in her eyes. "Not angry," she repeated in a trembling voice. "It's hatred, Sindri."

Slowly, Sindri pushed himself to his feet. "Giving pain for pain won't bring her back. You disappoint me, Miss Brigid. I had thought your thirst for vengeance would have been satisfied by forcing me to stay behind on the Aurora."

He straightened, rubbing his midsection. "If you follow me, perhaps I can show you something that might make the flame of hate burn a little less bright."

Grant smiled crookedly. "Maybe she'd prefer dislocating all your major joints instead."

"Maybe I would," Brigid said tightly.

Sindri favored her with a sad smile, then turned, marching toward an aisle formed by a double row of glass-fronted mainframes. "Kicking around an opponent half your size is something I would've expected from Mr. Kane, not from you.''

Anger rushed heat prickles to the back of Kane's neck and warmed his cheeks. The situation was entirely too reminiscent of the time when Sindri played their host on *Parallax Red.* He had been posing then to conceal his real agenda, and there didn't seem to be a good reason to believe he was doing anything other than that now.

''Hold it,'' he barked. ''We're not going anywhere with you until we get some answers.''

Sindri's pace didn't falter. Over his shoulder he said breezily, ''That's truly unfortunate, Mr. Kane—because the only way you'll get any answers, much less some, is to come with me.''

''There's another way,'' Grant grunted. He thumbed back the hammer of the Smith & Wesson. ''Unlike you, I'd have no problem shooting one or both of your legs out from under you.''

Sindri kept walking. ''That would be the act of an unregenerate ingrate, Mr. Grant...to even contemplate crippling the man who quite literally snatched your beloved little albino from the jaws of certain death.''

Grant's normally immobile face contorted, molding itself into a rictus of soul-deep pain. With a long-legged bound, he shouldered between Kane and Brigid and jerked Sindri to a violent halt by

clamping a hand on his right shoulder. He spun the
little man as if he were a doll.

Sindri tried to slap Grant's hand away, his eyes
shining bright with first anger, then fear when he
looked into the hollow bore of the revolver. "Get
your hand off me, Mr. Grant. You don't want to do
this."

In response, Grant dug in his fingers and Sindri
bit back a cry of pain. He nearly went to his knees.
Glaring up at the man towering giantlike over him,
Sindri said in a tone sibilant with repressed fury,
"Yes, it *was* me, Mr. Grant. I did it. I mentioned
before that you owed me a debt."

"Why'd you do it?" Grant demanded, his voice
husky and thick. "You don't know her."

"What difference does it make why I did it? She
obviously means something to all of you."

Sindri gazed past Grant to Brigid. "If you must
slap a motivation on my actions, then let it be my
way of atoning for what happened at the Anthill."

"If that's the case," Brigid replied, "then we owe
you nothing. We're even."

Sindri grimaced under the relentless pressure of
Grant's grasp. "Perhaps that's so. But you don't
know how I did it or what else I can do. That's
really the whole crux of the matter, isn't it? That's
what has kept me alive since I disarmed."

Grant released the little man. "I have a feeling

that if we really tried to kill you, this place is rigged to stop us.''

Sindri didn't voice a denial. He rubbed his shoulder and scowled up at Grant.

"Furthermore," Kane interjected, "you need our help for something...otherwise we'd be dead by now."

"Two of you would be at least," Sindri muttered sulkily.

"So what is it you want us for?" Grant challenged. "And skip the bullshit about being a master of space and time. We already know this is an Operation Chronos facility and that you've been dicking around with it. We've been here before, as you damn well know."

Sindri pursed his lips as if he tasted something sour. "Don't try to pretend I've done nothing more impressive than find an old automobile and tinker it back together. In most ways, Operation Chronos was the most crucial undertaking of the Totality Concept.''

Grant, Brigid and Kane knew Sindri spoke the truth, at least as much as they knew from Lakesh, who claimed that not only was the nuclear holocaust preventable, but also it was not supposed to happen. The temporal dilation of Operation Chronos had disrupted the chronon structure and triggered a probability wave dysfunction. An alternate event horizon had been created.

A year or so before, Lakesh had tried to dispatch Kane and Brigid back through time to a point only a month before the nukecaust so they could hopefully trigger a second alternate event horizon and thus avert the apocalypse.

Though they were translated into a past temporal plane, they came to learn it was not their world's past, but another world's almost identical to it. Any actions they undertook had no bearing on their reality's present and future.

Lakesh could only engage in fairly futile speculation on what had happened, and on the system of physics at work. If the chronon theory was correct, then time itself was made up of subatomic particles jammed together like beads on a string. According to the theory, between each bead, each individual unit of time might exist in an infinite series of parallel universes, fitted into the probability gaps between the chronons.

"Besides," Sindri went on, "you're wrong."

"About what?" Kane asked.

"About this being an Operation Chronos installation."

Three pairs of eyes regarded the little man with skepticism, suspicion and outright hostility. Still, his declaration captured their undivided attention, which apparently was his intent.

"If it's not a Chronos facility," Brigid said, "then what is it?"

With a chuckle lurking at the back of his throat, Sindri announced, "It's *the* Operation Chronos site."

In a tone ragged with impatience, Grant demanded, "Just what the hell does that mean? That this is the main headquarters of the Chronos subdivision?"

"It's that," Sindri conceded, "but it's far more. This is indeed the place where the final attempts to coordinate all the experiments and the breakthroughs in time travel were made. It's here where the debugged and fully functional temporal dilator was built. A pity the nukecaust came along before it could be put to its full use."

"You said it was more," Kane pointed out.

"Yes, I did." Sindri turned smartly on his heel. "And since you will require proof of my words, I'll need to provide visual aids."

Sindri strode down the aisle between the computers, not bothering to check if the others were following him. Kane ran an impatient hand through his hair. To Grant and Brigid, he asked, "Is there any point to us pretending we're not going along with this?"

Brigid shook her head. "Not one I can see. If he really can operate a temporal dilator, we'd be too stupid to live not to take it away from him."

"Or him away from it," Grant grunted.

The three people fell into step behind Sindri.

Kane sidemouthed to Brigid, "What's with the sha-dowsuit, Baptiste?"

She looked down at herself distastefully. "He forced me to put it on. He said it was for my own protection."

Kane arched an eyebrow at her but said nothing. The shadowsuit hugged every curve and bulge like a second skin. He could think of plenty of places where wearing such a thing would put her in a po-sition of requiring protection, certainly not the other way around.

They followed Sindri through a door and into a short hallway. To the left, a sign hung above a va-nadium alloy door. The faded lettering read, Not An Exit. No Unauthorized Personnel. A red-and-black hourglass symbol was stamped at the bottom of the sign.

Sindri punched a six-digit sequence into the key-pad on the door frame, and the computer-controlled lock clicked open.

The door slid aside, revealing only an empty land-ing and a stairwell. Painted on the wall was a red down-pointing arrow, and the words To Confine-ment Section. Sindri led them down the wide con-crete steps, fingers tapping out a ditty on the metal banisters.

They reached another landing, another door, an-other inverted arrow on the wall, but they kept walk-ing down. At the next landing, they came to a heavy bulkhead framed within a recessed niche in a double-baffled wall. The door bore the emblazoned warning Only Operation Chronos Personnel Beyond This Point! Must Have MAJIC-Ultra Clearance To Proceed! Deadly Force Is Authorized!

Sindri tapped in a code on the keypad lock and with a squeak and a hiss, the bulkhead slid into its slots between the double frame.

They faced a narrow, uncarpeted passageway, long and low ceilinged. A dim glow filtered from its far end. Cool air fanned their faces, and they heard a rhythmic drone of turbines and generators.

"Where are you taking us?" Grant demanded gruffly.

Sindri entered the corridor saying cheerily, "That you'll see in short order...pun intended."

"He knows we've come too far to back out now, so we might as well finish out this charade," Brigid murmured.

They moved on, toward the light. Kane's and Grant's combat senses were on full alert. The mechanical throb grew louder, a sound that all three recognized. The passageway took on a downward slope, and the floor changed from bare concrete to metal plates ridged and flaking with rust.

The passage ended abruptly at a door made of glass. It bore a sign stating, Radiation Danger Beyond This Point! Entry Forbidden To Personnel Not Wearing Intermolecular Uniforms!

Beyond the door was a small booth. From hooks on the wall hung a number of black shadowsuits with hoods and transparent Plexiglas faceplates. Sindri held the door open for them and they stepped in. The generator throb grew considerably louder.

"Please do as the sign says," Sindri said. "There are high levels of radiation beyond the door."

Kane and Grant recalled on their prior visit they had seen evidence of deadly electromagnetic radiation pulses, but the two men weren't convinced.

Grant pinched the sleeve of a black suit, rubbing it between thumb and forefinger, frowning doubtfully. "They don't feel like they could protect you from a gnat bite, much less radiation."

"In actuality," Sindri replied, "they can protect you from a number of different dangers, including biological contagions. Each suit is climate controlled for environments up to highs of 150 degrees, and as cold as minus ten degrees Fahrenheit. Microfilaments control the temperature."

"What are they made of?" Kane wanted to know.

"A weave of spider silk, Monocrys and Spectra fabrics."

All three people turned their heads toward him, faces registering incredulity. "Spider silk?" Brigid echoed.

Sindri nodded. "Nylon has about twice the tensile-strength-to-weight ratio of silk and Kevlar has about three times the tenacity of Nylon. Monocrys is about eleven percent better in its tenacity than Kevlar, and Spectra is about thirty percent better than all three. Natural spider silk has about six times the tenacity of Spectra."

"How do you know so much about it?" Grant asked gruffly.

Sindri fluttered his black-gloved fingers through the air. "All the information was stored in the database. Apparently, predark genetic engineers succeeded in developing a way to copy spider silk. A compiled weave of all those materials resulted in a two-phase, single-crystal metallic microfiber with a very dense molecular structure. The outer Monocrys sheathing goes opaque when exposed to most wavelengths of radiation, and the Kevlar and Spectra layers provide protection against blunt trauma. The spider silk allows flexibility, but it trades protection for freedom of movement."

Grant knuckled his chin thoughtfully, eyeing the suits. "How did the night-gaunts—the Furies—get hold of them?"

"That's a story for another time," Sindri replied. He grinned and added, "Once again, pun intended."

Kane uttered a wordless grunt of impatience. "Let's drop the fashion discussion and just get on with it."

Sindri shrugged. "As you wish. But when your flesh blisters and drops off your skeleton and your teeth fall out and you begin hemorrhaging in a most distressing fashion from your ears, nose and rectum, remember how the untrustworthy Sindri tried to save .you.''

Grant and Kane glared angrily at the dwarf, then with resigned shakes of the head, began disrobing. They stripped down to their undershorts and pulled on the suits. Both men were surprised how the fabric molded itself to their bodies, adhering like another layer of epidermis. They smoothed out the wrinkles and folds by running their hands over their limbs. Although they were impressed by how comfortable the garments felt, they kept their comments to themselves.

Following Sindri's actions, the three people donned the hoods and followed him out the opposite door of the booth. They walked across a steel-grated catwalk. Some twenty feet below a strangely shaped generator droned. It was at least twelve feet tall, and looked like a pair of solid black cubes, the smaller balanced atop the larger. The top cube rotated slowly, producing the steady drone of sound. An odd smell, like ozone blended with antiseptic, pervaded the air.

All of them had seen generators of that type before in various and unlikely places around the world. Brigid and Lakesh speculated they were fusion reactors, the energy output held in a delicately balanced magnetic matrix. When the matrix was breached, an explosion of apocalyptic proportions resulted.

Sindri led them through an open archway and traversed yet another broad hall lined on either side by niches inset into the walls. The little man looked straight ahead as he strolled past a niche containing two stone tablets engraved with ten sentences in Aramaic. Another niche contained a litter of ancient weaponry, swords, maces and battered shields. One shield bore likenesses of crouching lions.

"What is this, Sindri?" Brigid demanded. "A museum?"

"Something like that," he answered. "An archaeologist's paradise, the clutter of past ages brought here and stored by the previous tenants of this complex."

They continued walking down the hall, passing niche after niche of incredible objects. Skulls, machines, even something that looked like a sheep's fleece dusted with gold, filled the niches. They were a gathering of relics from fact, fable and even fantasy.

Up ahead a shimmering radiance drove away the shadows, like rays of sunlight as viewed through thick cloud cover. The passageway terminated at a railed gallery encircling and overlooking a metal-walled shaft thirty feet across. The cavity was barely fifteen feet deep, but a borealis-like glow exuded from the walls in waves.

At first all they saw was the dancing veil of amber light. They felt subtle energies tingling their flesh, like a weak static discharge. Kane, Brigid and Grant looked through the pulsing glow, stared past it, focusing their eyes on the shapes that lay beyond it.

"A stasis field," Brigid announced.

Sindri smiled at her fleetingly, appreciatively. "Exactly. And behind it are selective samplings from many different eras, many different centuries." He swept his arm toward the cavity. "This part is less a museum than a tomb of time."

All three people stared, fascinated. Down below, within a recessed niche behind the glimmer, they saw a man in a starched blue uniform with a yellow neckerchief and gauntlets. On the crown of his broad-brimmed blue hat they could just make out an insignia patch that depicted a pair of crossed sabers. Although he was as immobile as a mannequin, he clutched at one of three arrows jutting from his torso. His right arm was bent at the elbow, his index finger crooked around empty air.

Grant rumbled, "You got the Smith & Wesson from him, didn't you?"

Sindri nodded, moving along the rail. "Where else?"

They followed the little man, looking down into the shaft at the figures frozen behind the stasis screen. They saw a bearded man wearing a dented metal breastplate and steel casque from the days of the conquistadors, and a slouching, heavy-jawed brute wearing only a pelt of shaggy hide. Then they stiffened as they saw two large creatures crouched motionless in the shadows cloaking the chamber. Reptilian monsters, their crocodilian heads didn't move, nor did their massive scaled bodies stir. They were like fragments of dreams, snatched from the imagination and encased in amber.

As they circled the gallery, Kane said, "This is all very interesting, Sindri, but we guessed quite some time ago you figured out how to trawl living creatures from the past. Some of them made it to New Edo."

Sindri nodded. "Quite true, although I wasn't responsible for everything that came tumbling through the time stream. However, it is New Edo I wish to discuss with you."

Grant blinked in surprise behind the transparent faceplate. "Why?"

Sindri stopped at the rail and made a downward gesture. "That's why."

Grant, Kane and Brigid followed his arm motion. They saw another niche and a dark-haired naked woman standing within it, her back against the wall. What appeared to be steel claws, little more than four curves of metal, held her around the arms and legs.

To their mutual surprise, the woman moved, lifting her head, shaking her hair out of her eyes. The woman gazed up at them, and an expression of mingled fear and joy appeared on her finely sculpted face.

A single word was torn from Grant's lips, half a snarl of fury, half a groan of horror. *"Shizuka!"*

Chapter 14

When the world blew out in 2001, more than the face of the Earth changed beneath the soaring fireballs and mile-high mushroom clouds. The physical world was vastly different. Ruins stood in place of gleaming towers, radioactive wastelands and toxic bogs existed where national parks had once played host to families of tourists. Cities teeming with life were swallowed by desert sands.

All the old cultures were gone, burned down to their foundations, so new societies were formed, with their own laws, their own rules, their own beliefs and even their own dialects.

In North America, the English language remained essentially the same, though the postapocalyptic vocabulary contained new words, combinations of abbreviations created by a new generation accustomed to acting, rather than talking.

Nuclear holocaust was melded into ''nukecaust,'' the nuclear winter was referred to as ''skydark'' and any time period before January 20, 2001, was spoken of as ''predark.'' Cities and towns and settlements were classified as ''villes.''

Even the definition of the word *Cerberus* had changed. To classicists, Cerberus was the three-headed, dragon-tailed hound who guarded the gateway to Hades, the Hell of Greek mythology. The monstrous creature permitted the spirits of the dead to enter, but none to return to the land of the living. Only one mortal ever defied Cerberus and that was Hercules.

As part of the bargain he struck with King Eurystheus of Mycenae, Hercules was charged with performing twelve labors. His final labor took him down to Hades itself to bring Cerberus to the upper world. He could use no weapons to subdue the terrible beast, but even so he forced the hellhound to submit and carried him, growling and snapping, all the way to Mycenae. When King Eurystheses saw the monster, he was so horrified he ordered Hercules to return him to the underworld.

By the midtwentieth century, scientists rather than scholars first redefined the word Cerberus, but it still possessed a tenuous connection to the creature of myth. Project Cerberus was considered to be an appropriate code name for an undertaking devoted to ripping open the gates between heaven and hell.

Under the aegis of the Totality Concept, utilizing bits of preexisting technology, Project Cerberus researched and engineered matter transmission. To streamline the mass production of the quantum interphase mat-trans inducers, the project was moved from the Dulce, New Mexico, installation and head-quartered in a redoubt on an exceptionally remote mountain plateau in Montana's Bitterroot Range. The trilevel, thirty-acre facility was built into the side of a mountain peak, and was constructed primarily of vanadium alloy and boasted design and construction specifications that were aimed at making the complex an impenetrable community of at least a hundred people. The redoubt contained two dozen self-contained apartments, a cafeteria, a decontamination center, a medical dispensary, a swimming pool and holding cells on the bottom level.

The plateau holding the redoubt and the road leading up to it were surrounded by an elaborate system of heat-sensing warning devices, night-vision video cameras and motion-trigger alarms. In the unlikely instance of an organized assault against the installation, an electric force field energized with particles of antimatter could be activated at the touch of a button. A telemetric communications array was situated at the top of the peak.

The redoubt's control complex contained five dedicated and eight shared subprocessors, all linked in a mainframe system. The advanced model used experimental error-correcting miniature microchips, which even reacted to quantum fluctuations. The biochip technology utilized protein molecules sandwiched between microscopic glass-and-metal circuits.

Although official designations of all Totality Concept-related redoubts were based on the phonetic alphabet, almost no one stationed in the facility referred to it as Bravo. The mixture of civilian scientists and military personnel simply called it Cerberus.

One of the enlisted men with artistic aspirations went so far as to illustrate the door next to the entrance with an image of a three-headed hound. Rather than attempt even a vaguely realistic representation, he used indelible paints to create a slavering hellhound with a trio of snarling heads sprouting out of an exaggeratedly muscled neck. The neck was bound by a spiked collar, and the three jaws gaped wide open. In case anyone didn't grasp the meaning, he emblazoned beneath the image the single word, Cerberus, wrought in ornate Gothic script.

Generations after the nukecaust and some thirty years after his revival from a century and a half spent in cryogenic stasis, Lakesh expanded the definition of Cerberus yet again. It now encompassed not only the matter-transmission process and the redoubt itself, but also the small group of exiles who lived in the installation as both a home and a sanctuary. It was no longer a manufacturing facility. It was full of shadowed corridors, empty rooms and sepulchral silences, a sanctuary for twelve human beings. It was possible that the handful of people who lived in the installation would be the last who would ever walk its hallways.

A little less than a year before, Cerberus had housed more than a dozen, but there had been casualties since then. First Adrian and Davis in the Black Gobi, murdered by the forces of the Tushe Gun, then Beth-Li Rouch, killed by one of the redoubt's own. The most recent casualty was Cotta, dismembered by a mind-controlled sasquatch in the Antarctic.

Since then, and the near death of Domi, the fear the redoubt would suffer more casualties had become almost a phobia. It hadn't reached a point where operations were crippled, but Reba DeFore could easily envision it happening in the future.

In the hour since she and Domi gated back into Cerberus, DeFore had done little more than shower, change into a white bodysuit, the unofficial uniform of the redoubt's staff, and stand in the central complex. A long room with high, vaulted ceilings, it was lined by consoles of dials, switches and computer stations. A huge Mercator relief map of the world spanned the far wall. Pinpoints of light glowed in almost every country, and thin phosphorescent lines networked across the continents, like a web spun by a rad-mad spider. The map delineated all the locations of all functioning, indexed gateway units all over the world.

DeFore paid no attention to the map. Her eyes

were fixed on the medical monitor. The telemetry transmitted from Kane's, Brigid's and Grant's bio-link transponders scrolled upward. The computer systems recorded every byte of data sent to the Comsat and directed it down to the redoubt's hidden antenna array. Sophisticated scanning filters combed through the telemetric signals and precisely isolated the team's current position in time and space.

The vital signs of the three people indicated stress, but Grant's blood pressure and heart-rate readings were nudging the far end of the high scale. The indicators were very unusual for the normally phlegmatic man. DeFore couldn't help but wonder what was upsetting him so deeply.

"What the hell is going on?" she murmured for the third time in the five minutes. "Where the hell are you?"

From behind her, Lakesh said with a touch of asperity, "As I thought I made clear, they're apparently somewhere in California...in the general vicinity of where Santa Barbara used to be."

She turned toward him, unconsciously crossing her arms over her breasts. "I'm just talking to myself. A kid like you wouldn't know how easily distracted we senior citizens can become."

Lakesh didn't respond to her sarcasm. Even after nearly five years, DeFore wasn't sure how she felt about him, particularly over the past couple of months. She attributed his demanding and rather

high-handed manner of late to his restored youth—
or rather his restored early middle age. She didn't
even pretend to understand how it had happened.
The process Lakesh described flew so thoroughly in
the face of all her medical training—as limited as it
was—that he might as well have relegated the cause
to a miracle.

All DeFore really knew was that a couple of
months ago she watched Mohandas Lakesh Singh
step into the gateway chamber as a hunched-over,
spindly old man who appeared to be fighting the
grave for every hour he remained on the planet. His
hair was so washed-out by time that it was ash-gray.
Thick spectacles looked like double-glazed windows
over the pale blue eyes that were incongruous with
the sallow, liver-spotted skin.

A day later, the gateway chamber activated and
when the door opened, Kane, Brigid Baptiste, Grant
and Domi emerged. A well-built stranger wearing
the white bodysuit of Cerberus duty personnel followed them. DeFore gaped in stunned amazement
at the man's thick, glossy black hair brushed back
from a high forehead. His olive complexion was
clear, his well-fed face split in a toothy, excited grin,
his big blue eyes alight. She recognized only the
long, aquiline nose as belonging to the Lakesh she
had known these past four years.

Lakesh claimed he had no idea how long his vitality would last. Whether it would vanish overnight

and leave him a doddering scarecrow like the fabulous One Horse Shay or whether he would simply begin to age normally from that point onward, he couldn't be certain. However, he wasn't about to waste the gift of youth, as transitory as it might be. DeFore didn't know who One Horse Shay had been or what was so fabulous about him, but she did notice Lakesh surreptitiously eyeing her bosom in a way he had never done before.

She had never felt very comfortable with him, despite the fact he fascinated her. Part of her enchantment with him, though, was a result of his history. Lakesh had been born back before skydark. He'd seen the world before it had died, had memories of times well before the nukecaust. He'd slept in the Anthill, the master center of the redoubts located in Mount Rushmore, for more than a century and been awakened fifty years ago to take his place in the plans of the nine barons. His major organs were replaced upon his resuscitation, including a new heart, a new set of lungs, knee joints made of polyethylene and even a second pair of eyes.

However, everything he'd seen and lived through, everything he remembered from the past, had served to alter Lakesh's alliances. Instead of remaining a conspirator with the Totality Concept's aims and goals, he'd become its most dangerous adversary. Over the years he'd put his plans into action. His chief strength lay in the fact that he'd known the

Cerberus redoubt was still active when all nine barons believed it was unsalvageable.

Despite making it the headquarters for a fledgling resistance movement, in fact the installation hadn't functioned as much more than a hideout, a bolt-hole for the various exiles from the baronies. Only with the arrival of Kane, Grant, Brigid and Domi had the Cerberus resistance movement initiated action of any sort.

Irritably, DeFore said, "It just galls me that we can't jump to where they are."

Lakesh indicated the Mercator map with a backward jerk of his head. "The transit lines have been closed off. It's happened before, once anyway."

She nodded. "I remember. By Sindri. But he's supposed to be dead."

"And I'm supposed to be pushing three centuries old," Lakesh shot back.

"You are," she said tersely.

He nodded. "The term 'supposed to be' is the operative one here. Sometimes events don't happen in the way we think they're supposed to."

DeFore suspected he was making an oblique reference to the events of the past few months, the so-called Imperator War. Rather than ask him for clarification and be drawn into a protracted and bewildering discussion about the person, creature or entity Lakesh called the imperator—or depending on his mood, simply Sam—she declared, "Kane and

Grant behaved as if they knew who was behind Brigid's abduction.''

He smiled sourly. "Another supposition?"

"Yes," she admitted. "But I'm still not clear on
why Grant was so adamant that me and Domi—her
in particular—didn't go with them.''

Lakesh tugged absently at his nose, a habit that
had not changed since his age reversal. "I can only
speculate on his motives, but more than likely friend
Grant feared that what Sindri—or whoever—giveth,
he could also take away.''

DeFore regarded him keenly. "So you think Sindri trawled Domi and saved her life? From what I've
heard of him, he doesn't seem to lean much in the
way of altruism.''

Lakesh lifted a shoulder in a shrug. "I have no
idea if Sindri did it or how he managed it, but he
certainly is the most probable culprit.''

"Culprit," she echoed. "You make it sound like
he committed a crime instead of saved a life.''

Lakesh favored her with a grave up-from-under
look, the same way he had done when he peered
over the rims of his spectacles. "Perhaps in a way
he did. Who knows if Domi was fated to die that
day? By interfering in the flow of time and events,
Sindri very well may have triggered another alternate event horizon. As it is, he didn't retrieve her a
microsecond before her death because of any Sa-

maritan impulses. No, it was either a whim or a component of a larger plan.''

DeFore didn't like what she was hearing. Chill fingers of dread stroked the base of her spine, and she shivered. ''Sindri deliberately lured us to the Operation Chronos facility in Chicago, is that what you're saying?''

Lakesh nodded. ''Precisely. During my short time spent in Sindri's company, I found him to be a brilliant, cunning...yet possibly the most hate-filled man I ever met. And I've met quite a few in my two-plus centuries of life.''

''I thought he fancied himself a scientist and a liberator.''

''Oh, I'm sure if Sindri was questioned on that point, he would deny his hatred. He would claim hate is not scientific, and therefore he is incapable of feeling that emotion.''

Lakesh's eyes acquired a faraway sheen, and his voice dropped to a husky whisper. ''He would never suspect, much less admit that under the surface of his intellect a hatred hot enough to set the world on fire smolders continuously. Nor would he guess that his dreams of setting the world aright had their roots hidden in his hatred.''

DeFore said quietly, ''Maybe hate is all he ever had.''

''No.'' Lakesh's voice was the rustle of coarse cloth. ''But it's all he has left.''

Suddenly, he seemed to mentally shake himself and he knuckled his eyes. "Forgive me, Doctor. When I'm tired I tend to wax philosophical."

"And psychological," DeFore interjected with a jittery smile. "I wasn't aware you had the time to analyze him."

Peremptorily, Lakesh stated, "Let's just say I know the type."

His tone closed the subject, but DeFore guessed he had been thinking of the source of his renewed vitality, the child god—or demon—who had assumed the title of imperator. Despite the explanations offered to her, not only by Lakesh but Brigid, as well, she had no idea of the true nature of the imperator. She knew he allegedly ruled some of the barons, but how many and for how long was still an open question.

Although all of the fortress cities with their individual, allegedly immortal god-kings were supposed to be interdependent, the baronies still operated on insular principles. Cooperation among them was grudging despite their shared goal of a unified world. They perceived humanity in general as either servants or as living storage vessels for transplanted organs and fresh genetic material.

The nine barons weren't immortal, but they were as close as flesh-and-blood creatures could come to it. Due to their hybrid metabolisms, their longevities far exceeded those of humans. Barring accidents, illnesses—or assassinations—the barons' life spans could conceivably be measured in centuries. Grant figured that even the youngest of them was close to a hundred years old.

But the price paid by the barons for their extended life spans was not cheap. They were physically fragile, prone to lethargy, and their metabolisms were easy prey for infections, which was one reason they tended to sequester themselves from the ville-bred humans they ruled.

The vast genetic engineering facility beneath the Archuleta Mesa in Dulce served as a combination of gestation, birthing ward and medical treatment center. The hybrids, the self-proclaimed new humans, were born there, the half-human spawn created to inherit the nuke-scoured Earth.

None of the hybrids reproduced in conventional fashion. They reproduced by a form of cloning and gene-splicing, but it hadn't seemed reasonable they would rely completely on the subterranean facilities beneath the mesa. And if that were so, if they did not have access to a secondary installation, then extinction for the barons was less than a generation away. Or so all the Cerberus exiles fervently hoped when the Dulce installation was destroyed.

That hope vanished quickly when Lakesh informed them of the Area 51 complex, and the body of legends that had sprung up around alien involvement with the top secret facility. The so-called aliens weren't referred to by name, but they fit the general physical description of Balam's people. If that was indeed the case, Lakesh theorized that the medical facilities that might exist in Area 51 would be of great use to the barons, since they would already be designed for their metabolisms. Baron Cobalt could reactivate them, turn them into a processing and treatment center, without having to rebuild from scratch. He could have transferred the medical personnel from the Dulce facility.

Baron Cobalt's forces had occupied the Dreamland complex in order to dole out the means of baronial survival as he saw fit. Kane and Domi were captured when they penetrated the enormous installation. During their two weeks of imprisonment in Area 51, they been told about a mysterious figure called the imperator who intended to set himself up as overlord of the villes, with the barons subservient to him. That bit of news was surprising enough, but it quickly turned shocking, when Kane said his informant claimed none other than Balam, whom they had thought was gone forever, supported this imperator.

Balam, the sole representative of the so-called Archon Directorate and therefore the masters of the baronial oligarchy and the entire hybrid dynasty, hadn't escaped—he had been set free.

In the months since the entity's departure, Lakesh had toyed with the notion that Balam had chosen to remain a prisoner in Cerberus for over three years until the resistance group was strong enough to actually make a difference in the war to cast off the harness of slavery. In essence he had made the Cerberus exiles participate in a conspiracy to manipulate a conspiracy.

Lakesh turned toward DeFore, forcing a smile. "There's no point in both of us standing here wondering what the biolink telemetry actually means. I think we should—"

A soft bong emanated from the monitor screen. Both people's heads swiveled toward it so swiftly their neck tendons twinged in protest. Hearts triphammering, they stared in horrified fascination as the icons symbolizing Brigid, Kane and Grant flickered and vanished from the screen.

Chapter 15

Lakesh focused on his ghostly reflection barely visible in the blank monitor. For an instant he saw a haggard and ancient face staring back at him—the face he had worn before meeting the imperator. The accusation in the blue eyes was firm, and it was just as firm in DeFore's voice. "Dammit, don't ignore me! I had enough of that from Grant today. What are we going to do?"

Inhaling a deep, calming breath, Lakesh turned to face the agitated medic. "There's very little we can do, Doctor." He deliberately addressed her by the honorific, despite knowing her education as a physician was woefully incomplete, at least by predark standards. "Our only option is the time-honored practice of serving by standing and waiting."

DeFore's eyebrows drew together at the bridge of her nose as she tried to reason out the meaning of the old bromide. Gesturing to the gateway, she demanded, "Isn't there any way to override the transit block from here?"

"I fear not."

"Didn't Sindri overcome your own security

blocks and beam his walking stick in here?'' she challenged. ''You were the Project Cerberus overseer, right? This is the first fully functional and debugged gateway, isn't it, the template for all the units in the network? Are you saying he can do things with them you can't?''

Despite knowing what the woman was doing, Lakesh bristled. ''Don't try to bait me with such an obvious ploy. Whatever methodology Sindri used to accomplish what he did was never made clear to me.''

In truth, the problem had vexed Lakesh for a long time. He could only speculate that once Sindri grasped the fundamental principles of the quantum inducer operations, he approached the problem from a direction Lakesh had yet to figure out.

''There are many reasons why we're not receiving the transponders' telemetry at the moment,'' he went on in a reasonable tone. ''It doesn't necessarily mean the jump team's life functions have ceased.''

She nodded. ''I know.''

''Besides, there are other matters to occupy me. Your intriguing account of the so-called nightgaunts for one. You weren't very precise about them.''

''I told you all I know,'' DeFore replied defensively. ''Domi was the one who called them that.''

His lips quirked in a patronizing smile. ''Yes, I'm aware of the Outlands superstitions of faceless soul stealers. But inasmuch as you said they spoke, it's apparent they have mouths and therefore faces, even if you couldn't see them.''

She frowned. "I don't know if it was an actual language or not. It sounded like gibberish to me. Linguistics isn't my field.''

"Can you reproduce some of the sounds you heard? If I hear the phonetics, I might be able the identify the root and therefore where the creatures came from.''

Lines of concentration furrowed on her smooth brow. After a thoughtful moment, she said, "*Di-ku.* That's what I heard most of all. *Di-ku.*''

Lakesh's eyes widened then narrowed. "You're sure?''

"Of course I'm not sure," she answered gruffly. "It was chaos in there." Slowly, as if he were dredging through his memory, he said, "During my investigations into the mythological origins of the Archons, I had occasion to read translations of Sumerian legend and lore.''

"So?''

"Theirs was an agglutinative tongue, its vocabulary, grammar and syntax are unrelated to any other language, living or dead. If it was Sumerian you heard, then no wonder it sounded like gibberish to you.''

Suspiciously, she asked, "I hope you're not getting ready to theorize that we ran into a bunch of time-trawled Sumerians.''

"Hardly. However, the word *di-ku* means 'to judge' or 'judgment determiner.' I find it very significant, particularly since we know that the Sumerian civilization was influenced by the Annunaki.''

DeFore put out a hand, palm outward. "Stop," she said sternly. "Don't go there, all right? Not now. You know how I hate all that ancient astronaut crap.''

Amused in spite of the situation, Lakesh inquired innocently, "Even if it's the truth?''

"We don't know if it's the truth," she shot back. "It's only what Brigid claimed she was told.''

Lakesh didn't deny it or argue with the woman. Even Kane had pointed out that all the history they knew of the barons, the nukecaust and even the Archons derived from secondhand and dubious sources, with very little empirical evidence to back it up. All they really had as a foundation was myth, often distorted and disguised out of all reasonable proportion.

DeFore passed a hand over her face and said wearily, "Sorry, Lakesh. I'm worn and wrung out.''

"Why don't you go the cafeteria?" he suggested gently. "You haven't eaten since your return, and I can tell you're exhausted. I'll apprise you of any change.''

She sighed heavily, loath to leave the control

complex. "It never gets any easier, does it? The waiting and wondering?"

"No," he answered bluntly. "I wish I could say it did, but it never does."

DeFore left the ready room, walking around the long table that served as its only furniture. Lakesh watched her go, once again thanking whatever mysterious fates had brought the woman to his attention. But at the same time he thanked them, he also feared them. If Reba DeFore ever learned the true circumstances of her exile from her ville, he would earn her undying hatred, and he knew he deserved every atom of it. Despite all the rationalizations and justifications he employed, guilt still consumed him, more so now that he was an exile himself.

Lakesh's usual method of recruitment was to select likely candidates from the personnel records of all the villes, then set them up, frame them for crimes against their respective barons. He had used the ploy to recruit Brigid Baptiste, Reba DeFore, Benjamin Farrell, Donald Bry and Robert Wegmann, knowing all the while that the cruel, heartless plan had a barely acceptable risk factor.

It was the only way to spirit them out of their villes, turn them against the barons and make them feel indebted to him. This bit of explosive and potentially fatal knowledge had not been shared with the exiles other than Kane, Grant and Brigid, and they had occasionally held it over his head, as both a means of persuasion and outright blackmail.

It wasn't as if Lakesh hadn't undertaken enormous risks himself in his covert war against the barons. Before, as a member of the Cobaltville Trust, he straddled the fence between collaborator and conspirator. Unfortunately, the suspicions of Salvo, a fellow Trust member and Magistrate Division commander, had been aroused by his activities. He pulled Lakesh off the fence and onto the side of a conspirator because he suspected him of not only being a Preservationist, but of arranging Kane, Brigid and Grant's escape from the ville.

Part of this suspicion was true, but the other part was a deliberately constructed falsehood. Salvo had bought into a piece of mole data that Lakesh himself had sent burrowing through the nine-ville network some twenty years before. Salvo was convinced of the existence of an underground resistance movement called the Preservationists, a group that allegedly followed a set of idealistic precepts to free humanity from the bondage of the barons by revealing the hidden history of Earth.

The Preservationists were an utter fiction, a straw adversary crafted for the barons to fear and chase after while Lakesh's true insurrectionist work proceeded elsewhere.

Salvo believed Lakesh to be a Preservationist, and that he had recruited Kane into their traitorous rank and file. When Baron Cobalt had charged Salvo with the responsibility of apprehending Kane by any means necessary, the man presumed those means included the abduction and torture of Lakesh, one of the baron's favorites.

Lakesh had been rescued and taken back to Cerberus, but the retrieval increased the odds the redoubt would be found. Although the installation was listed on all ville records as utterly inoperable, Lakesh extrapolated that Baron Cobalt would leave no redoubt unopened in his search for him.

After all, the baron had witnessed a group of seditionists using his own personal gateway to transport elsewhere, so logically, his quarry had to have a destination. The matter stream modulations of the Cerberus unit were slightly out of phase with other gateways so they couldn't be traced. The baron's only alternative was a physical search of every redoubt. In spite of Grant, Kane, Brigid and Domi's efforts to lay false trails in other redoubts, Lakesh knew far too many things had happened since his rescue to be able to return to any of the villes, either as a conspirator or collaborator.

War had come to the baronies. Baron Cobalt had disappeared, and the imperator was setting into motion momentous events that would eventually result in a violent climax or a terrifying synthesis. The doctrine of unity had been decisively shattered, and Lakesh had no idea what might take its place. For the majority of the ville-bred citizens, the concept of a living outside of a narrow, structured society would be akin to insanity. Lakesh knew the people of the baronies would not be as resilient as Kane, Grant and Brigid Baptiste when their entire belief system collapsed into the rubble of lost dreams and meaningless dogma.

For most of their lives, Kane, Grant and Brigid had subscribed to the doctrine of unification. In the case of Kane and Grant, they had dedicated their lives to serving those ideals. As Magistrates, the two men enforced the many and contradictory laws of the villes, enjoying their reputations of being both ruthless and incorruptible. Both men followed a patrilineal tradition, assuming the duties and positions of their fathers before them. They did not have given names, each taking the surname of the father, as though the first Magistrate to bear the name was the same man as the last.

As Magistrates, the courses their lives followed had been charted before their births. They were destined to live, fight and die, usually violently, as they fulfilled their oaths to impose order upon chaos. Kane's life had taken a different route, but he learned later he was following the secret path laid down by his father.

When Kane, Grant and Brigid were reclassified as outlanders, or nonpersons, they could never return to Cobaltville. As far as Kane was concerned, the war was over. The nukecaust made the planet the property of someone—something—else, and humans like himself were exiles on the world of their birth.

Only Lakesh's theory that the nukecaust happened because of an alteration in the probability wave gave him even a dim light of hope. If the Archons turned the wave in a direction it was not supposed to flow, then perhaps the course could be redirected.

It was a small, almost ridiculous hope, but neither Kane, Grant nor Brigid had anything else on which to base a reason to continue living. Faced with the choice of bleak acceptance of the reality or a faint chance of salvaging humanity's future, they chose the faint chance.

According to Kane, it was the only human choice to make. Fortunately, the crucible of spiritual fire did not destroy Kane, Brigid and Grant. It cleansed them even as it scorched them, driving them forward, keeping them from accepting or surrendering to the forces arrayed against them. They declared war on the dark forces devoted to maintaining the yoke of slavery around the collective necks of humankind. It was a struggle not just for the physical survival of humanity but for the human spirit, the soul of an entire race.

Over the past two years, they scored many victories, defeated many enemies and solved mysteries of the past that molded the present and the future. More importantly, they began to rekindle of the spark of hope within the breasts of the disenfranchised fighting to survive in the Outlands.

Victory, if not within their grasp, at least no longer seemed an unattainable dream. But dark clouds arose from the nuke-scoured caldron of the hellzones, building to a critical mass. The war that ended a civilization and began another two centuries before had entered a new and far more deadly phase—and it was one that Kane and his friends had unwittingly brought about.

Lakesh started to walk into the control center and grimaced at a stabbing pain in his right knee. The pain was brief, but it was familiar. He knew the symptoms of arthritis and with a sinking sensation in the pit of his stomach he realized the imperator's gift of restored vitality was no more substantial than the dogma of unity.

He saw Bry seated at the main ops console and Farrell at environmental station. They were engaged in a casual conversation, talking of matters mundane and ordinary. Lakesh fervently wished he could join in, but he couldn't force his mind away from the crisis. He knew he should have anticipated Sindri's involvement in Domi's resurrection and taken precautions. But he had not, and now he feared disaster for all of humankind was afoot in the night.

He strode up the aisle between computer stations.

Usually the sublime hum of computer noise comforted him, but tonight it ate at his nerve endings. Once again, renegade technology cast a threatening shadow on a world that already had seen its fair share of darkness.

Somewhere out there existed an immensely powerful tool for mass destruction, and it was in the hands of a madman possessed of an overwhelming need to avenge his own birth.

Chapter 16

Grant heeled away from the railing as the echo of his cry still vibrated in the air. Sindri didn't move, didn't so much as flinch as Grant lunged toward him. He met the big man's expression of bare-toothed, wild-eyed, homicidal fury with a bland smile.

Too maddened by rage to even think of unleathering his Sin Eater, Grant closed his hands around Sindri's upper arms and hoisted him up effortlessly, holding him at eye level.

"Let her go!" Grant roared out the words, his breath fogging the faceplate of his hood. "Let her go, or I'll rip your fucking arms off and hammer them down your throat!"

"I have no doubt you could do so," Sindri replied, his voice calm. "And I always intended to release her. Under a condition, of course."

"Of course," Brigid spit angrily. "What is it this time? More of your 'bow, yield, kneel' shit?"

The occasion was rare when Brigid used profanity and when she did, it meant she was stressed-out indeed. Kane, although equally angry, wasn't partic-

ularly surprised by Sindri's ploy. As Brigid had
pointed out earlier, Sindri never did anything without holding out an ace. He glanced down into the
shaft at Shizuka in the alcove. Her dark eyes silently
implored him, but he wasn't sure what she wanted
him to do.

Growling deep in his throat like a lion infuriated
beyond all sense of self-preservation, Grant roughly
reversed his grip on Sindri, spinning him and dan-
gling him over the railing by the ankles. He shook
him, bellowing, "I'm not playing these games with
you, pissant! Let her go, or I drop you straight on
your head!"

"You can do that," Sindri agreed, still striving to
sound unruffled and in control of the situation. "But
you'd kill her, too."

Grant opened his hand around Sindri's right ankle
and the little man cried out involuntarily in fear,
kicking at the air. His voice trembling in anger at
the indignity of being held upside down like an infant, Sindri shouted, "Oakshott!"

Grant's brow furrowed in confusion. He exchanged a swift glance with Kane and Brigid.
"What does that mean?"

"It means," Sindri retorted, "the process of killing Shizuka has already begun. Look."

Even behind the amber shimmer, they saw Shizuka's body tauten, and she bit her lower lip as if
stifling a cry of pain. She strained against the curves

of metal holding her to the wall. A crimson trickle ran down her left thigh from beneath a claw.

"I gave the signal to tighten the restraints," Sindri announced. "Even if you kill me, you won't be able to breach the stasis field in time to free her— not before she's dismembered."

"We'll take our chances," Grant snapped, but he didn't sound very confident. Still, he lowered Sindri a foot or so.

"The best you could hope for is that only one of her limbs will be amputated." Sindri's voice rose, hitting a shrill note of panic. "For a woman like her, that would be worse than death."

Shizuka squeezed her eyes shut and with mounting horror, Kane and Brigid saw threads of blood inching down her forearms. Grant stared unblinkingly at the woman, then with a snarl, pulled the little man back over the rail and dumped him unceremoniously onto the floor.

Sindri picked himself up quickly, his cheeks bright red from the blood that had rushed to his head. He stumbled dizzily. "If I'd known the extent to which I was going to be abused by you three, I would've let both bitches die."

Grant's desire to kill the little man by any means possible was so overwhelming he could barely speak. He clenched his hands around the top bar of the railing so tightly Kane fancied he heard the metal creak.

"Get her out of there," Kane directed Sindri, "or he'll break your neck, regardless of the consequences."

Sindri said, "All right, Oakshott. Enough." He clapped his hands as if dusting them off. "Done and done. Now we can be friends again."

Some of the tension went out of Shizuka's body as the pressure of the claws decreased. Her lips moved, but they couldn't hear what she said.

"She'll be fine," Sindri declared curtly. "I'll have her brought around so you can speak with her. She's not hurt. Those restraints weren't designed to perform such unpleasant tasks as dismemberment anyway."

"You mean they don't meet your high standards of instruments of torture," Brigid grated.

Sindri shot her an icy-eyed, searching stare. "They were apparently built to retrieve and hold dangerous items that were trawled from the time stream, much like the mechanical arms used in predark nuclear power plants."

"Fascinating," Kane said with undisguised contempt. "We're always astounded by the uses you find for old predark junk. Space stations, gamma-powered lasers, molecular destabilizers, stealth aircraft—you're the king, Sindri. Of scavengers."

Sindri showed his teeth either in a grimace of outrage or a savage grin of defiance. In a silky soft voice, he said, "Mr. Kane, you don't know the half of it. I've not even *begun* to astound you."

Kane, Brigid and Grant all realized he wasn't making a promise but issuing a threat.

ONCE THEY WERE out of the stasis chamber, Sindri took off his hood and told his three companions to do the same. They followed him through a narrow door and went silently along an ill-lit corridor. The dim blue glow of the occasional neon light provided the only illumination.

Grant was still too agitated to speak, fury seething in his eyes. Kane, walking abreast of Sindri, asked, "Are you going to tell us how Shizuka became your prisoner?"

"Certainly, " he answered smoothly. "She and a contingent of samurai came here several times over the past couple of months. Apparently, they were searching for you three. I was content to let them prowl around the perimeter of the installation, since they were obviously loath to enter it. Finally, she came in alone."

"So you were here when we tracked the Magistrates down?" Brigid demanded.

Sindri nodded. "I was indeed." He pointed to a vid spy-eye on the ceiling. "I watched it all from a safe remove. When you got into this section of the complex, I decided it was time to go. I used the mattrans to jump to Redoubt Echo in Chicago. When I returned a few days later, I found a considerable amount of damage had been done to the dilator.'' He cast a reproachful glance toward Kane. ''And you left a body for me to dispose of. That was very uncouth, Mr. Kane.''

After several baffling turns, the corridor began to slant downward. ''How'd you even find out about this place?'' Kane asked.

Sindri smiled slyly. ''I had unrestricted access to the database in the Anthill, remember?''

Kane nodded and said nothing more. Since the vast Anthill complex had been intended to be the seat of all Totality Concept divisions, it stood to reason the computer system there contained all the gateway destination codes for redoubts relating to the Concept projects.

''I didn't come here immediately, of course,'' Sindri went on. ''I was injured, as you might recall.'' His voice became flinty and he glared accusingly over his shoulder at Brigid. She met his glare with one of her own. ''I jumped to *Parallax Red* and stayed there long enough to heal. Then I came here.''

''Speaking of *Parallax Red*,'' Kane remarked, ''where are your helper elves, the transadapts?''

Sindri waved a hand through the air as if the matter was of little importance. ''They're waiting for me, never fear.''

Grant finally deigned to speak to the little man.

"You don't usually work alone. You need followers and worshipers."

"Like Megaera and her Furies who think you're the smiling god," Brigid interposed. "Where are they?"

"Not here," Sindri retorted with a studied nonchalance.

"Why not?" Brigid challenged.

"Because like all fanatics, they're too unpredictable to make reliable help."

"Where'd they come from?" Kane asked.

"Would you be surprised to learn that I really don't know? During the course of my investigations here, I accidentally brought them through and then transported the whole bunch to Redoubt Echo."

"'Through'?" Kane repeated. "What do you mean by that?"

"Apparently, the dilator's focus-conformals were already preset on a target. So when I—"

"Forget the technobabble," Grant snapped impatiently. "Where's Shizuka?"

Sindri turned a corner and paused at an open doorway. He bent at the waist in a mocking bow. "'Hope against hope and ask till you receive,'" he quoted. "But please disabuse yourself of the notion that once you're reunited with her you can make good on your threat to insert my arms down my throat."

Grant grunted as if the comment were of no con-

sequence and pushed past him into a wardroom or
small galley. It contained several tables, chairs, a
stove and refrigerator. Seated at one of the tables,
head bowed and hugging herself, was Shizuka.

Her normally glossy black hair was dull and disarrayed. Her face was drawn tight over a smoothly
curving bone structure. Her complexion, normally a
very pale gold with roses and milk for an accent,
was more milk now than gold. The almond-shaped
eyes didn't glint with fierce pride. Instead they were
mirrors of suffering. Looking at the dispirited warrior, Kane felt a painful clenching in his chest.

She wore a thin cotton shift that left most of her
arms and legs bare. Red welts showed starkly
against the flesh. Grant started to rush toward her,
but then checked the movement. A gigantic man in
black loomed over Shizuka. He looked to be seven
feet tall if he were an inch, and probably tipped the
scales at three hundred pounds. His round moon face
was dead-white, like that of a bled-out corpse. His
tiny baby's mouth glistened with saliva. Bushy side-
burns adorned both jaws, and his dark hair, gleaming
with pomade, bore a white part right down the middle.

His thick black suit with its long frock coat, old-
fashioned celluloid collar and cravat tie made him
look like a store-window mannequin from the late
nineteenth century. He regarded the newcomers
without a flicker of emotion. In one hand, held close

to his belly, he gripped a tiny wooden pistol, carved in the shape of a revolver. Kane saw a transceiver plug nestled in the man's right ear.

Brigid, Kane and Grant all felt a chill a fear when they looked into the giant's lusterless, pewter-colored eyes. Sindri gave a jaunty little laugh. "This is Oakshott. He's my right-hand man at the moment. Aren't you, Oakshott?"

The man leaned forward a little, peering down at Sindri. His flesh-bagged eyes flicked from the little man to Brigid then to Grant and finally settled on Kane. The expression on his face was not entirely vacuous—there appeared to be a laborious form of thought going on.

When Grant stepped toward Shizuka again, Oakshott shuffled forward as if to block his path. "It's all right, Oakshott," Sindri said soothingly. "He's one of the friends I told you would be visiting. That's a good fellow."

Oakshott stared at Grant mistrustfully and grunted. "Yes. Yes. I understand. Yes."

His voice, though thick and deep, carried an unmistakable British accent. He moved stiffly away. Shizuka rose as Grant reached for her, embracing him tightly. In a voice barely above a whisper, she said, "I feared you were dead. You never returned."

Grant stroked her hair, kissed the top of her head and murmured, "I'm back now, Shizuka."

She said faintly. "*Hai*. Yes."

"Yes," Oakshott echoed. "Yes. I understand."

Kane looked the big man over. He saw white puncture scars in the man's eye sockets. Oakshott looked as if he had been stabbed at the corners of each eye with an ice pick. "Where the hell did you find him?"

Sindri laughed nervously. "He was already here. Sort of. I retrieved him from the matrix."

Kane wasn't sure what he meant, but before he could ask for clarification, Brigid inquired, "Do you know where he's from at least?"

"As a matter of fact, I do," Sindri answered. "He was trawled from the year 1899, snatched from a private mental institution in Manchester, England. The dossier I found in the database described Mr. Sherrinford Oakshott as a stark, raving lunatic. He was classed as incurable. The doctors of the day couldn't do a thing with him or for him, and they tried everything in their limited repertoire.

"Poor Mr. Oakshott used to fall victim to periods of what they called 'catatonic excitement,' which from what I gather was a Victorian euphemism for a rampage of killing and raping. In any event, they gave him a prefrontal lobotomy."

Sindri fingered his eye orbits. "In those days the procedure amounted to little more than jamming a knitting needle into his brain."

Nausea surged in Kane's belly. Even Brigid looked a bit sick. He covered his suddenly upset stomach by saying, "He appears to be the perfect servant for you, Sindri. Not as high maintenance as your transadapts."

Sindri did not appear to be offended by the observation. He touched the high collar of the black bodysuit. "You speak very truly. I keep in touch with him through a comm. He obeys simple orders exceptionally well."

"Particularly," Brigid pointed out dryly, "if they involve torturing women."

Sindri chuckled. "Apparently," he went on, "Mr. Oakshott's sudden disappearance from his cell in the asylum didn't receive much publicity. The authorities didn't report it, and were probably relieved when he simply vanished."

"If you found him in the matrix," Brigid said, "that means he was time-trawled. Why would a lunatic be pulled from the nineteenth to the twentieth century?"

Sindri gave her a macabre grin. "Especially when there were so many in that time period. If you care to take seats, I'll explain everything...including why I need your help."

"Why should we believe anything you 'explain'?" Grant demanded angrily, Shizuka still enfolded in his arms. "Why shouldn't we just shoot your slagging ass dead and go on our way?" He nodded toward Oakshott. "Lunatic bodyguard or no lunatic bodyguard."

Sindri sighed like a teacher forced to deal with a rowdy student. "Mr. Grant, I could have just as easily killed your precious Shizuka as imprison her. But I spared her. Nor did I mistreat her while she was here. Ask her if you don't believe me."

Shizuka pushed herself away from Grant and combed nervous fingers through her hair. She seemed to have regained some sparks of her old inner fire, the ferocity that had driven her to put down a rebellion and command the forces that beat back an invasion of New Edo, all in a single night.

"That is true," she stated. "He didn't harm me, but only because I cooperated with him. The *zurui chibi* tricked me into believing he would destroy New Edo if I tried to escape."

"*Zurui chibi?*" Kane repeated, stumbling over the pronunciation. "What's that mean?"

Brigid smiled coldly. "Sneaky dwarf."

Sindri flushed in anger. "Very droll. But make no mistake, any of you—I wasn't lying to her when I threatened to destroy New Edo. I certainly can do that...and for that matter, destroy anyone or thing I pretty much please."

He took a deep breath and forced a smile to his mobile mouth. "But enough boasting. Let's sit down and discuss matters like civilized people."

Brigid and Kane snorted at the same time.

Chapter 17

It was almost like a replay of their first meeting with Sindri. As the four people took seats, very aware of the looming, intimidating presence of Oakshott, Sindri rummaged through a refrigerator, murmuring about refreshments. Neither Kane, Grant nor Brigid was fooled—one of Sindri's favorite impostures was that of the congenial host.

He withdrew a carafe of reddish-purple liquid, placed it on the table and busied himself finding glasses. Grant eyed the carafe distrustfully. "What's this? The same drugged wine you slipped us on *Parallax Red?*"

Sindri shook his head mournfully. "As big as an elephant and with the same long memory for wrongs. I apologized for that."

Sindri placed three tumblers on the table. "No, actually, this is a different vintage—plum wine from Miss Shizuka's very own New Edo."

He tipped the carafe, pouring the wine into Shizuka's and Brigid's tumblers first. He served Kane last, who gave the little man a mirthless smile. "Many thanks. Whenever you get tired of being a psychotic asshole, you can always find work waiting tables."

Sindri smiled disarmingly. "I've already pulled my tour of being a servant, Mr. Kane. Those days are gone and will never return, regardless of what the future may bring."

Once again, Sindri's tone held an undercurrent of a threat.

None of the four people touched the wine until they saw Sindri take a long gulp from his own glass. His face screwed up and a prolonged shudder shook his slight frame. Sounding half-strangled, he husked out, "Smooth."

Kane took an experimental sip and had the impression of drinking a fruit punch mixed with battery acid. "Let's get down to the business at hand, Sindri. But first of all, don't for one second delude yourself into believing we'll allow you to stay here."

Sindri lifted his eyebrows. "Actually, I'd prefer *you* stay here with me. Like I said, this was apparently the seat of Operation Chronos, code-named Redoubt Yankee. It was built on one of the Santa Barbara or Channel Islands, disguised as a satellite campus of the University of California."

None of the Cerberus team was particularly surprised to hear that. When they first saw the buildings housing the Chronos technology, Brigid opined it resembled pix she had seen of predark universities.

"This was one of the finest and most secret research establishments in the world," Sindri continued. "Its engineering and computer centers were second to none, and I doubt its accomplishments in the field of physics could have been matched, much less exceeded. It was here the personnel cracked the cosmic code."

Sindri paused expectantly, waiting for the inevitable question about the meaning of his statement. When it was not forthcoming, his upper lip curled in a disdainful sneer. Flicking his gaze over the faces of Brigid, Shizuka, Grant and Kane, he declared, "Don't try to persuade me you know what I'm talking about."

Without hesitation, Brigid stated, "The cosmic code is vernacular for the unified field theory. It refers to the mathematical reconstruction of the first few seconds of the big bang, when the universe was a primal monobloc without dimensions of space."

Kane didn't bother suppressing an appreciative laugh when disappointment passed over Sindri's face like a cloud. Brigid's eidetic memory made her something of an ambulatory encyclopedia, since she retained just about everything she ever read, particularly during her years as an archivist. A vast amount of predark historical information had survived the nukecaust, particularly documents stored in underground vaults. Tons of it, in fact, everything from novels to encyclopedias, to magazines printed on coated stock that survived just about anything. Much more data was digitized, stored on computer diskettes, usually government documents.

Although her primary duty as an archivist was not to record predark history, but to revise, rewrite and often completely disguise it, she learned early how to separate fiction from the truth, a cover story from a falsehood and scientific theory from fact.

A little sullenly Sindri said, "Yes, well...do you know how the application relates to the overall objective of this facility?"

"Time travel," Grant bit out. "We know that already."

"Time manipulation," Sindri corrected smoothly. "The possibility of going back and forward in time had long been discredited by most scientists, but the project overseer of Operation Chronos discovered a means of doing so. A man named Silas Torrance Burr."

"We know," Kane said. "It wouldn't have been possible without Lakesh's breakthroughs with the gateway units."

Sindri regarded him mockingly. "Breakthroughs that of course wouldn't have been possible without his access to the findings of the so-called Philadelphia Experiment."

"What the hell is that?" Grant demanded gruffly. "I never heard of it."

"I'm not surprised," Sindri answered. "I doubt

your Dr. Singh would want to credit an accident with providing him with the foundation of his career. Essentially, back in 1943 during the height of World War II, an experiment was undertaken to make warships invisible through the selective bending of light. Rumor has it that Albert Einstein himself was involved.

"Whatever energy source was employed caused not only the USS *Eldridge* to vanish into a bank of green fog, but within seconds it was teleported from the Philadelphia Navy Yards to Norfolk, Virginia, and a moment after that, it reappeared in Philadelphia. Legend also had it that the *Eldridge* was not only be transported from point to point in linear space, but briefly to another time period.

"In my estimation, the Totality Concept's Operation Chronos and Project Cerberus were nothing more than efforts to re-create what had happened by accident."

Sindri smiled smugly, adding, "So the high esteem in which you hold Dr. Singh's genius may be misplaced. I think Dr. Burr deserves the lion's share of credit."

Brigid said coldly, "Most of Burr's time-trawling experiments were failures. The living tissue of whatever was trawled forward from the past broke apart. It wasn't until Lakesh made the first fully functional gateway unit operational that Burr was able to assemble the trawled subjects in the mat-trans without organic decohesion.''

Sindri waved away her words. ''The personnel here overcame that handicap, as all three of you witnessed yourselves.''

Puzzled, Shizuka asked, ''What's he talking about?''

Grant shook his head. ''I'll explain later.''

Sindri laughed. ''That should be interesting. Let me know when you do. I'd love to hear it.''

''It doesn't really matter who did what,'' Kane pointed out, feeling a little strange to be defending Lakesh even in a backhanded way, ''since everything relating to the Totality Concept was filtered down from another source.''

''Ah.'' Sindri nodded. ''The so-called Archons. Or to be more precise, their forebears, the Annunaki and the Tuatha de Danaan.''

Shizuka cast her dark eyes from Sindri to Grant. ''Who is he talking about?''

''That's an excellent question, madam,'' Sindri retorted. ''And it has yet to be satisfactorily answered even now.''

Grant pushed the wine tumbler away from him with such force the liquid sloshed out of it. Harshly, he said, ''How long do you expect us to sit through another one of your dissertations? No matter what you yammer about, you're still outnumbered.'' He touched his holstered Sin Eater. "And outgunned. So get to the goddamn point, Sindri."

Oakshott stepped forward, pointing his wooden revolver at Grant. "Behave yourself, sirrah. Understand? Yes, yes, you understand."

Sindri waggled a finger at Oakshott. "Never mind, never mind. That's a good fellow. I'm not being threatened."

"The hell you're not," Grant growled menacingly.

Sindri scowled at him, then arranged his face into a smirk of superiority. "You evidently paid very little attention to Miss Brigid's statement that I never do anything without an ace. I assure you that's true."

No one responded for a long, awkward tick of time. Then Kane yawned, as if ennui were settling over him. In a disinterested tone, he asked, "And what might that be?"

"And—" Sindri broke off, took a breath, then jumped out of his chair and walked toward the door. "Follow me, please. Visual aids are so much more conducive to cooperation than, as Mr. Grant described it, another one of my dissertations."

Oakshott folded his arms over his chest and stared impassively at the four people until they pushed back their chairs and stood. They walked out into the corridor, trailing after Sindri with Oakshott bringing up the rear. The little man stopped in front of a heavy metal door without a knob or latch. He tapped in a sequence on the keypad on the wall. Machinery clanked, and with a prolonged hiss of pneumatics, the door slid to the right. Sindri entered a room dominated by a huge flat-screen vid monitor. The screen was divided into twelve square sections, each one showing different black-and-white views from a variety of perspectives.

One screen showed a high-angle view of rough seas upon which a little sailboat pushed through the waters, skipping on the chop like a flat stone on a pond. The craft approached a dark landmass rearing out of the ocean like a massive cube of black volcanic rock. Green vegetation was apparent on the summit of a small peak. Atop it stood the outline of a watch or bell tower. Castellated cliffs loomed at least a hundred feet above the surface of the Cific. Thundering waves crashed and broke on the bare rock, foaming spray flying in all directions. All of them recognized the scene.

In a voice tight with wonder, Shizuka said, "That is New Edo."

Sindri chuckled. "That it is. Take a closer look." His hand manipulated a knob on the console and the view changed.

The little sailboat navigated a narrow channel between the high walls. The sea heaved under the boat as a rawboned man operated the sweep. Several other people could be seen hunkering down in the wave-tossed craft.

"That's Dubois!" Grant exclaimed. Dubois was a fisherman who had transported the Cerberus team from Port Morninglight to New Edo months before.

"Is that his name?" Sindri seemed to be enjoying himself thoroughly. "Maybe you'll be so good as to identify his crew."

Once more he manipulated a knob, and the perspective on the screen tightened. Kane, Grant, Brigid and Shizuka stared at Kane, Grant and Brigid in the boat.

As they watched in bewilderment, the fishing boat plunged into the strait between the slick, seaweed-draped walls of the narrow channel. It pitched and jumped as it followed the twisting passage. The boat picked up speed, shooting forward, threading its way between upthrusts of pitted rock. The strait widened and the boat plunged into a lagoon. Even within the inlet, the sea was turbulent and swells threatened to pile the vessel up on the rocks. The boiling sea calmed the farther the ship moved from the throat of the strait.

With an overwhelming sensation of déjà vu, Brigid, Grant and Kane gazed at Dubois unfurling the sail. When a breeze filled it, he steered the ship toward a stone jetty on the far side of the lagoon. Several quays and docks were built around a spit of volcanic rock that jutted out into the blue waters. A cluster of vessels was tied up there, mainly barges and skiffs, but he saw three large vessels that had all the characteristics of warships.

They were all of a type, riding high above the waterline, consisting of sharp angles, arches and buttresses. The sails didn't look like broadcloth. They reminded him of window blinds made of a waxed and oiled paper.

He, Kane and Brigid had seen similar craft before, on the island of Autarkic. As he recollected, the ships were called junks. Beyond the ships and the docks, he saw a crescent moon of a white sandy beach, bracketed by stunted palm trees and tropical ferns.

Kane turned away from the screen and addressed Sindri. "Are we supposed to be all shook up by a vid record of what we did a few months ago?"

"Actually," Sindri answered mildly, "you should be. Do you recall seeing anything like a camera on the high seas or even...here?" He flicked a switch and another screen flickered with movement.

They watched as a squad of Tigers of Heaven marched toward the images of themselves. They were attired in suits of segmented armor made from wafers of metal held together by small, delicate chain. Overlaid with a dark brown lacquer, the interlocked and overlapping plates were trimmed in scarlet and gold. Between flaring shoulder epaulets, war helmets fanned out with sweeping curves of metal. Some resembled wings, others horns. The face guards, wrought of a semitransparent material, presented the inhuman visage of a snarling tiger.

Quivers of arrows dangled from their shoulders, and longbows made of lacquered wood were strapped to their backs. Each samurai carried two longswords in black scabbards swinging back from each hip. None of them carried firearms, but their skill with *katanas* and the bows was such that they didn't really need them.

A roan horse suddenly cantered through the line of armored men, and they quickly gave ground. A small, lithe figure sat on its back, easily controlling the horse with an air of authority. Shizuka reined her mount to a halt and vaulted lightly from the saddle. She spoke a stream of rapid-fire Japanese to the samurai, who instantly began drifting away as if all of them had suddenly remembered something else they needed to do.

The screen next to it blurred with a jagged pattern of pixels, then the fortress of Lord Takaun appeared, stretching like a slumbering animal among gardened terraces. The structure was not particularly tall, but it sprawled out with many windows, balconies and carved frames. The columns supporting the many porches and loggias were made of lengths of thick bamboo, bent into unusual shapes. The upcurving roof arches and interlocking shingles all seemed to be made of lacquered wood. It was very well laid out with deep moats on three sides and cliffs on the other. At the top of the walls were parapets and protected positions for archers and blastermen.

Abruptly, the sky darkened, turning the deep purple of twilight between one eye blink and another. The screen showed the sprawling, landscaped lawn at the rear of the fortress. Through an open gate came a surge of Tigers of Heaven, their armor glinting in the sunset.

From almost every shadowed point on the lawn between the bathhouse and the castle rushed a horde of black-garbed and hooded figures wielding swords and lances. They struck the Tigers from both flanks, pushing them toward the rear of the fortress.

Shizuka inhaled a sharp breath, her eyes glinting in anger. She recognized, as did Brigid, Kane and Grant, the attempted insurrection orchestrated by the Black Dragon society. According to Takaun, the roots of the society stretched back three or more centuries to the last days of Japan's old feudal system. A group of *soshi,* disenfranchised and rabidly xenophobic samurai, formed an underground organization to fight the spread of Western influence. In reality, they were terrorists and later they became Nippon's pioneers of organized crime.

The Black Dragon society was revived in New Edo, hiding in plain sight, since most of them were recruited from the ranks of the samurai trainees. They did not want any commerce or contact with the mainland at all, and they were particularly incensed when Grant, Kane and Brigid arrived on the island.

Because he feared alienating the samurai, Lord Takaun did not take action against the Dragons. He claimed that even offering hospitality to the three outlanders was risking a rebellion, perhaps even a coup. Bitterly, Grant realized the daimyo's fears were grounded in reality.

There was almost no room to maneuver, and the *katanas* of the Black Dragons penetrated chinks in the Tigers' armor and sank deep into eyes through the slits in the visors. The gloom lit up with little flares as blue sparks flew from impact points.

The Black Dragons did not wear armor, only ebony kimonos. He saw that most of them wore wide headbands, which Shizuka had called *hachimaki*. The foreparts were augmented by strips of chain mail. Grant and Kane had learned through painful experience they wore chain mail beneath their robes, as well.

Sindri tapped a sequence of buttons. "As interesting as all that is, for sheer entertainment value, I prefer this."

The view of the battle shimmered away, replaced by a panoramic view of a dark jungle clearing. Rain pounded down the foliage, and streamed from the fernlike fronds of trees. Four figures crept out of the underbrush, all of them armed. Moisture gleamed on

the black armor of the Magistrates like a coating of
oil. The armor was close-fitting, molded to conform
to the biceps, triceps, pectorals and abdomen. They
wore face-concealing helmets, their eyes masked by
red-tinted visors. The only spot of color anywhere
on them was the small, disk-shaped badge of office
emblazoned on the left pectoral. It depicted, in crimson, a stylized, balanced scales of justice, superimposed over a nine-spoked wheel.

The badge symbolized the Magistrate's oath, of
keeping the wheels of justice turning in the nine
baronies, but now the only emotional resonance it
carried was one of bitter betrayal. All of them were
armed with Sin Eaters.

The quartet of armored men huddled together in
the clearing to confer. Behind them, a shadowy
shape shifted out of the gloom. Even watching from
the safe remove of time and distance, Kane couldn't
repress a shiver.

Grinning jaws bared rows of glistening yellow
fangs. A saurian snout bore a pair of flared nostrils
that seemed to dilate and twitch. The head, bigger
than that of a horse, was set upon an extended,
scaled neck.

Huge cold eyes, like those of a serpent a hundred
times magnified, stared unwinkingly from beneath a
pair of scaled, knobby protuberances. Two huge
legs, almost as big around as some of the palm trees
they'd seen, supported the massive, barrel-shaped

body. A long tail trailed from behind, disappearing into the undergrowth. Its wet hide bore a pebblelike pattern of dark brown scales. Clawed forelegs were drawn up to its chest, almost in an attitude of prayer.

Then, with incredible swiftness, the monster bounded out of the foliage and landed among the four Magistrates. They fired their weapons in a frenzy, the muzzle-flashes smearing the murk with bursts of light. One of the Mags ran pell-mell toward the jungle, fleeing like a panic-stricken deer.

The dinosaur caught up with the running man with one spring-steel legged leap. Huge jaws closed over the Magistrate's head, and the creature's neck jerked back and forth. The arms and legs of the armored man flopped bonelessly, like those of a disjointed marionette.

Sindri laughed delightedly as the four people watched the sequence in horrid fascination. The scaled monstrosity clutched the Mag in its underdeveloped claws as it chewed through his vertebrae. The man's helmeted head fell from the blood-flecked mouth of the dinosaur and rolled across the muddy ground like an awkward ball. Clutching the decapitated corpse to its chest, the creature gathered itself and bounded from sight into the jungle.

Kane wiped at the clammy film of cold sweat that had gathered at his hairline. He retained an exceptionally vivid recollection of coming across the man's head. Since he, Grant and Brigid had

glimpsed the creature earlier, he had guessed how
the hapless Mag had come to be beheaded, but to
actually witness it made his mouth fill with sour
saliva.

Sweat glistening on his own brow, Grant turned
toward Sindri, looming over the little man like a
black colossus, ignoring the presence of Oakshott.
"How'd you accomplish this?"

"Simplicity itself." Sindri depressed a button and
pointed to another screen. On it they saw a trunk
made of metal, but overlaid with glass wedges. The
lid suddenly split smoothly in two until the halves
were in vertical positions. A small object, halfway
between a sphere and a child's top, rose straight up
from the exposed recess and hovered. Sindri rotated
a joysticklike control, and the globe rose up and flew
around the trunk.

Another screen lit up but showed only blank, featureless walls that seemed to be spinning like a cen-
trifuge. On the monitor beside it an image appeared
that looked strangely familiar. Kane's nape hairs tin-
gled when he realized it displayed a rear view of
themselves.

He pivoted swiftly. Gliding into the room, only
inches beneath the ceiling, came the sphere. A misty
white radiance emanated from it. Now that it was
closer, he saw a framework like tiny wire filaments
sectionizing it.

"A vid scanner," Brigid announced, sounding not the least impressed.

"It's that," Sindri conceded, "but it's more appropriately a targeting scanner. The Chronos techs never returned bodily to any past or future epoch, or at least there is no record of any of them doing so. They contrived these devices to do that. They could and did, travel the time stream."

"How do they work?" Grant asked, eyeing the sphere suspiciously.

"They select a subject to be trawled or monitored and 'tag' it with a microwave pulse. That acts as a tap conduit to the control computers here. From what I've been able to ascertain, there are outposts of these remote scanners at all predark scientific installations, particularly those that dealt with the Totality Concept experiments. I even patched into the one at Area 51."

Sindri touched a dial on the screen, and on it appeared Domi, scooping up the fallen implode gren. Then she disappeared in a white blaze of incandescence. "With barely three-quarters of a second to spare," he said pridefully, "I pulled her out of there. And what to do I get for my trouble? Physical and verbal abuse."

"Just why *did* you do it?" Grant asked, trying to keep his voice from quavering.

Sindri shrugged. "I'm entitled to my whims. Of

course, indulging my whim wouldn't have been worth the effort if not for you three.''

The scene wavered and coalesced into a high-angle view of the very room they occupied. Brigid, wearing a partial suit of samurai armor, sat at the console, looking at the screens. Kane and Grant, their bodies encased in Mag black polycarbonate flanked her. Her voice, sounding strained but enthralled, filtered out of a speaker. ''The quantum interphase matter confinement channels are on-line with the chronon wave guide. The wave function and state vectors are all in sync—the coordinates have already been programmed and locked in…it's only waiting the final sequence to initiate retrieval.''

''Retrieval?'' Kane heard himself echo incredulously. ''Retrieve her from where? Or rather when—that particular day, that very second?''

Brigid watched herself comb nervous fingers through her hair, noting how tangled it appeared. Her voice stated, ''No. In my estimation, she's already been retrieved, but not yet rematerialized. The trawling process hasn't been completed. She's in a state of nonexistence, reduced to her basic energy form, not too different from a gateway's quincunx effect.''

The quincunx effect referred to a nanosecond of time during gateway transit when lower dimensional space was phased into a higher dimension.

''This is all guesswork,'' Grant declared suspiciously. "You can't change the past by pushing a few buttons."

They all stared, fixated on the drama of the scene, as the image of Brigid swiveled sharply in the chair. "What's the nature of time anyway, Grant?" she challenged. "Can you describe it to me, when the most advanced physicists of the predark world barely understood it? Before the nukecaust, modern science was just beginning to perceive that subatomic particles and quantum events made no distinction between space and time.

"The laws of physics are fixed only by our perception. According to Lakesh, that was the major problem both Project Cerberus and Operation Chronos personnel constantly grappled with. Another was computing the precise temporal transfer points. Cerberus moved things from place to place. Chronos had to deal with moving things from place to place and time to time.

"In certain circumstances, photons—the particles of which light is made—could apparently jump between two points separated by a barrier in what appears to be zero time. The process, known as tunneling, was even used to make some of the most sensitive electron microscopes.

"If the very existence of time depends on the presence of space, then time is only a variable, not an absolute. Therefore you can have more than one event horizon, which means you can have more than one outcome from an event—"

"Are you always like that?" Sindri murmured to her.

Repressing a smile, Kane replied, "Most of the time."

He watched his image lift a hand to stem a further floodtide of scientific principle. "Nobody's arguing with you on this point. You're way smarter than we are, all right? We settled that a long time ago. But there are still a couple of areas we need to explore."

"Like what?" Brigid wanted to know.

Kane glanced around uneasily. "First of all, the microwave pulse. It's obvious whenever this temporal dilator thing is turned on it sends out the burst."

Brigid nodded. "We should be safe from it behind the shielding. You know enough of the properties of armaglass to know that it goes opaque when exposed to certain levels and wavelengths of radiation. That's one of the reasons it's used in the mat-trans gateways, to block energy overspills."

"Fine," Kane retorted brusquely. "One area dealt with. That leaves us with the second—who the hell set up all of this for us? How do we know this isn't bait to trick us into pushing a button and blowing us, and maybe this whole region of the Cific, to atoms?"

"Who would do that?" Grant demanded.

Kane shrugged. "I can think of a couple of past sparring partners who might have the know-how, but they're dead—I hope. But you can't deny this entire arrangement is just a little too convenient for us to accept at face value."

Sindri cast Kane a wry smile. "I presume I was one of the past sparring partners who crossed your mind that day. Who was the other?"

Kane didn't answer him. He watched as the image of Brigid on the screen declared tersely, "Whoever set this up offered us two choices—we do nothing and Domi is lost to us forever. Or we can engage the final sequence, and at least initiate a chance to have her returned. I personally think that's worth taking the risk of blowing ourselves up...but then that's me."

Sindri touched a knob and the scene froze on Brigid in a very unflattering pose, with her mouth open and her eyes half-closed. "We all know which choice you made," he declared.

Grant started to speak, then cleared his throat. "What happened—I mean, what would have happened if you hadn't made that choice?"

Sindri's eyes flashed with a combination of merriment and fascination. "Excellent question. My answer is, I don't know. Once I performed the action of trawling her, we had a definite cause and effect. Was I fated to rescue her in that three-tenths of a second, or was it truly a spur-of-the-moment decision that resulted in an alternate event horizon and therefore a paradox? Which came first, the girl's death or my decision to prevent it?''

"I didn't see any floating scanner that day," Kane pointed out. "Or any of those other days, either."

Sindri grinned. "I would have been surprised if you had. The devices pack what was known in the techno vernacular as 'cloaks'...for all intents and purposes invisibility screens, but in reality, they are more like low-observable camouflage screens. Within the scanners are a series of microcomputers that sense the color and shade of the background and exactly mirror the background image. It automatically blends in with its surroundings.'' He paused and added, "Still, they didn't always work."

"Why do you say that?" Brigid asked.

Sindri gestured expansively. "I don't say it—history says it. Think of all the reports from every culture since the dawn of time about lights in the sky, flying phenomena. Small radiant, spherelike objects were observed during pivotal points in many civilizations, from the ancient Egyptians to the so-called foo fighters reported by Allied pilots during World War II.''

Shizuka regarded him with inscrutable eyes, but the tone of her voice was doubtful. "You expect us to believe those remote scanners have been dispatched throughout history from here?"

As an answer, Sindri's nimble fingers clattered

over the buttons on the console, as if he were a
pianist warming up to play a sonata. All the monitor
screens flashed with a flowing panorama of images,
appearing and disappearing so quickly they were little more than glimpses of people, places and things.
Semblances of savages and protohumans, of pyra-
mids and castles, of Renaissance artists and steam-
engine operators flickered by in dizzying rapidity.

Kane watched as history unfolded on the screens,
but he wasn't moved to awe. The concept of such
power at Sindri's command rooted him to the spot
in terror.

Chapter 18

Sindri leaned against the railing of the catwalk, resting his chin on his forearms. He smiled down at the two-forked pylon as if it were his child. He nodded fondly to it. "And there it is—the absolute pinnacle of quantum mechanics. The temporal dilator."

He turned to face the people arrayed on the walkway around him. His brow furrowed as if he were troubled. "Which, of course, you caused to be damaged during your last visit." His tone was less accusatory than genuinely puzzled. "To this day I have no idea how you managed it."

"We didn't," Brigid replied stolidly. "It was a feedback pulse from a secondary energy source. The electromagnetic discharge of the two signatures meeting and merging caused the damage."

Sindri's brow furrowed. "Really? From where did the secondary energy pattern originate?"

Brigid opened her mouth to speak, then she caught Kane's eye. He shook his head and she stated, "It doesn't really matter."

Sindri's eyes slitted with suspicion. "I have a

feeling it definitely does matter, particularly if the interception was deliberate.''

No one responded to his conversational lead-in. Even though Lakesh had explained the event to her, Brigid wasn't certain of what happened on that day. According to Lakesh, Sam—the self-proclaimed imperator—could manipulate the energies of what he called the Heart of the World, an encapsulated packet of the quantum field.

Buried beneath the Xian pyramid in China, the Heart was described as containing the energies released in the first picoseconds following the Big Bang, channeling the matrix of protoparticles that swirled through the universe before physical, relativistic laws fully stabilized. It existed slightly out of phase with the third dimension, with the human concept of space-time. From this central core extended a web of electromagnetic and geophysical energy that covered the entire planet. Sam himself claimed he had transported from Thunder Isle to Xian by opening a localized wormhole in the energy web.

When Sindri realized a response to his query was not forthcoming, he shook his head in exasperation and returned his attention to the pylon. ''As distressed as I was initially, the damage was mainly superficial, even though some of the secondary systems had to be replaced. Most of the failures were software, not hardware.''

"That makes me feel a lot better," Grant muttered.

Sindri ignored the remark. "The actual structure itself remained completely intact."

Kane eyed it critically. "What's it made out of?"

"A blend of conductive alloys and ceramics, which make it virtually indestructible. Believe it or not, the dilator is essentially a giant electromagnet. It creates two magnetic fields, one at right angles to the other. Both of the fields represent one plane of space. But since there are three planes of space, a third field is produced through the principle of resonance."

Sounding slightly surprised, Brigid asked, "Sound?"

"Exactly."

Kane eyed the pylon again, realizing that even if Brigid seemed startled, she shouldn't have been. He thought back to the infrasound wands wielded by the hybrids at Dulce, to the instrument played by Aifa in Ireland, and a similar device Sindri claimed had been found on Mars, a relic of the Tuatha de Danaan. They all seemed related, devices operating on the same principle of manipulating sound. The infrasound wands converted electricity to ultrahigh sound frequencies by a miniature maser.

He recalled how Sindri had described the Danaan harp as producing energy forms with balanced gaps between the upper and lower energy frequencies. He explained if the radiation within particular frequencies fell on an energized atom—like living matter—it stimulated it in the same way a gong vibrated when its note was struck on a piano. Harmony and disharmony.

Sindri went on to describe scientific precedents cloaked by myth and legend such as the Ark of the Covenant bringing down the walls of Jericho when the Israelites gave a great shout. He claimed the walls were bombarded and weakened by amplified sound waves of the right frequency transmitted from the Ark. Sindri also cited Merlin, who was reputed to be of half-Danaan blood, and had "danced" the megaliths of Stonehenge into place by his music.

"From what you said earlier, I'm guessing you haven't been here but for a few months?" Shizuka said.

Sindri nodded. "That's right."

Two vertical lines of consternation appeared between her nose. "Then you couldn't have been responsible for the phenomenon that we of New Edo witnessed almost from the day of our arrival on the main island."

"How long ago was that?" Sindri asked.

"Over eight years now," she replied.

New Edo had been settled by the House of Mashashige, fleeing political unrest in Japan. The daimyo of the House of Mashashige, Lord Takaun, made one last attempt to not only reclaim his clan's power, but also to restore some semblance of order and dignity to his country. He failed, and had no choice but to flee, to go into exile. Taking with him as many family members, retainers, advisers and samurai as a small fleet of ships could hold, they set sail into the Cific. Their destination was the island chain once known as the Hawaiians.

But the heavens broke open with the unchained fury of the *tai-fun*, the typhoon. The storm drove the little fleet far off course. The ships had no choice but to make landfall on the first halfway habitable piece of dry ground they came across.

This turned out to be a richly forested isle, the tip of a larger landmass that had been submerged during the nukecaust. Evidently, it had slowly risen from the waters over the past two centuries and supported a wide variety of animal and vegetable life. Lord Takaun decreed it would support theirs, as well. The exiles from Nippon claimed it as their own, and named it New Edo, after the imperial city of feudal Japan.

Of course there were many problems to overcome during the first few years of colonization. Demons and monsters haunted the craggy coves and inland forests. They had a malevolent intelligence and would creep into the camp at night to urinate in the well water or defecate in the gardens. More than one samurai was slain during that time, their heads taken. The depredations were the acts of creatures who had made their way from Thunder Isle to New Edo.

When Brigid, Grant and Kane made landfall on the isle, they found evidence of radiation poisoning that extended out from the Chronos facility in a parabolic shape. Brigid theorized the affected area was regularly subjected to short bursts of high-power microwave radiation.

Sindri lifted his shoulders in a shrug. "The chronon wave guides seemed to activate random intervals, either reconstituting trawled subjects from the matrix or snatching new ones from all epochs in history. When I arrived, I installed a governor to keep that from happening."

"Except," Shizuka snapped, "when it suited you."

"Yes," the little man said agreeably. "Except when it suited me."

"What about Megaera and her Furies?" Brigid demanded. "Were they trapped in the matrix, or did you intentionally trawl them from somewhere?"

Sindri pursed his lips. "I honestly know no more about the where the Furies came from than you do. During my investigation of all Operation Chronos connected installations, I found a special encoded program that was linked, but separate from Chronos. It was code-named Parallax Points. The subhead was Alternative Three."

The dwarfish man looked expectantly into their faces. "Does that mean anything to you?"

"Should it?" Brigid asked.

"Perhaps not. Alternative Three was a conspiratorial premise that begins with a virtual epidemic of mysterious abductions of ordinary people. The theory postulated that they were lifted off to build secret bases on the Moon and even Mars. Does that strike a familiar chord?"

"As a point of fact," Kane answered, "it does. You claimed your ancestors were forcibly abducted to Mars to serve as slave labor. What does the Parallax Points program have to do with it?"

Sounding a little ashamed of himself, Sindri replied, "I haven't been able to overcome the encryption." Defensively, he added, "But only because I've been too busy repairing the damage to the dilator."

Shizuka stepped to the rail and gazed down at the pylon. "You mentioned earlier something about Archons and root races. What did you call them?"

"The Annunaki and the Tuatha de Danaan," he promptly responded.

"What did they have to do with this?"

"In a way," Sindri declared smoothly, "just about everything. I know very little about the Annunaki, but I'm familiar with the Danaan, since evidence of their culture still exists on Mars."

"The Danaan are long gone," Grant rumbled.

"Yes," Sindri agreed. "But much of their science remained, particularly that which was interpreted as magic. One thing that had been realized by the Danaan at the very dawn of their scientific maturity, was the indivisibility of space and time. The mystery of space had seemed easily solvable at first—there was matter and there was energy, but the problem of determining which was which became more and more complex.

"They eventually discovered that matter and energy could be interchangeable—one turned into the other and vice versa, according to the application. The deeper the Danaan probed into the minutiae of matter—the building blocks of material objects—the more they found energy and complexities of energy at the bottom of everything."

When the little man paused to take a breath, Kane interjected, "That's the entire template for Project Cerberus."

Sindri nodded, saying waspishly, "Of course it is. Please be a little more like Miss Brigid and don't state the obvious. Burr and the other Operation Chronos scientists proceeded from the same principle as the quantum interphase inducers, the gateways. Both Cerberus and Chronos were seeking a form of rapid transit along hyperdimensional paths. But temporal dilator caused an overlapping of the third and fourth dimensions—a mingling of spatial and temporal distance."

"There was a bit more to it than that," Brigid said dryly. "Balancing out the energy-exchange ratios, for one thing."

Sindri bobbed his head impatiently. "That was one hurdle, but leaping over preconceived notions was another. There were those who insisted that ultimately everything resolved into electromagnetic charges, and since electromagnetic charges were apparently without physical substance, it could be claimed that everything that existed was nothing, simply a matter of subjective perspective."

The little man began pacing nervously back and forth across the catwalk, first to one end and then the other. "Pursuing this train of thought, if the universe and all of its manifestations were nothing, then the universe was all in the imagination. Whether the imagination in question was supposed to be that of a being prior to and superior to the whole of existence, or was supposed to be that of each individual, was still under debate. The essential point here was that if all existence was in some way imaginary, then it need not necessarily adhere to any definite laws.

"Unfortunately for this view, the universe did seem to follow discoverable and even predictable patterns. It obeyed specific laws, and an action did indeed beget a reaction. Therefore, the problem remained unresolved."

Sindri drummed his fingers on the handrail as he paced, a staccato accompaniment to his speech.

"Then there was the factor of the passage of time. Nothing remained at a standstill. What did exist— all that was known to the Danaan and humanity— was in a state of motion, of vibrational change. Perhaps the answer to the riddle lay in electromagnetic energy in the process of change and movement. Possibly the meaning of time was a universal motion, a glue that maintained the universe in apparent existence.

"The Danaan had grappled with space, but time was not so easily mastered. How could a fly lift itself from flypaper? How can those who are fixed in the motion of time extricate themselves from a stream that surrounds them on all conceivable sides?"

Sindri stopped his pacing and speaking. After a long moment of silence, as if he were pondering a truly weighty problem, he announced somberly, "The answer, said the Danaan and their descendants, the so-called Archons, lay in the mystery of entropy. That was the method used in crossing time, and of the principles that were rediscovered here."

Grant massaged his temples. With his eyes closed, he intoned, "Sindri, if you don't get to the goddamn point, you'll be rediscovering a principle of my own creation. How a size-14 foot can fit into a size-2 rectum."

Sindri smiled without mirth. "Very humorous, Mr. Grant. Droll and vulgar at the same time. But I doubt Oakshott would allow you to put it into practice. The least you can do is not to interrupt. If you don't have the intelligence to follow my reasoning...very well then, that is not your fault. But will you please refrain from making impotent threats and allow me to continue? Thank you.''

Anger stirred in Grant's eyes, and he clenched his fists. Shizuka noticed and laid a hand on his arm, saying quickly, ''Let's not argue the point. Let's hear him out.''

Sindri looked at her blankly and said, ''Entropy describes a process by which the universe is slowly running down, so slowly that it can only be measured in terms of aeons. Every particle of matter is losing energy, and this energy in the form of heat and light gradually accumulates throughout the universe. The rate at which bodies lose their energy is the entropic gradient. It appears that this process is also part of the process that we call the passage of time, or our perception of its passage. The entropic gradient is steady, incessant and inexorable.''

Kane thought about asking for a clarification about the difference between a perception of time passage and the passage itself, but decided to let the little man continue. This was Sindri's show, and he liked nothing better than to strut in the spotlight. Such dedication to being the center of attention would eventually make him careless.

Sindri went on, ''The physical constituents of the

universe—oh, let us say in the year from which Oak-shott was trawled, 1899—were quite different than those constituents at any other time. That's a fundamental bit of physics, both quantum and relativistic.''

"In other words," Brigid commented, "you can't step into the same river twice."

Sindri clapped his hands together. "Exactly! The implications of that old bromide are clear enough—it means there's a difference in entropic measurements in regard to capacity for energy. And the differences between the universal constituents in 1899 and 2199 add up to a substantial amount. Now we reach the truly fun part—what entropy means to me."

"Whatever it means," Grant grunted, "it can't mean anything good—at least not anything good for the rest of us."

His lips stretched in a grin, displaying his perfect teeth, Sindri said, "You could be so wrong, Mr. Grant, that you would cease to be even pathetic. If the entropic gradient of any piece of matter can be reversed, either organic or inorganic, if it can be restored to the status of matter of say, three hundred years ago, we don't just have a temporal dilator."

He wheeled toward Brigid, stabbing a finger at her. "Quickly, Miss Brigid—what would we have?"

She frowned and unconsciously nibbled at her un-

derlip. Kane watched her face and was surprised by
the expression that suddenly crossed it. It wasn't
only comprehension; it was horror. Her lips moved,
and it took her two attempts before she was able to
husk out, "Immortality. You would have, for all intents and purposes, a machine to make anything—
or anyone—immortal."

Sindri nodded in smug triumph. "Precisely, Miss
Brigid. A god machine."

Chapter 19

Sindri's pronouncement brought all conversation to a complete halt. A number of things popped into Kane's mind to say, but he knew Sindri wouldn't appreciate any of them.

Shizuka broke the silence by demanding, "Why should we believe anything you say, particularly an insane boast like that? You're not only a madman—you're a liar."

Anger made a mask of the face of the dwarf. He turned as if to summon Oakshott. Ever so slightly, Kane shifted position, readying himself to kick the little man full in the face before he could verbalize an order.

With a visible effort, Sindri regained control of his temper. "Immortality is the one dream that always haunted man yet eluded him. He has hungered after immortality in the same way he hungered after great power." He waved toward the forked pylon. "That is the source of both."

"I won't dispute you on one score," Brigid said. "But how do you know entropic reversal works on organic matter? The physical body is a chemical machine. It wears out. Corrosion eats away at cell structures, at the nervous system, at the marrow of the bones. Going back in time a thousand years, and then returning to this time period won't insure you'll live for a millennium. There's no way you can prove your theory."

"Actually," Sindri said with a sly smile, "I have empirical evidence...but I need more. That's where you three enter the equation. I'd hoped you'd bring your little pet albino with you, since she has already been exposed to the chronon radiation, but I can make do with the material I have here."

Kane, Grant and Brigid gaped at him as Sindri pointed a finger at them, one by one. "You I'll send to the Triassic Age, you to the Bronze. And you—" he chuckled, a sinister rattlesnake laugh that stood the short hairs on everyone's neck at attention "—you, Miss Brigid, I owe a bloodletting and therefore a lesson in humility. Perhaps I'll send you to Caligula's Rome or inject you into the fall of Troy. If you survive, you'll have some interesting tales to bring back."

With a whir and a click, Kane's Sin Eater sprang into his hand. Coldly, he stated, "Perhaps I'll send you to hell, Sindri. And you *won't* have any interesting tales to bring back."

Grant flexed his wrist tendons and his own autoblaster slapped into his waiting palm. Sindri regarded both weapons with inscrutable eyes. Sardonically, he murmured, "I suppose now would be the best time to play my ace."

"You'd better do something," Grant said grimly. "I know I've run out of reasons to keep you alive."

Oakshott lumbered forward, aiming his wooden pistol at Grant. "Bang, bang. Behave yourself, sirrah. Bang, bang."

Grant grimaced in annoyance, lifted the Sin Eater and squeezed off a single shot. The cracking report was painfully loud. The round centerpunched Oakshott in his exceptionally broad chest and slammed him backward. He dropped his toy gun, and his huge arms windmilled in a clumsy attempt to keep his balance. He fell heavily onto his back. His huge hands balled over his sternum, scarlet squirting between the fingers.

Training the pistol on Sindri, Grant growled, "What was that about an ace?"

Seemingly not the slightest bit perturbed by the shooting of Oakshott, or the gun inches from his forehead, Sindri held up two gloved fingers. "Two aces actually. The first is the tried and true tactic of holding a hostage."

"And who might that be?" Kane asked.

"Everyone in New Edo."

Shizuka's shoulders jerked in reaction.

"Explain," Brigid snapped.

"Gladly. During the late 1990s, there was an epidemic of disappearing nuclear warheads from arsenals all over the world, in particular the small, 'squeeze yields' ones.''

Brigid frowned, sifting through her memory. ''Yes, I remember reading about it. They called them backpack nukes. Evidently they were stolen and sold to small nations without nuclear weapons capabilities or to terrorist groups.''

''That was one theory,'' Sindri agreed. ''And I'm sure that happened to a few of them. But not all.'' He widened his eyes in mock fear. ''I wonder, oh, I wonder what happened to the others.''

''Bullshit,'' Grant spit contemptuously. ''You're bluffing.''

Sindri crooked challenging eyebrows at him. ''Oh, really? If I can snatch a human being literally from the jaws of death, don't you think it would be easier to snatch up stationary objects from the past? Like missiles in silos?''

He paused to let his words sink in, then continued. ''I confess I managed to make only one functional, but it's more than sufficient to obliterate this island and New Edo. The warhead is fairly small, around 200 kilotons, but it's exceptionally dirty—a mixture of cobalt and iodine. If I detonate it, the yield effect is roughly three miles. Within one mile of the hypocenter of the explosion, this entire island would be vaporized instantly. Within two and a half miles, ninety percent of the population of New Edo would be killed, and all the buildings leveled.''

Shizuka's face paled, but she only compressed her lips.

"How do you control it?" Kane asked casually.

"That will be my secret."

"And the other ace you mentioned?"

Sindri gestured toward the fallen Oakshott. "The empirical evidence of reverse entropic immortality." He raised his voice. "Oakshott! You may get up now."

Grant made a noise of disgust deep in his throat. "He's not going to get up, you little—"

A deep, gargling groan rose from the black-clad body. Kane felt his skin prickle and clammy sweat form on his face. The body of Oakshott stirred, his hands came up, the bloody fingers twitching fitfully. Grasping the railing, he pulled himself to a sitting position. Grant, Kane, Brigid and Shizuka stared in incredulous horror as the giant reeled upright. His small eyes were glassy. Blood glistened wetly on his shirtfront, and his face was screwed up in pain.

"Hurts," he said hoarsely. A coughing fit overcame him, and he bent at the waist, his body shaking violently. A jet of scarlet spewed from his lips, and a little metal cylinder clattered on the grillwork. Kane, his heart turning to ice, realized it was the flattened bullet Grant had fired into the giant's chest.

Gasping for air, Oakshott straightened. He dragged a sleeve across his blood-flecked lips. Sindri said reassuringly, "You'll be as right as the mail soon enough, Oakshott. That's a stout fellow."

Smirking into the astonished faces of the four people standing around him, Sindri declared, "I can only speculate on the extent of entropic reversal on organic matter, but as you have witnessed, Oakshott's cellular structure renews itself from moment to moment. It rejects all foreign bodies from bacteria to bullets."

His hand trembling perceptibly, Grant raised his Sin Eater and aimed it Oakshott's head, who merely blinked at him. "And what happens if I blow his brains out? Will that be reversed?"

"I really couldn't say," Sindri answered. "I was saving that experiment for one of you three. However, if you do that to Mr. Oakshott, I'll have no choice but to retaliate with a nuclear detonation. A bit of overkill, I can't deny, but you would leave me no option."

Very slowly, Grant lowered his arm. In a quiet, even tone Sindri said, "Very good, Mr. Grant. Now you and Mr. Kane will disarm."

Kane didn't move. "Why should we?" he demanded. "We refused to do it earlier."

"Then you didn't have an inkling of the kind of power I control. Even if you're ninety percent certain I'm running a bluff about the warhead, surely you don't want to gamble the lives on New Edo."

"I'm sure this has occurred to you at some

point,'' Brigid pointed out sardonically, "but you'd die along with them."

"I'm not afraid to die, Miss Brigid," he retorted sharply. "Not in the least. That's one thing about me you should be certain of." He gazed up at her unblinkingly. "Don't force me to prove it."

Sindri's voice had acquired a raspy undertone of conviction. Kane understood that somewhere inside of the man's diminutive frame was a soul that had lived with pain since the day he was born—and whose focus in life was to find a way to end it.

"So much for your promise you meant us no harm," Brigid said darkly.

"I mean to keep my promise. I'm offering you immortality. How is that harming you? I may hurt you, but I won't permanently harm you. Not if you cooperate."

Grant cast a questioning glance toward Shizuka. "It's your home at stake here, so it's your call. Yes or no?"

Shizuka hesitated and nodded in resignation. "*Hai*. Yes. We cannot take the chance."

Kane and Grant pushed their pistols back into their holsters and stripped them off. They pushed them into Sindri's arms. He inclined his head in a parody of a gracious nod. "Thank you, gentlemen. I always knew you could be reasonable...at least when you're forced to be."

He turned, marching back toward the control room. "Come with me now."

The four people slowly followed him along the catwalk. As they did so, Kane bent his head close to Brigid and whispered, "I'm betting you remember how to activate the dilator."

Her lips barely moved as she breathed, "You'd win."

Kane said no more. He lengthened his stride to step in front of her. When they entered the control room, he positioned himself in such a way that Brigid was blocked from Sindri's view. As it was, the little man was pushing the still-dazed Oakshott ahead of him. Imperiously, he ordered, "Step lively, now."

As the giant obeyed, Brigid slid to one side, standing at the edge of the console. She ran her eyes over the buttons and toggle switches. Her fingers flew over them like a concert pianist's. The throbbing vibration of the generator suddenly climbed in scale and pitch, becoming almost painful. Sparks flashed through the facets of the prisms on the arms of the pylons.

Sindri spun, arms full of pistols and holsters. His face twisted in shock. "What are you doing? The chronon wave guide doesn't have a target—"

Grant lunged forward in a diving tackle. He ducked under an arm Oakshott flung out and closed his hands around Sindri's throat, slamming him off his feet. As he grappled with the little man, the momentum of his leap carried him into Oakshott's legs and sent him staggering backward. With Grant on top of him, Sindri squalled in pain and anger.

Grant snatched up the little man, left hand cupping his chin, while his right forearm came across the windpipe and hauled back. Sindri uttered a small, aspirated gurgle. "Tell your lobotomized valet to back off, or you're dead in about two seconds," Grant snarled.

Sindri clawed impotently at Grant's arm, then waved at Oakshott. The giant, in the process of lumbering forward, froze in midstep. Shizuka glided forward and picked up the Sin Eaters. Carefully, Grant got to his feet, holding Sindri in front of him. Kane was irresistibly reminded of a ventriloquist and dummy he had seen in an old predark vid.

"Tell him to back all the way off," Grant said.

Sindri squirmed. "You idiot, you don't understand. You've got to cut the dilator's power—"

Grant cinched his grip tighter, increasing the pressure on the dwarf's neck. Sindri yelped in pain. "Tell him," Grant repeated.

Current crackled loudly between the forks of the pylon. From the curving arms hissed bolts of lightning, which whipped and snapped along the network of wires like serpents made of blue plasma.

Exhaling a pain-choked breath, Sindri shouted,

"Oakshott! Go to the corner and stay there until I say otherwise."

The giant hesitated. "Do as I say, damn you!" Sindri shrilled.

Ponderously, Oakshott followed Sindri's command, stepping to the far wall and jamming himself into the corner. Grant edged toward the door. His companions followed him, keeping their eyes on Oakshott.

They entered a corridor, dimly lit by neon strips on the ceiling. They had traversed it before and Brigid took the lead, since she remembered all of its twists and turns. Sindri tried to speak several times, but Grant clapped a hand over his mouth. After a few minutes they pushed their way through a glass-and-chrome door and entered a large lobby. The floor was thickly layered with concrete dust. The walls were black-speckled marble and showed ugly crisscrossing cracks. A litter of office furniture was half covered by broken ceiling tiles.

A big reception desk occupied the far wall, and it was nearly buried by plaster and metal electrical conduits. On the right side of the room, a hallway stretched away, lined on both sides with wooden doors. Past the desk lay the entrance door. Beyond it they saw only a murky semidarkness, as of late afternoon on an extremely overcast day.

"What's the plan?" Kane asked.

"How the hell do I know?" Grant retorted stiffly.

"I'm open to suggestions. I'm sure as hell tired of carrying this slag-ass midget around."

Tersely, Shizuka said, "There may still be landing boats at the beach, ones we used to get here from New Edo."

"One problem," Brigid said. "Once the temporal dilator builds up a charge, it releases a microwave pulse. If we're not out of the effect radius, we'll be cooked."

Sindri began squealing wordlessly behind Grant's muffling hand, kicking his legs violently. His eyes shone with wild, frantic light. "Let him talk," Kane suggested.

Grant removed his hand and after dragging in a noisy breath, Sindri said, "It's worse than the microwave pulse! I've got to cut the power. Let me do it and you can go on your way."

Kane stared into Sindri's face, looking for any signs of duplicity. He gave it up after a moment as a pointless exercise. "What's worse than the pulse?"

Sindri struggled in Grant's arms. "Put me down and I'll tell you."

Kane nodded. "You'd better do it."

Scowling, Grant released the little man, allowing him to drop none too gently to the floor. He stumbled and would have fallen if Kane hadn't steadied him. "Explain," he snapped. "And make it fast."

Words tumbled out Sindri's mouth. "Critical mass—critical mass!"

"What?" Grant grunted.

Sindri squeezed his eyes shut, his body trembling. "There's a critical mass for certain elements—plutonium, for instance—beyond which no increase in energy is possible without a release. It's the same with some subatomic particles."

Green eyes bright with worry, Brigid demanded, "Like chronons?"

Sindri bobbed his head. "And photons. Once critical mass is reached, it can only resolve itself by a venting of energy. There has to be an escape."

"You mean an explosion?" Shizuka asked.

"Yes!" Sindri blurted desperately. "Possibly even a dimensional cross-rip. I wasn't lying about possessing an atomic warhead—the dilator is running wild without a target conformal. If its energy builds to critical mass, it'll touch off the bomb. A hole half a mile deep could be blasted through the bottom of the Pacific Ocean."

"And you can keep that from happening?" Grant asked.

"Yes, if you let me go right *now!*"

Kane and Grant looked toward Brigid in unison. She met their questioning gaze with one of angry frustration. "Don't look at me! I don't know enough about Operation Chronos to confirm or deny anything he's saying."

Kane hissed out an obscenity. To Grant he said, "We can't afford to take the chance."

Grant's lips peeled back over his teeth in a snarl. "I know—damn him to hell."

Kane stepped aside and waved toward the door. "Go. We'll settle up with you later. Count on it."

Without another word or a backward glance, Sindri immediately broke into a sprint, running as fast as he could, slamming open the door with a squeal of rusty hinges.

Watching him go, Shizuka asked apprehensively, "What should we do now?"

Kane handed Grant his Sin Eater and began strapping his own onto his forearm. "What we always do when we're in a situation like this."

Shizuka cocked her head at him quizzically. "What's that?"

Balancing herself on the balls of her feet, Brigid spoke a single word: "Run."

Chapter 20

In their rush to get away from the Operation Chronos installation, the four of them simply ran—away, anywhere, beyond the effect radius of the microwave pulse.

Grant slammed open the door and they plunged down a short, wide set of stairs and out into the complex of structures. Dusk shrouded them, yet the semidarkness was a blessing. They were, after all, in enemy territory, in Sindri's playground where the possibility of any threat couldn't be discounted.

Kane glanced back at the building they had just left. It was the largest structure and showed little signs of wear. It was an almost perfectly square block, appearing to be hewn from a single monstrously huge chunk of stone. He had named it the Cube on their prior visit. Its dark facade had no windows, and when he looked at it, he again sensed a subliminal aura of evil radiating from the structure.

All the looming buildings of the Operations Chronos base were made of blocks of a dark, stained stone that reflected no trace of light. Some of the smaller buildings had eroded so much they had fallen completely into ruin. Roofless arches reared from the ground, and a few storage buildings were scattered around the outer perimeter of the walls.

They clambered over walls, concentrating more on what lay behind them than ahead. Kane, Shizuka, Brigid and Grant ran across a broad courtyard filled with great chunks of concrete and blocks of basalt that had fallen from buildings. As the fleetest of foot, Kane had to hold himself back, so as to not outdistance his companions, and he chafed at the delay.

They reached a broad blacktop avenue that ran outward from the Cube. The asphalt had a peculiar ripple pattern to it, and weeds sprouted from splits in the surface. Kane, Brigid and Grant had seen the rippling effect before, out in the hellzones. It was a characteristic result of earthquakes triggered by nuclear bomb shock waves.

Lampposts lined the road, most of them rusted through and leaning over. Secondary lanes stretched out in all directions, like the spokes of a wheel. Legs pumping, lungs laboring, the four people sprinted through the empty streets, bordered by the empty husks of buildings. One of the structures had collapsed entirely, folded in on itself like a house of dominos, with the fallen rear wall knocking down all the interior sections one by one.

Once beyond the complex area, a bitter, acrid odor stung their nostrils and coated their tongues.

Their pounding feet churned up ash and grit. They had entered the dead zone, a flat, sandy plain at least half a mile across wherein the microwave pulses had rendered the soil sterile. What little grass grew was thin and brown, little more than stubble.

Even in the fading light they could see the circle of demarcation. On the far sides of the circle grew thick, lush grasses and ferns. Sprinkled across the barren and sere landscape were the browned skeletons of birds, their featherless wings outstretched as if they had dropped dead in midflight. Here and there were smaller collections of bones, like those of rats and other animals.

Light gleamed dully through the layer of ash, and when they drew closer, Shizuka couldn't swallow a sob of grief and a groan of horror. She slowed her pace, rocking to a stop, her small breasts heaving beneath her cotton shift. Grant grabbed her by the arm. "Come on," he wheezed.

She refused to move, and her three companions followed her gaze downward. All of them recoiled in revulsion. Two nearly fleshless faces grinned up at them from the soot-covered ground. Radiation and exposure had turned the faces into mummified travesties. They wore full suits of samurai armor and had apparently been caught in a microwave burst. It had literally cooked them inside their armor, like lobsters in their shells.

"They came looking for me," Shizuka murmured

in a congested voice. "I ordered them to stay with the boat, but they—"

She swallowed hard, bent and pulled a pair of bladed weapons from one of the corpses, a long *katana* sword and a shorter-bladed *tanto*. Kane relieved the other corpse of his pair of weapons, handed the *katana* to Brigid and they started running again.

When grass swished against their ankles, the four people realized they were out of the dead, defoliated zone. Shizuka panted, "When can we—"

The rest of her question was lost in a distant thunderclap. They skidded to a halt, twisting their heads as a deafening, concussive blast cannonaded up from the complex of buildings behind them. A consecutive series of brutal, overlapping shock waves rolled over the ground like invisible breakers, hurling up dust and ash and knocking the four of them flat.

The ground heaved violently, and they heard a clash of rending rock and a distant shriek of rupturing metal. They saw the Operation Chronos complex seeming to shake itself to pieces. Cornices and basalt blocks toppled, crashing and colliding. All of them shared the same terror—that a chain reaction caused by the dilator's energies would touch off the atomic warhead and a mile-high mushroom cloud would swallow not just Thunder Isle and New Edo, but most of the Cific coast.

A reverberating, extended thunderclap rolled as
they saw the walls of buildings folding in on themselves and cascading down in a contained avalanche.
In the dim light, veiled by swirling clouds of dust,
the entire complex seemed to implode. Finally, the
cataclysmic sounds began to fade, replaced by the
crunch and grate of settling stone. Planes of dust and
ash rose toward the sky.

Kane squinted through the vapors and saw the
dark edifice of the Cube still towering in the distance
but its facade was riven through with cracks from
which shimmers of light glowed. He spit some of
the sour ash from his mouth and asked, "What the
hell happened?"

"I don't know," Brigid said. "Maybe the dilator
reached a point of critical mass and Sindri was able
to contain it before it touched off the warhead. I
don't know whether to be relieved or worried."

Grant pushed himself to his feet, pulling Shizuka
with him. "For right now, let's be relieved. It's still
at least a forty-minute walk to the beach. Sindri will
do whatever he can to stop us from reaching it."

Shizuka threw him a startled look and gestured to
the complex with a *katana*. "Surely you don't think
he survived all of that!"

Flatly, Kane declared, "He had as much time to
escape as we did. Don't assume anything about that
little man—particularly that he's dead."

Shizuka gazed at him steadily, then flicked her

gaze to Brigid. "You respect him, don't you?" Her voice carried a note of incredulous challenge.

Neither Kane nor Brigid responded to the query, but Grant intoned, "I don't."

They walked toward the jungle as the sun dropped lower in the sky. Twilight deepened over the island. This close to the dead zone, the fronds of the palm trees and leaves of shrubbery were stained and spotted with livid streaks of yellow. The sweet, fetid stench of decay was so thick it was almost sickening. Breathing through their mouths didn't help much, since the air tasted like a compost heap. Only Grant didn't appear discomfited by the odor.

They strode among the close-set palm trunks, draped with loops and curves of flowering lianas hung down like nooses. Kane's point man's sense felt danger, and the feeling increased so it was almost tangible. On every hand, wherever they looked, there were growing plants, most of them ferns. The size ranged from tiny seedlings to monstrous growths the size of oak trees. Tangles of creeper vines carpeted the jungle floor. The atmosphere was like that within a greenhouse—impregnated with the overwhelming odor of vegetation and nearly impenetrable with water vapor.

Grant's, Kane's and Brigid's bodysuits kept them cool, as the internal thermostats adjusted to the heat and humidity. Shizuka suffered in silence, her face and limbs sheened with perspiration, her hair hanging limp and damp.

They stopped for a moment to rest and get their bearings. They couldn't hear the crash of breakers on the shoreline, but the gurgling of running water, either a river or a stream came to them faintly. Another sound reached their ears, a grunting, snuffling noise. The four people froze in place, rooted to the spot.

The foliage shook, the leaves rattling. Behind a tangled screen of greenery they glimpsed a shaggy, lumbering beast. "What the hell—" Grant began, but Shizuka shushed him into silence.

The creature suddenly reared up, standing at least ten feet tall. The black, curving claws of the forepaws were at least three inches long, as were the yellow, saliva-slick canines revealed by black-rimmed lips. Its shaggy coat was a dark brown in color, tipped in silver.

"It's a bear," Shizuka breathed in disbelief. "A bear on an island in the Pacific?"

"It's a cave bear," Brigid whispered. "Extinct for at least fifty thousand years. It must have been trawled here and released—"

The bear sniffed the air, blinked its tiny eyes at them in utter disinterest and dropped back down behind the wall of shrubs. The four people waited, not daring to relax, to move, speak or even breathe hard.

After a minute, Kane said lowly, "I think it moved on."

With an explosion of leaves and twigs, the bear burst through the wall of foliage, giving voice to a prolonged, eardrum-compressing roar. Grant and Kane instantly snapped their right arms up, flexing their wrist tendons against the holsters' actuators to pop the Sin Eaters into their waiting hands. Nothing happened.

With a jolt of fear, Kane realized the microwave pulse might not have damaged him organically, but it had fried the tiny electric motor that activated the spring and cable mechanisms in the holsters. He came to an immediate and, on the face of it, insane decision. Hefting the *tanto* sword, he lunged in front of his companions, shouting, "Hah!"

The cave bear changed course, its claws tearing up clots of soft ground. Kane held steady. "What are you doing?" Brigid cried.

"Run!" Kane yelled. He sprang to one side just before the animal was on him and slashed a backhanded stroke at its hind legs that missed narrowly.

Roaring in maddened fury, the bear dug in all four paws and skidded to a clumsy halt, loose leaves and loam cresting up in front of like a wave. Kane bounded away from his companions, shouting again, "Run! I'm the fastest! I'll draw it away and meet you on the beach!"

"Kane, you goddamn—" Grant bellowed.

The rest of the diatribe didn't reach Kane's ears as he sprinted into the jungle. Snarling slobberingly, the bear pounded after him. He began a flat-out run through the tangled green hell, ducking and dodging along paths that zigged and zagged like the trail left by a broken-backed snake. He could hear the animal's crashing progress through the undergrowth and its panting grunts of exertion.

He hazarded only one quick backward glance. The bear was only three or so yards behind him, loping along with a clumsy rocking gait, but not faltering at all. Foam flew from its open mouth, its red tongue lolling out between the fanged jaws.

Kane did what he could to increase his speed, slashing through overhanging branches and vines. The skin between his shoulder blades itched in anticipation of a taloned paw tearing into his spine. He splashed through many shallow pools of stagnant water and jumped over a narrow channel that cut across his path. As he did so, he glimpsed the black water beneath him roil and bubble ominously, as if something large moved off the bottom toward the surface. However, the cave bear plowed through it without being molested.

The pain of a stitch stabbed along Kane's left side, the muscles of his legs felt as if they were pressed between the jaws of a tightening vise and his vision fogged. Nevertheless he kept running, even though the blood thundered in his ears and his lungs noisily labored to suck in oxygen. He began to hope he had outdistanced his pursuer. With its greater weight, it couldn't really have the same stamina as him. As he contemplated slowing, the ground disappeared beneath his feet. He caught only a glimpse of the surface of a wide ribbon of water.

The drop to the river was ten to twelve feet. He tried to align his body into a vertical position so he would enter the river in a dive. Instead, he half belly flopped against the surface, and it was all he could do to keep the air in his lungs. Water gushed up his nose and filled his sinus passages, trickling into his throat.

Resisting the impulse to stroke for the surface, Kane allowed the weight of his Sin Eater and short sword to keep him submerged and out of sight of the bear. The current tugged at him and he kicked and pushed with it, since it was carrying him in the direction he wanted to go, toward the ocean. During his Magistrate training, he used to practice holding his breath under water, and rarely had he managed to exceed four minutes, even when he hyperventilated after the fashion of Polynesian pearl divers. Though he wasn't exerting himself and expending oxygen, his lungs were already aching with the strain.

He opened his eyes and saw a school of small fish all around him, the silvery moonlight glinting from their delicate scales. He hoped they weren't carnivorous. The water buffeted him, making him lose all sense of direction and time.

Kane stayed beneath the surface until the thundering of blood in his temples and the fire in his chest became intolerable. He kicked upward, a little surprised by how much effort it required. His head broke the surface and he fought the impulse to cough and gasp.

The current carried him around a bend, where the waterway narrowed. Tree limbs, like gnarled fingers, reached down toward the river from both banks. Blinking the water from his eyes, Kane tilted his head up and back, scanning the pale indigo sky. He saw nothing but the rising moon and a scattering of stars above the tree line.

Kane knew better than to put the double-edged *tanto* blade between his teeth. The current was so strong it could slam him against an obstacle and cut half of his head off. With one arm, he stroked for the right-hand bank, reaching up to grasp a low-hanging limb. Using the branch and roots as hand- and footholds, Kane clambered his way up the muddy bank until he reached the top.

He sat down to catch his breath. After a couple of minutes, he got up and walked inland, *tanto* in hand, moving quietly through the brush. The Sin Eater in its holster was a waterlogged encumbrance, and he contemplated removing the pistol from it but he knew it would take time. The sound of a something—or someone—moving swiftly, if not noise-lessly, through the foliage reached him and he im-mediately sank to his knees beneath a leafy bush. He tried to penetrate the dark, overgrown tangle with his eyes, searching for any movement. Leaves crunched somewhere on the other side of the bush. Holding his breath, he waited for another sound. It came in the next few seconds, a hoarse, liquidy pant-ing interspersed with grunts.

Although he couldn't see it, Kane knew it was the cave bear, stalking along the riverbank, loath to give up its prey.

He saw the shaggy beast lumber to within ten feet of him, turning its huge head to and fro like a fox-hound casting for a scent. It padded forward another few steps. Kane lay flat and could only hope his recent dousing had muted his scent.

The cave bear moved on, the shadows between the tree ferns swallowing up its monstrous bulk. Kane waited three minutes to be sure then slowly rose in a crouch. He was turning when the foliage behind him rustled violently. The bear surged over the ground in a juggernaut-like charge. Its lips were drawn back from its fangs in a contortion of rage, its eyes glistening. Kane threw himself backward, but the animal lashed with a paw the size of his head. Even as a thick-soled paw slammed into his left shoulder, his blade lashed out and he felt it sink briefly into yielding flesh.

The impact of the blow jarred through the bones of his upper body, down to the small of his back. He didn't try to resist the kinetic force or keep his footing. He allowed himself to fall into the brush, reflexively slapping the ground to absorb the momentum and minimize the chances of having the wind knocked out of him. Shoulder throbbing, he rolled and got to his knees, knife still in his fist. The tapered tip gleamed with wet crimson.

The cave bear thrashed on the ground, blood shooting from his severed neck arteries in a jet. It was in too much pain to even think of charging Kane again. It forced itself up on all fours and ran blindly until it rammed its head into the bole of a tree. It collapsed there, snarling until it choked on its blood and died.

Slowly, Kane rose, his back throbbing with intense pain. His slash with the *tanto* had been exceptionally lucky and wouldn't have been so effective if the blade were not so sharp. He inhaled a deep breath, wondering if he should feel pride in his accomplishment or pity for the bear, which had not asked to be snatched from its native environment and forced to survive in a strange new world.

After a moment, Kane decided a little pride wouldn't hurt. Then he heard an ululating, croaking bellow from right behind him.

Chapter 21

A trumpetlike cry pierced the murk, followed by a deep-throated bawling. All of it was overlaid by the crack of branches and the hollow snaps of green timber. The dull reverberations of a heavy weight slamming repeatedly against the marshy earth made a racket that sent a shiver up Kane's spine, despite the heat and humidity. He dived into a hollow between intertwining ferns and lay there, fisting the *tanto* and cursing himself for not using it to cut the Sin Eater free of its holster.

Vegetation swished and crashed from somewhere behind him, and the ground shook incessantly. A dark shape loomed out of the gloom, propelled by a pair of massively muscled rear legs. The clawed forelegs were small in proportion to the rest of its body, but the curving, steel-hard talons tipping each of the three fingers were at least six inches long. They were drawn up to its chest almost in an attitude of praying. Grinning jaws bared rows of glistening yellow fangs. The saurian snout bore a pair of flared nostrils that seemed to dilate and twitch. The head, twice the size of that of a horse, turned this way and that upon an extended scaled neck.

Huge cold eyes like those of a serpent's a hundred times magnified stared unwinkingly from beneath a pair of scaled knobby protuberances. Two huge legs, almost as big around as some of the palm trees he'd seen, supported the massive, barrel-shaped body. They were enormously overdeveloped. A long tail trailed from behind, disappearing into the undergrowth. It apparently used its thick tail to balance itself. Its damp hide bore a pebblelike pattern of dark brown scales.

The revolting odor of rotted meat and the sour stench of reptiles clogged Kane's nostrils. So great was the monster's weight that its huge, three-toed feet sank deep into the damp ground with each hopping step.

Despite its size, the most frightening aspect of the creature was its fangs. They gleamed in the blunt, scale-armored maw that gaped wide to allow a long black tongue to dart to and fro. Kane guessed that like a snake, its tongue was extremely sensitive, and it tasted the coppery tang of the bear's blood. Kane didn't know if the thing was a medium-sized Tyrannosaur or an overly large Dryosaurus, and at the moment he didn't give a damn. He assumed it was the same monster that had bitten off the head of the hapless Magistrate. The dinosaur bounded past him, then stopped abruptly, standing spraddle-legged over the dead cave bear. Its tongue continued to flicker in and out of its mouth as if it were tasting the air.

Then, it opened its jaws and voiced a roar that combined the worst aspects of a siren, steam valve and the howl of a dying dog. The massive creature spun toward Kane's hiding place. Its tail lashed back and forth, shredding shrubbery and ferns. As it lowered its head, the flaring nostrils dilated. His blood running like ice water, Kane realized the creature had scented him, and it either perceived him as a threat to its meal of dead bear, or it preferred human meat to ursine. The monster rushed him.

Kane sprang to his feet and ran as he had never run before, starting to dash to the left, then wheeling over to the right, lunging into a bed of ferns. The dinosaur clumsily turned and wallowed confusedly in the copse of vegetation for a moment. Kane guessed it was unaccustomed to having quarry evade it by the process of strategy. The monster appeared to be slow in getting itself organized.

Lungs straining with the effort of breathing in the thick, humid air, Kane warred with the fear that threatened to engulf him. Complete panic gnawed at his nerves. He had an almost overwhelming desire to surrender sanity and plunge shrieking madly through the jungle.

The ground trembled underfoot as the Tyrannosaur changed course and pounded after him.

Through the mist, Kane glimpsed a branch of a tree fern arching over the path he had taken. His steel-spring legs propelled him upward in an adrenaline-fueled leap. The fingers of his left hand grasped, closed around it and with a back-wrenching twist got himself atop it.

He had only a second to wonder if the monster had seen the maneuver when it came blundering through the murky mist like an out-of-control locomotive. He realized the dinosaur wasn't as large as he had initially thought, maybe twenty-five feet long and between twelve and fifteen feet tall.

Still, it weighed in the vicinity of three tons, if not more, and it crashed into the trunk of the tree fern with a splintering impact. Kane slapped his hand around the branch, but because of the damp, smooth surface, he failed to cling and he fell from his perch. The Tyrannosaur was directly beneath him, and he landed astride the monster's neck.

More frightened than at any time in his life, feeling as if he were trapped in a hideous, ongoing nightmare, Kane clamped his legs about the creature's throat, wrapping his arms under its lower jaw and locking his ankles together.

The Tyrannosaur was bewildered, astounded and even a little outraged. It shook its head furiously from side to side in an attempt to dislodge its rider, but Kane clung tightly to keep from being hurled off. He knew if that happened, his life could be measured in seconds. A sweep of a clawed foot would disembowel him or a snap of the jaws would decapitate him.

The gigantic reptile attempted to rub him off by bending almost double and scraping its head against the turf, then against the trunks of the tree ferns. Even though the jungle growths had fairly smooth bark, his skin felt abraded despite the fabric of the bodysuit. Kane gritted his teeth against the pain and kept his legs locked at the hinges of the monster's jaws.

The creature spun in a tight circle, twisting its head around to snap at him, performing a little spinning dervish dance like a dog chasing its tail. Its clawed feet tore up huge chunks of jungle floor.

Then, in a wild panic, the scaled monster went charging through the jungle, hissing, bawling and roaring. As the monster's fear grew, Kane's receded just enough so he could think tactically, if not necessarily rationally. He realized that though the gargantuan reptile's body was sheathed in powerful muscle, armored in a coat of thick scales, the flesh under its jaw was comparatively tender. It wasn't covered by the scales.

Taking a deep breath, Kane clamped his thighs tighter around the monster's gullet and removed his right hand from where it had gripped his left wrist. He drove the eighteen-inch steel blade of the *tanto* to half its length into the dinosaur's throat, as close to the jaw hinge as he could manage.

The Tyrannosaur screamed and exploded in a wheeling, writhing fury, tail thrashing like a whip through the undergrowth. Kane tightened his legs around the monster's neck while he stabbed again and again with his long blade.

Hot, thick blood spilled over his hand and wrist, soaking his sleeve halfway to the elbow. The Tyrannosaur crashed through the jungle, battering its head blindly against trees. Kane was shaken and struck and leaf whipped, but he continued thrusting with the razor-keen sword.

He caught a glimpse of a long branch drooping in the Tyrannosaur's path as the dinosaur bounded beneath it. The blunt head cleared it by less than a foot. Kane released his *tanto* and relaxed his scissors-lock around the reptile's neck. In the same instant he threw his arms up and caught hold of the limb.

The limb sagged beneath his weight, but the dinosaur continued its thundering charge, its sluggish brain not immediately registering the fact that the presence of the prey turned tormentor was gone. By the time it did, Kane had dropped to the jungle floor, retrieved his knife and glided into the undergrowth.

He knelt down, breathing heavily, his heart pumping hard. He tried to repress his trembling. He bit his lips and clutched the handle of the *tanto*. After a few minutes, when the crash and thud of the Tyrannosaur's mad flight had receded in the distance, he slowly got to his feet. His limbs still shook with a tremor, but he wasn't ashamed. He couldn't think of any reason to be, not after the past half hour.

IF BRIGID, GRANT and Shizuka had spent a more uncomfortable hour in their lives, they couldn't easily recall it. Blood-curdling screams echoed from one end of the island to the other.

They could hear vast bodies slogging and crashing through the dense vegetation, some moving with great hops, others lumbering on all fours. Finding a place in the jungle to hole up and rest was completely out of the question. The three people waited in expectation of sudden death at any moment.

A heavy rain began to fall, a tropical downpour that lasted only a few minutes. But it was sufficient to raise the humidity level and create clouds of fog. Water dripped from the low branches. Damp-feathered birds sat hunched in the trees making sad clucking sounds. They sounded as though they all suffered head colds.

At one point, they came across a four-legged lizard sitting in the middle of their path, eating at the carcass of some small dead creature. It hissed at them, and they gave it a wide berth. None of the three spoke much. Brigid's and Grant's thoughts were with Kane and what he might be going

through. Even when they heard the rhythmic boom
of the surf, they didn't smile with relief.

They came out of the wall of palm trees and labyrinth of underbrush onto a rocky beach. They also
saw, moored to one of the tree trunks, a twelve-foot-
long landing boat from New Edo. Grant quickly inspected it, making sure it still had its oars. Its keel
looked intact.

Shizuka went to his side. "How long do we wait
for Kane?"

Brigid answered for him. "For as long as it
takes."

Shizuka glanced at her a bit reproachfully. "I was
not implying otherwise. I was about to suggest we
wait until daybreak. If he's not back by then, we
make our way to New Edo and return with a much
larger and better armed party."

Grant knuckled his chin thoughtfully, then he
stiffened, eyes narrowed as they fixed on the jungle
perimeter. Brigid and Shizuka followed his intense
stare. "What?" Shizuka asked in a tense whisper.
"What did you see?"

"I'm not sure. I thought I saw something moving." Grant stepped slowly forward, feet crunching
on the gravel. He stopped and listened. He didn't
hear a sound, and he searched the dark spaces between the trees with his eyes and saw nothing.

Then Sherrinford Oakshott stepped out of the
shadows. His baby mouth glistened with saliva. He

stood quite still and looked impassively at Grant. His huge shoulders hunched, and he raised an arm. He gripped a double-bladed hatchet in his enormous balled fist.

"Shit," Grant said softly.

Shizuka tossed him the *katana* she had retrieved. Grant snatched it out of the air and lunged forward, driving the curved point of the blade at Oakshott's chest. The giant slapped the blade contemptuously aside.

Oakshott, in a surprisingly swift movement, swept a leg into Grant's ankles. Taken completely off guard, Grant couldn't jump away. He was bowled over and cracked the back of his head sharply on the rocky shoreline. Multicolored pinwheels spun behind his eyes and he clung to consciousness, groping for the *katana*. He thought he heard Shizuka scream his name.

"Stay back!" he shouted. Abandoning the sword, he managed to get to his feet just as Oakshott closed with him, trying to bury the blade of his hand ax in the crown of Grant's head. The former Mag hit him with all the strength he could muster, the heel of one hand under the giant's chin. It was like punching a granite statue. Oakshott swiped overhand blows with the hatchet at Grant's head, trying to split his skull.

He deflected two of the blows, feinted with his right fist and smashed his left into Oakshott's face. Pain seared up Grant's knuckles into his wrist, as bone crunched beneath his fist. He sidled away. Oakshott remained standing, blinking a bit in mild bemusement, ignoring the blood trickling from the two-inch cut on his cheek. He dropped the hatchet at his feet as if he had forgotten it.

Oakshott didn't move for a long moment. Grant prayed he was suffering from a delayed reaction to his blow and would simply drop over unconscious. It didn't happen. His head twitched from side to side, his little eyes searching for his weapon.

Grant jumped for the fallen hatchet, but the giant moved to cut him off. He dodged aside and eluded the great grasping arms. As Oakshott came after him, Grant rammed the crown of his head into the man's face.

Oakshott stumbled and tottered but kept his feet. He blew scarlet bubbles from his split lips. He grinned, exposing red-filmed teeth. "You behave, sirrah."

"Where's your keeper?" Grant asked him, letting a taunting smile play lazily on his face. "He send you out here or did you take the initiative?"

Oakshott acted as if he hadn't heard. He bent and picked up the ax and spun it skillfully around by the handle, the double-bladed head dancing like a cobra preparing to strike. His familiarity with the weapon was apparent.

Grant watched his opponent as they circled on the beach. He darted forward, feinting to the left. As

Oakshott swung the hatchet, Grant dived under the edged steel, plucked up the sword and lashed out with it one smooth motion. The blade razored along his stomach, slicing through his coat and shirt and opening a long, shallow cut. Oakshott gazed down at the wound with dispassionate eyes.

Grant closed with him, not bothering with the feint, trying for contact with the *katana*. Oakshott blocked with his hatchet, and steel rang on steel. He was strong enough to stop Grant's knife, then brought the ax down in a sideways slash.

Once again surprised by the giant's speed, Grant narrowly avoided the blow. The hand ax whistled through the air, missing Grant's shoulder by a fractional margin. The huge man came at him at once, exploding into motion. Giving ground before the charge, Grant kept the *katana* flashing, meeting a half-dozen attacks in a row, sparks skidding in all directions as he met a dozen more.

He listened to Oakshott's breathing, hoping with all the weight he carried he would get winded quickly. He wasn't sure if it made any difference. A man who could cough up a 9 mm hollowpoint slug in his lungs and recover from hydrostatic shock inside of a couple of minutes wasn't likely to tire easily.

Grant launched a front stab-kick that caught Oakshott in the chest. Oakshott staggered backward, then set his feet and charged again, holding the ax high.

Staying loose, bouncing on the balls of his feet, his breath ragged in his own ears, Grant danced with death. Glittering steel edges slashed by his face, missing by scant millimeters, turned or parried by Grant's weapon or his forearms. Perspiration beaded his forehead. Oakshott brought the hatchet down in a vicious overhand blow, aiming at Grant's upturned face. Grant sidestepped, using all of his Mag skills and experience to avoid the giant's rush.

Grant leaned in, closing his fist around the ax's haft. He slipped his forearm in front of Oakshott's wrist, blocking the blow with bone-jarring contact, hoping to knock the weapon free. But Oakshott's grip held. Concentrating on his moves, keeping the weapon locked down, Grant brought a knee up and slammed Oakshott in the groin.

The kick knocked Oakshott backward, but he managed to lift the hand ax. Grant dived in again, driving his opponent back with sword slashes and thrusts. Oakshott managed to avoid them.

Grant lashed out again, turning the huge man's hatchet away, but was not able to beat through Oakshott's defenses. He landed three kicks against the bigger man's side and stomach, but before he could disengage, Oakshott's ax sliced a thin, shallow furrow along his right temple. Grant felt the flow of blood running down his neck.

Oakshott came for him, a juggernaut of flesh and blood and glittering steel. Grant's sword moved mechanically, blocking the attacks, feeling the man's incredible strength, listening to the quick flicking scrapes of steel.

Oakshott lunged at him, but Grant sidestepped easily. He rammed the long *katana* blade through Oakshott's ribs, hoping to drive it home into the man's heart. Oakshott turned enough to make him miss his heart, and the blade was locked in the clutch of ribs. Oakshott swung the hatchet in a backhand blow.

Ducking, Grant caught himself on his left hand in a crouch, then shot his right foot out at his opponent's knee. He aimed the kick from the side, with Oakshott totally exposed and vulnerable. Oakshott grunted but didn't go down. Droplets of blood sprayed from his lips, and Grant knew the knife might have missed the man's heart, but it was buried deep in a lung. An ordinary man would have drowned in his own blood as his lungs filled.

Oakshott grasped the handle of the long sword and drew it from his body, the length of steel carmined. He groaned between clenched teeth as he did so. He glanced at it, as if surprised to find it in his hand and dropped it to the beach.

Grant bounded to recover it. Oakshott pistoned out his left arm and his right hand grasped Grant around the neck. Gagging, Grant pried at the fingers crushing flesh, tendon and cartilage into bone. Oakshott lifted him from the ground and slammed him down, putting his weight on Grant's throat to hold him in place. He lifted the hatchet for a skull-splitting blow. Either Brigid or Shizuka or both screamed.

"Son of a bitch!" Grant snarled. He drew up his knees in a protective gesture and shot both heels upward with a pistoning force into the giant's crotch. Lifted in the air, Oakshott sailed backward. He hit the ground hard on the back of his head and neck, the ax blade chiming against the rocks.

Grant staggered to his feet, vision clouded, breath clogging in his throat. Oakshott rose, as well, hatchet in hand. Without looking behind him, Grant rasped, "Brigid, Shizuka, push off in the boat. If I can—"

Whatever else he intended to say was drowned out by a grunting roar. The stamp of heavy feet propelling a monstrous body filled Grant's ears. He dimly heard Shizuka shouting a warning in Japanese.

Propelled by gargantuan legs, a creature lunged out of the jungle. Before Grant, Brigid and Shizuka could move, the monster landed on the beach right behind Oakshott. He turned, chopping at it with the hatchet. The mountainous mass of muscle that made up most of the bulk of the dinosaur did not even flinch as the blade rebounded from its hide. Even in the feeble light, Grant saw blood gleaming darkly on its throat. The creature was wounded, in a frenzy of pain and attacking anything that caught its eye.

The creature lowered its head, its great jaws opened, then closed with a loud snap. Caught by the head and shoulders, Oakshott was lifted high in the air. His legs kicked in a futile spasm. The monster bounded away, its huge fangs shearing through flesh, crunching through bones. Grant saw the lower half of Oakshott's body fall to the ground. Then the dinosaur was gone.

Grant, Shizuka and Brigid stood rooted to the spot, staring in wide-eyed shock. Brigid was the first to speak. "Entropic reversal isn't going to help him now."

"No shit," said Kane's voice. He came limping out of the jungle. Brigid ran to him but he waved her away. "I'm all right. I'm all bloody, but it's not mine. It's that dinosaur's. He's been after me for the last half hour. I'm glad somebody else caught his attention."

"I'm just glad it was that madman," Shizuka said, going to Grant's side. They looked thoughtfully at each other in silent surmise.

Feeling suddenly awkward, Kane said, "We can always go back to the installation and see if the gateway unit survived."

Grant didn't even look at him when he said, "I've got a better idea. Let's go back to New Edo—at least for a few days. Then we can decide how to get back to Cerberus...or even if we really want to.''

He cupped the side of Shizuka's face and she embraced him. They kissed passionately. Brigid and Kane stepped away, toward the edge of the jungle. She gazed into it without really seeing it. Kane guessed she was looking beyond the vegetation to the distant Operation Chronos complex—or what was left of it.

''I think we should stay in New Edo for a while,'' she said softly. ''We should check out the Chronos base. There are too many secrets there just to turn our backs on.''

''What kind of secrets?'' he asked suspiciously.

''The secrets of creation,'' she said dreamily. ''The secrets of the beginning of life on Earth.'' She glanced over at Kane questioningly. ''You understand me, right?''

Kane looked down at the deep, three-toed imprints of the dinosaur's feet in the sand. His voice was flat when he said, ''Not in a million years, Baptiste.''

In a ruined world, the past and future clash with frightening force...

JAMES AXLER

DEATHLANDS®

Sunchild

Ryan Cawdor and his warrior companions come face-to-face with the descendants of a secret society who were convinced that paradise awaited at the center of the earth. This cult is inexorably tied to a conspiracy of twentieth-century scientists devoted to fulfiling a vision of genetic manipulation. In this labyrinthine ville, some of the descendants of the Illuminated Ones are pursuing the dream of their legacy—while others are dedicated to its nightmare.

Even in the Deathlands, twisted human beliefs endure....

Available in December 2001 at your favorite retail outlet.